PRAISE FOR WORKS OF

"Rocket-boosted action, brilliant ~~~~~~~~~, and the recreation of a horror out of the mythologic past, all seamlessly blend into a rollercoaster ride of suspense and adventure."
-- James Rollins, New York Times bestselling author of JAKE RANSOM AND THE SKULL KING'S SHADOW

"With THRESHOLD, Jeremy Robinson goes pedal to the metal into very dark territory. Fast-paced, action-packed and wonderfully creepy! Highly recommended!"
--Jonathan Maberry, NY Times bestselling author of ROT & RUIN

"Jeremy Robinson is the next James Rollins"
-- Chris Kuzneski, NY Times bestselling author of THE SECRET CROWN

"If you like thrillers original, unpredictable and chock-full of action, you are going to love Jeremy Robinson..."
-- Stephen Coonts, NY Times bestselling author of DEEP BLACK: ARCTIC GOLD

"How do you find an original story idea in the crowded action-thriller genre? Two words: Jeremy Robinson."
-- Scott Sigler, NY Times Bestselling author of ANCESTOR

"There's nothing timid about Robinson as he drops his readers off the cliff without a parachute and somehow manages to catch us an inch or two from doom."
-- **Jeff Long, NY Times bestselling author of THE DESCENT**

"Greek myth and biotechnology collide in Robinson's first in a new thriller series to feature the Chess Team... Robinson will have readers turning the pages..."
-- **Publisher's Weekly**

"Jeremy Robinson's THRESHOLD is one hell of a thriller, wildly imaginative and diabolical, which combines ancient legends and modern science into a non-stop action ride that will keep you turning the pages until the wee hours. Relentlessly gripping from start to finish, don't turn your back on this book!"
-- **Douglas Preston, NY Times bestselling author of IMPACT**

"Jeremy Robinson is an original and exciting voice."
-- **Steve Berry, NY Times bestselling author of THE EMPEROR'S TOMB**

"Wildly inventive…fast, furious unabashed fun."
-- **Publisher's Weekly**

ONSLAUGHT

(BOOK 5 OF THE ANTARKTOS SAGA)

JEREMY ROBINSON

For the real Solomon, my son and inspiration

ACKNOWLEDGEMENTS.

I must once again thank a small group of people who make the Antarktos Saga some of the best books I've written. Kane Gilmour, your edits continue to improve my books, and as you've come to know my stories better than anyone else, your guidance and opinions are invaluable.

My wife, Hilaree, and my two girls, Aquila and Norah, your imaginations and energy keep this family imagining, passionate and pushing the boundaries of creativity.

And Solomon, my son, upon whom The Last Hunter is based... When I began this series, I wondered if the attributes you possessed as a three year old—kindness, gentleness, forgiveness—would remain as you aged. You're now six, and I am astounded by the person you are becoming. Solomon Ull Vincent is a fictional character, but you, my son, are very real and are even more compassionate, kind and gentle-hearted than the character I've created. I hope that when you're old enough to read this story, you will approve of how I've used your name.

FICTION BY JEREMY ROBINSON

Stand Alone Novels
SecondWorld
Project Nemesis
Island 731

The Antarktos Saga
The Last Hunter - Descent
The Last Hunter - Pursuit
The Last Hunter - Ascent
The Last Hunter - Lament
The Last Hunter - Onslaught

The Jack Sigler Thrillers
Pulse
Instinct
Threshold
Ragnarok

Callsign: King - Book 1
Callsign: Queen - Book 1
Callsign: Rook - Book 1
Callsign: Knight - Book 1
Callsign: Bishop - Book 1
Callsign: Deep Blue - Book 1
Callsign: King - Book 2 - Underworld
Callsign King - Book 3 - Blackout

Origins Editions (first five novels)
Kronos
Antarktos Rising
Beneath
Raising the Past
The Didymus Contingency

Writing as Jeremy Bishop
Torment
The Sentinel
The Raven

Short Story Collection
Insomnia

Humor
The Zombie's Way (Ike Onsoomyu)
The Ninja's Path (Kutyuso Deep)

THE LAST HUNTER

PROLOGUE

"Belgrave Ninnis, come inside this instant, before Death himself decides you are too easy a target to pass by."

Lieutenant Ninnis leaned back in his chair, "Just a moment more." He took a slow drag from his pipe, allowing the warm smoke to thaw his lungs a touch. Momentarily relieved of the cold air's sting, he set his charcoal to the page once more and lost himself in the image.

He didn't notice that the gray cloud coming from his lungs with each breath wasn't pipe smoke. He didn't notice the brightness of the stars overhead or the thin crust of ice forming atop his water glass. The cold suited him. Always had. It was part of the reason he'd been selected to join Douglas Mawson's Antarctic expedition—that and his father of the same name was the Inspector Surgeon General of the Royal Navy and a member of the Vice-Admiral's Arctic expedition that explored the coasts of Greenland and Ellesmere Island. His father's legacy was more inspiration than pressure, but Ninnis couldn't deny a desire to outdo his father. Antarctica was further, colder, more dangerous and far less explored.

The charcoal, reduced to a nub, crumbled between his fingers. He lifted it from the page and looked down at his hands.

"Lord," came a sweet, but concerned voice. "You're shaking."

Ninnis watched his hand twitching back and forth, stricken by the cold. "So I am."

"I don't understand why you're out here, tonight of all nights," she said.

Ninnis turned back to his wife of four hours and smiled. She was wrapped in blankets. Her brown hair hung in ringlets, recently freed from a braid. Her deep brown eyes mesmerized him. "To prepare myself," he said.

"A full year will pass before you leave my side," she said. "Prepare yourself when winter returns."

"I was not speaking of my future adventures at the bottom of the world, or of the frigid lands that await me there," Ninnis said. "Rather, I was speaking of the warmth this night yet promises."

A grin formed on her lips, followed by a shiver that ran up through her body. "Devil."

"The devil could not love one as fair as you," Ninnis said, and then leaned to the side, revealing his drawing. "For you, dear, sweet Caroline. My wife."

When her hands went to her mouth, the blankets fell, revealing that the braid was not the only wedding decoration she had shed. She now wore delicate undergarments that both hid her body and accentuated it. Stunned by the sudden revelation, he was still in a stupor when she took the page from his hands and stepped inside, off of the balcony and away from the chilled London air.

He watched her walk away with the sigh of a man who knew, without a shred of doubt, that he had somehow won a lottery in Heaven and had been given one of God's finest creations. He lifted his water glass to his lips and tipped it back. When no fluid reached his mouth, he looked down, saw the layer of ice and laughed.

Shaking his head, he stood and looked out from the Cavendish Hotel's penthouse balcony. The lamp-lit streets, homes and businesses of London surrounded him, a sea of orange lights beneath a sky of white stars. Normally, he might gaze at the view, searching for interesting details or listening to the late night revelers defeating the cold with liquor, but the woman waiting for him inside was far more interesting. He spun on his heels and entered the suite, closing the doors to the balcony behind him.

The heat greeted him first, prickling his skin. The room felt like an inferno, though he knew it was just because he was so chilled. The fire had dwindled to a small flicker, and a new log would be needed to accommodate a late night. Half way to the fire, he paused when the heat became unbearable. Scratching his itching his skin, he turned to his new wife and watched. Noting his attention, Caroline met his gaze.

"How did you do it?" she asked, holding up the portrait. "It looks so much like me, but I wasn't posing."

Ninnis tapped his head. "There isn't a detail of your face I do not have committed to memory. That is my true preparation for the expedition. When I miss you, and I will, I can recreate your face on the page. In pretending you are gazing back at me, as you are now, I will find peace…" He shivered and grinned. "And maybe a little warmth in that barren world."

His grin widened when Caroline all but swooned at his words. She placed the page on the nightstand and lay back on the thick blanket. He moved to the fireplace, adding two more logs to the fire, and prodding the embers with a wrought-iron poker until the fresh wood caught. Satisfied that the fire would burn through the night, he turned to the bed.

Caroline smiled at him. "It's nearly time."

He smiled widely. "I know."

"You have to go," she said.

Ninnis paused, his shirt half lifted. "Go? Where?"

"Back," she said.

"Did you leave something in the hall?" he asked. "At the church?"

"Belgrave," she said. "You *know*. You remember."

Tears pushed at his eyes. An invisible hand clutched his throat. He sat down on the side of the bed. "I hoped it had been a nightmare. A very long, detailed nightmare."

She sat up next to him, hand on his back, tracing the contours of his shoulder blade. "I wish it were so."

Ninnis looked at her, his tears running freely. "And you? Are you real?" He looked up at the sketch, a perfect memory of his Caroline. "Or are you just a memory?"

"Look at me," she said. "Do you think you can remember me this well?"

His eyes traveled up and down her form. Every part of her was perfectly realized. "You're right," he said, "I'm not Solomon."

Ninnis gasped. Saying the boy's name solidified that this was a fantasy and the very bleak reality, where Caroline was long since deceased and his body had been kidnapped by an evil spirit, awaited him. His head sagged toward the floor.

"Chin up, Belgrave," Caroline said in a tone that was far more chipper than seemed appropriate.

Ninnis stood and stepped away from her, offended. "My own fantasy taunts me?"

Caroline frowned while still maintaining some form of smile on her face. The expression was new to Ninnis. She slipped from the bed and stood before him, reaching out a hand.

Before her fingers reached his chest, Ninnis stepped back. "This isn't real. The boy is real. The masters are real. It's all darkness. And death! And evil! And—"

Her hand reached his chest, flattening over his heart. He collapsed to his knees, wracked by sobs. She fell with him, clutching his body to hers, steadying him. "I *am* real, Belgrave. I am not a conjuring of your imagination. We are not even within the confines of your mind."

Ninnis snapped to attention at this, wiping the tears from his eyes. "Where are we then?"

"Where you needed to be."

Ninnis looked around his honeymoon suite. He had never felt as loved and safe as he had on the first night he spent in this room. He thought he understood, but a question nagged. "If I must leave, will I see you again?"

"I...do not know," she replied. "All I know is that it is possible."

"But...how?" he asked. "I am...my life is..." He shook his head. "I do not deserve any of this."

"You're right," she said, "you didn't deserve to be taken from me, or to be broken and made into a monster, or to be the architect of Solomon's transformation." When it was clear that Ninnis was far from convinced, she added, "Do you think the boy is the only one capable of forgiving you?"

Ninnis raised his eyebrows and looked her in the eyes.

"You have lived a long life, Belgrave Ninnis, but you still have so much to learn."

Tears, now of hope, fled from his eyes. "Then teach me."

She reached out and took his hand. "There is no time for that. I can only show you."

He resisted her pull toward the balcony door. The cold now reminded him of his frigid prison. But she didn't relent, and soon, he found himself standing before the door.

"Open it," she said. "And look."

He found himself reaching for the door handle. When his skin touched the metal handle, it did not sting of cold. Instead, it felt warm to the touch. He twisted the handle and pulled.

Warm air washed over him.

The night was gone, replaced by a brilliant, deep blue.

He stepped onto the balcony.

London was gone. In its place was—

"An army," Ninnis said.

And at the army's core stood a man—barely a man now—who was at once intimately familiar and wholly alien. Ninnis pointed to him. "There I am."

Caroline stepped up next to him, resting her hands on the railing. "Not you. Him. Ophion."

"*Nephil*," Ninnis said.

Caroline nodded.

He looked at her. "Tell me what to do."

1

"Gone? How could she be gone?" It's a stupid question with a thousand different answers.

Kainda picks the most obvious reply. "She has legs."

She's right, of course. Mirabelle Whitney, daughter of Merrill and Aimee Clark, has legs. She could have walked out on her own, but when I saw her here, through the eyes of Amaguq the shifter, who had impersonated Mira and who would have killed me if not for the sacrifice of Xin, she didn't seem hale enough to get far. The shifter had beaten her, near to death, before taking her form. That she survived is a testament to her strength, but escaping this cave in her condition doesn't seem possible. Still, it did take us three days to reach the cave. A lot could have changed in that time.

Part of me is angry at myself for not arriving sooner, but we really couldn't have traveled any faster. Grumpy and Zok, a pair of large cresties—my personal term for the green with maroon striped Crylophosaurs that populate the continent—moved at a sprint for a full day before nearly collapsing. Kainda and I considered continuing on foot, but the ground covered by the cresties was far further than we could go on foot, even without resting. So we stayed with our dinosaur companions, traveling faster and conserving our strength.

The cave is a quarter mile below ground—a shallow hole by hunter standards, but it's slick with moisture and moss, and it's coated in jagged stones. If she managed to climb out, she will have left a trail.

I sniff the air first. The scent of vegetation decomposing is the strongest, followed by a faint trace of human blood—Mira's—and then something else. A lingering odor that is unfamiliar to my nose. I sniff again. "What is that?"

Kainda breathes in, long and deep, through her nose. She lets the air out, looking confused. "I have no idea."

This is disconcerting. Kainda has been a hunter far longer than me and has experience with everything this continent has to offer, both natural and unnatural.

"Something from the outside world?" she asks, smelling the air again.

I shake my head. The scent is decidedly non-human. "It's not Amaguq, either." I got a big whiff of him before I removed his head. I can detect traces of the shifter, but they're not strong. "I don't think it's just one scent." I try to separate the commingling tang. It's a bouquet of stink unlike anything I've smelled before—part Nephilim, part animal—like rotten milk and musk. It's far too well mixed for me to sift through.

"There were at least eight of them," Kainda says.

Surprised that she could get this out of the scents, I turn and find her crouching over a patch of moss.

"They weren't too careful, either."

I squat next to her and look at the moss. It's been trampled. But the marks are confusing and unfamiliar. "What are they?"

Kainda just looks bewildered.

Looking more closely, I spot something familiar, but out of place. "That looks like a hoof."

She nods. "Like Pan's feet."

We nod in unison. Pan, the Greek god of shepherds, flocks and music had goat-like legs and hooves. In that way, he was unique from other warriors I have seen. He kept a flock of human prisoners, eating them one by one until we freed them, gave them guns and sent them to the U.S. forward operating base. But Pan didn't leave these footprints. The first indicator is that these prints are far too small. The second is that Pan is very dead. After Wright removed the protective metal band from Pan's forehead, Em buried one of her blades in it—the Nephilim's only weak spot. The only other way to kill them is to drown them...or cut off their heads entirely.

Thinking of Wright and Em twists my gut for a moment. Wright was a U.S. Army Captain who joined my small strike force along with his wife, Katherine Ferrell, a freelance assassin who worked, off the record, for the same government Wright served openly. Wright gave his life for our quest to locate the Jericho shofar, staying behind to fight an army of hunters and Nephilim while the rest of us fled. Katherine, who prefers to be called Kat, managed to forgive me for leaving him and was eventually identified as my *Focus*, by the Kerubim, Adoel, guardian of Edinnu, the mythological Garden of Eden.

Then there is Em—my *Faith*, whose full name is Emilee, or so we thought. Adoel also told us her real name—Rachel Graham, which led to the startling revelation that Kat's true maiden name was also Graham and that the pair were long lost sisters. And since Em is kind of my adopted sister, I suppose Kat is, in a way, my sister and Wright my brother-in-law. The bond between us all is too uncanny to ignore. There is a design in it.

As there is with Mira, my *Hope*. She and I were short-lived, but very close friends—kindred spirits, I suppose. A photo of the two of us kept me sane during several of my years underground. She doesn't know it, but I owe her my life. I will do everything I can to save her, not just because of our friendship, but because the angel, who gave names to my hope, focus, faith and passion, made it clear that I would need all four to overcome the war about to be waged. Mira, my Hope, is all that remains.

And it is with Kainda, my *Passion*, that I will find her.

Kainda's muscles flex as she leans out over the moss. "Three claws," she says, inspecting a second footprint. "These aren't the same creatures."

She is one of the strongest hunters. As the daughter of Ninnis, the most renowned hunter of all, she had the best and harshest teacher for much of her life. She also had the most pressure to excel, which in hunter culture translates to brutality. But she, like many hunters, has shed some of her Nephilim corruption and even managed to fall in love.

With me.

And I with her.

We're an unlikely couple—me a former nerd, klutz and bookworm, her a lifelong killer born out of darkness and hate—but we've both been broken and reformed. We are new together and we're better for it. I was not sure how she would feel about risking everything to find Mira, who I admit, I loved in my younger years, but she was the first to volunteer. This revealed not just her deep trust in me, but also a keen understanding of what needs to be done to not just survive the coming war, but also to win it.

"There are no human prints here," she says, then inspects another patch of moss that would be impossible to avoid while exiting. "None."

When my head starts to hurt, I realize I'm clenching my teeth, and I try to relax. This is bad news. No human footprints, or boot prints, means that Mira didn't walk out of this cave.

She was carried out.

And neither of us know who, or what, took her.

"More," she says, pointing at another, larger print.

"It looks like a horse hoof," I say.

"What is a horse?" she asks.

I shake my head in confusion. "A domesticated animal. People ride on them."

"Maybe she rode it out?"

"Maybe," I say, but neither of us believe it. All signs point to Mira being taken. She might have been on the horse's back, but I doubt she went willingly. For a moment I think she's been kidnapped by a herd of random farm animals, but then I recognize another print that's not been trampled by the others.

Four wide toes, each tipped with a long claw, and a thick pad, twice the width of my hand. "This one is a lion."

She nods. Apparently lions are known to the underworld, probably because they're renowned killers. Horses, not so much.

We follow the trail up through the cave. I'm kicking myself for not seeing it on the way in, but I wasn't looking at the floor. I was too busy rushing to the last spot where I saw Mira. Seeing the trail earlier wouldn't have really changed anything, but it might have saved a minute or two.

When we reach the cave exit and step out into the light of day, we're greeted by our dinosaur companions. They look up from the river where they're drinking and then they look back at us. They're massive creatures, stretching thirty feet from snout to tail tip. Grumpy's green skin shimmers, like new growth leaves in the sunlight. The maroon stripes over his neck, back and tail seem to absorb the light, creating a pattern of contrasting color and brightness that helps him blend into the jungle. But it's the tall crest over his eyes that distinguishes him from other dinosaur species—well, that and the fact that most other dinosaurs are now extinct. I say most, because this continent is full of surprises, the most recent of which is whatever took Mira.

The cresties go back to their refreshment when we walk past without speaking to them. The trail is easy to follow. It's a mash of footprints, a mix of species, following what appears to be a game trail through the jungle. Whoever has Mira is either so confident that they don't fear being tracked, or they're completely naïve to what is going on. I realize there is a third option a moment before Kainda speaks it aloud.

"This feels like a trap."

She's right. The trail is too easy to follow. But that's also the problem. "It's a really bad trap."

She frowns. "Obvious."

"Right." I look at her. "Not that it changes anything."

"Trap or not," she says. "We push forward."

I stop and take her hand. "Thank you."

She looks back, meeting my eyes with hers. Her dark brown eyes look almost black, perfectly matching her tied-back hair. "You would do far more for me." She scrunches her nose and then corrects herself. "You *have* done far more for me."

I want to kiss her. The moment is perfect. Her face looks soft. And her tan body, clad in the scant coverings of a hunter, has a sheen of sweat mixed with humidity that makes her glow. *Focus*, says the voice of Kat in my head.

Focus, I tell myself. *Mira is in danger.*

I pull my eyes away from Kainda and search the jungle around us. The trees—a species unknown to me—rise hundreds of feet into the air, their branches twisting and splitting into a thousand different directions. They remind me of when I used to drop ink onto a page and blow it with a straw. But the diamond-shaped leaves are sparse, and large patches of sunlight beam to the ground, allowing thick vegetation to grow. Moving through this jungle on anything but this path would be very time consuming...unless...

I look up. "Let's take the high road."

Scaling the tree's craggy bark is a simple thing. Soon we're moving through the jungle faster, more silently and without any fear of being set upon by an ambush. Not that we see one. It appears that whoever left the tracks is just sloppy.

Twenty minutes and a little more than a mile later, the trail splits ninety degrees in either direction, skirting the base of a cliff. We climb down to the jungle floor and inspect the tracks.

"They head in either direction," Kainda says. "And they're all equally fresh."

"She could have been taken in either direction," I say.

"We need to split up."

I don't like this idea, at all. Not because I don't believe Kainda is capable of rescuing Mira on her own, or that I don't trust she really wants to. But there are some things in the jungle that she can't handle alone, and if I manage to find Mira, but lose Kainda, I won't be any better off than I am now. Before I can say any of this, I spot something that keeps me from having to.

I quickly inspect the tracks on one path, and then move to the second.

"What is it?" she asks.

I ignore her, and move back to the path leading up to the T-junction. "There they are," I say.

"What?"

"The lion tracks." I point to the large paw print.

"I've been thinking about that," she says, while I move to the path leading to the right. "Do you think this could be the lion from Edinnu? What did you call him?"

"Ookla," I say, before pointing to the path. "No lion prints."

I move to the path leading to the left.

"Do you think this could be Ookla?" she asks. "And other creatures from Edinnu?"

"No," I say. I point to the path. "No lion prints."

"How do you know?" she asks, sounding frustrated at being dismissed so quickly.

"Because," I say, stepping closer to the rock wall and looking up. The cliff rises higher than I can see, stretching up into a bank of clouds. "I don't remember Ookla being able to fly."

2

"Fly?" Kainda says. She's about to ask what I'm talking about, but then seems to understand. She glances at all three trails. "The lion tracks stop here."

"And since there are no tracks through the jungle, no tracks heading back or into the trees, there is only one direction left to go." I look up.

"I don't see how this helps," she says. "Now we have three choices instead of two."

"We need to go up," I say.

"Is that what your instincts tell you?" she asks.

"Yeah," I say, hoping she doesn't hear the lie.

The truth is, lions have sharp claws and big teeth. If Mira is with the farm animal gang, I'm a little less afraid for her, but if she's with the flying lions, well, that's a bigger problem.

Kainda steps up to the wall and lifts herself up.

"What are you doing?" I ask.

"The climb will take most of the day," she says. "I don't want the sun to go down while I'm a thousand feet above the ground, do you?"

"Who said anything about climbing?" I say. She flinches when I pluck her from the wall and put her back on the ground. If I'd been anyone else, I'd be dead right now. The look on her face says I still might be.

I put my hands on her hips.

"You're testing my patience," she says.

"You love it," I say.

She tries to squelch a smile, but fails.

"Hold on," I say.

She puts her hands on my shoulders. When a sudden wind kicks up around us, she's pressed up against me. My hands slide around to her back and her arms wrap around the back of my neck. The embrace distracts us both and by the time I open my eyes, we're a hundred feet off the ground and climbing.

I hear a gasp in my ear. Kainda's arms squeeze a little tighter. That this hardened woman can feel fear pleases me. She'd once been numb to anything but hate, and now, she is so much more. It's one of the things I like best about her. The softening of one's heart is not an easy thing to do. I'm not sure I could have done it myself without Aimee's help.

Aimee, Mira's mother, held me in her arms just moments after I was born. It was her face that greeted me into the world and her face that returned me to it. And now, Merrill, her husband and my friend, has returned to save her, only now they've lost their daughter. And the majority of that is my fault. All the more reason to hurry.

The wind becomes an upward moving cyclone. My long blond hair whips around, stinging my skin. The air tugs at my clothing, which is not much more than Tarzan's loin cloth, a belt full of pouches, and Whipsnap—my weapon—wrapped around my waist, but a quick adjustment dulls the effect of the wind on our bodies.

My control over Antarctica's elements is more honed than ever. I can control the air, water, land and other natural elements of the continent as though they are part of my own body. Performing an unnatural feat, like flying, still wears me out, but summoning a storm or shifting the wind is almost second nature. I don't understand how I'm able to do these things. All I know is that my connection to the continent is a supernatural ability given to me at my birth, which was not too far from our current location. I was the first and only child born on Antarctica to non-Nephilim corrupted humans. That somehow bonded me to the land. Cronus, the Titan who resides in Tartarus, would probably say it was a gift, bestowed on me by a higher power. Actually, Adoel the angel would probably agree. And it's hard to argue with powerful beings that are not only ancient, but also genuine.

I've thought a lot about this during my time here. Certain events and the connections between people, and beings, times and places stretching back through time are hard to ignore. On one hand are the Nephilim, soulless half-demon, half-human monsters who want to eradicate the human race. On the other hand is a ragtag group of redeemed hunters, teachers, Titans, clones and even a traitor Nephilim willing to sacrifice himself to protect humanity. This war has been waged for thousands of years and is coming to a head...because of me.

A kid.

Sure, in surface years, I might be thirty-something years old, and yeah, I have a full beard, but I'm really just an eighteen year old who wouldn't be allowed to drink a beer.

And *now*, Nephil, aka Ophion, the first Nephilim whose spirit now resides in Ninnis, wants to claim my body for himself, something he came very close to doing. *Now*, the human race is looking to me for leadership against a supernatural army. And *now*, I'm doubting. Not in my purpose here. Or in my abilities. Or even in my ability to lead, or fight, and maybe even win.

But in the rightness of it all.

I've come to believe in God. I've even prayed. Twice. I've seen things, and spoken to creatures, and experienced other worlds that leaves no doubt that some kind of architect or mastermind is sitting behind the curtain, pulling our strings, directing us all to some sort of destiny. But there had to have been another way.

Billions died when Nephil used my body, and my connection to the land, to rotate the Earth's crust around its molten core, bringing Antarctica to the equator and destroying entire countries in the process. And then there are the more personal losses: Elias, Xin, Hades, Cerebus, Wright—even Ninnis, whose memories of his true self were returned for just a moment before Nephil took over once again. And what about the hunters—Kainda, Em, Elias, Zuh, and thousands more who have been tortured, corrupted and turned into monsters? How can all of this darkness, and hate, and death be allowed?

And why do I have to be at the center of it all?

"Solomon!" The voice is faint, barely reaching my consciousness. Then it repeats, louder, "Solomon!" I recognize the voice. Kainda. I open my eyes, not realizing they'd been closed, and I see the cliff face, streaking past, just a few feet away. We're traveling as fast as a missile and I've nearly crashed us into a rock wall.

I slow until we're hovering. My breath is ragged. The first pangs of exhaustion clutch my muscles. Lost in my anger and confusion, my powers took on a life of their own, reflecting my mood.

"Are you alright?" Kainda asks.

I nod. It's my second lie and I feel a pang of guilt. I don't want to lie to Kainda, about anything. "Actually, I'm not sure."

Before she can reply, I see the top of the cliff and forget all about my doubts and waning energy. "Look."

I spin us around so we can both look at the cliff. We're just thirty feet from the top, but the most remarkable aspect of the wall isn't the rock, but what's been built upon it.

"Those are nests," Kainda says.

"Really big nests," I add. I count twenty of them. Each is made from a combination of branches, leaves and random pliable objects. I see tents, ropes, blankets and large feathers in the mix. The oval shaped nests are at least fifteen feet long, half as wide and deep. They cling to the cliff face, resting on ledges and glued in place by something white and goopy. At the top of each nest, the cliff is carved away, forming paths to the top as though formed naturally by some ancient waterfall or glacier.

I bring us close to the wall and land just above one of the nests. Once Kainda is out of my arms, she scrambles up the stone path, headed for the cliff's precipice. I linger behind for a moment, looking into the nest. I'm expecting to see more feathers. Eggs perhaps. What I find instead surprises me. Really, nothing should surprise me anymore. I've seen a two headed, flying gigantes. But when I see golden lion hair coating the bottom of nest, I'm taken aback. True, I'd already surmised that the lions could somehow fly, but roosting like birds? Why? It doesn't make any sense. Then again, I just flew up the side of a thousand foot cliff and I don't have an S on my chest.

A chirp from above catches my attention. It sounds like one of the many species now populating the jungles of Antarctica, but the subtle urgent tone is all Kainda. I turn up and see her up above me on the slope, lying flat on her stomach. Without looking back she waves her hand, motioning me to join her.

I climb the stone in silence, still preferring bare feet to boots. Half way to the top, I see that Kainda is holding her battle hammer, which is a human-sized version of Mjölnir, the Nephilim Thor's hammer. He'd once been Kainda's master, just as Thor's father, Odin, was Ninnis's, and Thor's son, Ull, was mine. The Norse clan of Nephilim warrior, while not the most powerful, had produced three of the most feared and capable hunters, two of which might be their undoing.

Knowing that the hammer is out because Kainda is preparing for battle, I reach down for Whipsnap, but stop short of freeing the weapon. There were two Whipsnaps. The one I built from bone, wood and stone, and the second, forged by the Nephilim with an amalgam of solid, but light metals. I took both with me from Edinnu, and although I felt nostalgic about the weapon I constructed, I had to admit it was the inferior of the two. Of course, the second Whipsnap has been my constant companion for years, in the underground, on the surface and in Tartarus. I'm pretty attached to it. So I've kept the Nephilim variant, which has a more rigid staff that springs open more quickly. The crack it makes when loosed from my belt would give us away. I crouch down as I near the top, peeking through the tall grass at the edge.

My eyes widen and I whisper. "You have *got* to be kidding me."

3

"Have you seen them before?" Kainda whispers.

"You haven't?"

She shakes her head, no. "But...I think I know what they are."

"Me too," I say, looking at the figures. I can't make out details from this distance—they're at least a quarter mile from the cliff's edge—but their bolder features make them easily identifiable to me. I point to a creature with the body of a lion, and the head and wings of an eagle. "That's a griffin."

She points to one of the myths made real, this one with the body of a horse and a humanoid torso. "That's a centaur, right?"

"Yup," I say, pointing out several more. "And there's a manticore, a gorgon, a minotaur." My finger lands on a strange chicken-like thing with the upper body of a woman. She pokes her head forward with each step, eyes to the ground. "And that must be a harpie." Several more scurry up behind the largest of the bunch. "Harp*ies.*"

It's a Greek mythological Who's Who, though it's clear none of the would-be gods are present. These are the lesser creatures of the Greek myths. The pawns. The castaways.

"We call them the Forsaken," Kainda says. "But I thought they were just a story told to scare us before we were broken."

Despite my inner Ray Harryhausen fan being thrilled by what we're seeing, the fact that these creatures are the living embodiment of what *hunters* consider scary children's stories is not very comforting. I don't really want to ask, but I need to know what we're dealing with. "Tell me about them."

"They're Nephilim," she says.

Of course *they are,* I think.

"But they didn't fit into any of the more powerful classes. They might have the features of a warrior, a gatherer or one of the others, but they're mixed, usually in disfiguring ways with lesser animals."

"How is that possible?" I ask. "The Nephilim are half-human, half-demon. How could they have the body of a—" Kainda's raised eyebrow stops me in my tracks. The mix of sarcasm and humor on her face seems to say something to the effect of, "My sweet, little, naïve, Solomon."

That's when the reality of these creatures hits me. "Ugh." Demons are not human. Not even close. So a demon having a Nephilim child with a human isn't any more unnatural than a demon spawning with, say, a horse. They're equally outlandish. Gross, sure, but plausible—at least where the Nephilim are concerned. As for the creatures with more than one species... I don't want to speculate—lest I throw up and give us away—but

I'd guess it has something to do with the thinker Nephilim class's penchant for genetic tinkering.

Kainda spares me from the horrors of my own imagination, saying, "Because they didn't fit into any of the true Nephilim classes and served no purpose in the eyes of the warriors, they were cast out."

"But not all of them," I say.

She looks at me, confused.

"Pan," I say. "He must have somehow proven himself."

She nods. "His thirst for human blood was unrivaled. But other than that, I'm not sure what could have set him apart. As for the rest of his ilk, they have lurked in the shadows and on the fringes of the underworld ever since, watching young hunters for signs of weakness and snatching them into the dark."

"What happened then?" I ask.

"What do you think?"

I shrug and guess. "Sacrificed and eaten?"

"How would you put it..." she says. "Yup."

I don't miss the fact that Kainda's mood has become strangely lighthearted. Then I realize why. We're about to do battle. The down, dirty and bloody kind. There are about fifty of the things out there, some look to be twenty feet tall. We are severely outsized and outnumbered. But Kainda wouldn't have it any other way and it has her charged up.

But now is not the time to leap out with a battle cry. We haven't even found Mira yet. "We need to get closer."

Kainda frowns, but agrees. Her thirst for battle isn't strong enough that she'll make poor tactical choices. We slide up over the crest, moving slowly through the tall grass, and work our way toward the jungle that wraps around the clearing where the mythological creatures have set up camp. Concealed by the dense foliage that frames the clearing, we're able to stand, but our movement is slowed by twisting branches, thorny shrubs and the need for stealth.

It's fifteen minutes before we close the distance to just over a hundred feet. As we close to within fifty feet, right at the edge of the jungle, I hear what seems to be an argument. There aren't any words to speak of, in English, Greek, Sumerian or any other dialect. They're just kind of grunting, but the tone sounds disagreeable. I can't see them yet, but the variety of noises insinuates that the quarrel involves more than one species.

I reach a hand forward and slowly lift a large green leaf. Water pours from the cup-shaped vegetation and trickles to the ground. I freeze. The sound would have been enough to alert a hunter to my presence. But I hear no alarm or even a shift in the conversation. These creatures aren't hunters. In fact, given the easy-to-follow trail they left behind, it's kind of a miracle they're alive at all.

I peer into the clearing as the now waterless leaf rises without any more sound. At first, it's hard to make out individual bodies, but when I do, it's hard not to gasp, or flinch in disgust.

These are not the noble creatures of Greek lore. There are no smooth coats, shiny horns or seductive female forms. These...things...are hideous. Those with hair resemble a cat after a few rounds in a washing machine spin cycle—matted, clumpy or with hair missing. Scars ravage most of the bodies, ranging from long slices to gnarled skin, swollen burns and bites of all shapes and sizes. Eyes are missing. Feathers are plucked. Horns shattered or removed. Hooves with seeping, pus-oozing wounds. Not one of them resembles the regal images I have in my mind. They're a ragged band of monsters. True monsters who seem to lack as much intelligence as they do hygiene.

But I see bits and pieces of the other Nephilim races in this lot. The harpies, feathered up to their armpits with the arms, upper torso and heads of women, have the black almond eyes of gatherers. The three horse-bodied centaurs I can see resemble warriors from the waist up, as do the seven minotaurs from the neck down to their waists—the rest resembling massive, muscle-bound bulls. The griffins, fifteen of them, are the only creatures who lack any kind of resemblance to a Nephilim species. That's not to say they're an improvement. Their eagle eyes glow with hatred and of all the species present, they are in the best condition. They also seem to be above the argument, circling the group, at the core of which is a gorgon, whose head snakes are either dead, sleeping or cut away, and a pair of worked-up harpies who are squawking angrily.

I lower the leaf and look to Kainda, who has just backed away from her own lookout position. She traces her finger across her arm and mouths the word, "Scars."

Scars? I'm not sure what the significance is. They have a *lot* of scars, but I'm not sure what that—I nearly jump up and shout "eureka," when I figure it out. Nephilim warriors don't have scars because they heal so quickly. The other species of Nephilim heal as well, though much slower, but their purple blood still gets the job done well enough that I've never seen a scar on a Nephilim.

That's what sets these Nephilim apart from the others. They can't heal. They might be just as old, but they can be killed. Easily. And that's reason enough to cast them out. While hunters are also susceptible to quick deaths, we're also small enough to be useful in the underground. These things, even the chicken-lady harpies, are too large to do much more than use up resources.

This is good news. Fifty to two becomes a lot more manageable when the dead stay dead. Of course, the same applies to Kainda and me. I shift forward, lift the leaf and take another look at this band of misfit Nephilim.

They're armed, but the weapons are crude. The most basic are sharpened tree branches. The most advanced are maces fashioned from large stones...tied to tree branches. But the weapons are wielded by strong arms, and I have no way to know how skilled they are at fighting. Most are equipped with weapons bestowed at birth—horns, talons, sharp teeth and hammer-like fists. We can't underestimate them and we can't act rash—

One of the harpies involved in the scuffle clucks its way to the side, pecking its human-like mouth at the gorgon's tail. The movement gives me a clear line of sight to the center of the gathering, but just for a moment.

Still, it's long enough to see what's got them all riled up.

Mira.

She's prone and motionless. Her head is turned to the side, her eyes closed. I look to see if her torso is rising and falling, but my glimpse is cut short by a circling griffin. Alive or not, I don't know, but it's clear that this argument will end with Mira being claimed by one side or the other, and I cannot wait for that to happen.

I start to rise.

"Sol," Kainda whispers.

My boiling blood blocks out her voice.

"Sol!" she says a little more loudly. "Wait!"

But her plea for patience fades behind me as I surge up and out of the jungle, yanking Whipsnap from my belt and alerting the mythological mob to my presence. As my wind-propelled leap crests at thirty feet and I drop toward a surprised looking harpie, I see what must have kept Kainda from leaping out of the jungle alongside me.

A thirty-foot tall centaur with an upper torso that has the bulk of a warrior and the pale gray skin of gatherer, focuses its massive, black eyes on me—

—and enters my thoughts.

4

It doesn't speak, but I can feel its consciousness humming inside my head. Despite the mental intrusion, I'm committed to my attack. I draw Whipsnap back, aiming to thrust the bladed end through the breast-bone of the harpie now letting out a panic-stricken squawk. But as my arm shoves the blade forward, the huge gatherer-centaur does something to my mind, severing the connection between my thoughts and my body.

My leap becomes a ragdoll tumble. I crash to the ground landing hard in the trampled grass.

Then, something in my mind pushes back.

Hard.

The centaur is repelled, and I regain control of my body as the giant rears back in pain.

What was that? I wonder, as I climb to my feet. I was so taken aback by the appearance and sudden mental intrusion of the Nephilim centaur that I didn't have a chance to put up some kind of cerebral fight. The force that pushed the centaur back wasn't me, and Ull, my former split personality with a bad temper, is now fully a part of me. *So what repelled the creature?*

A question for another time, I decide as a griffin lunges.

The griffin ripples with lion muscles. Its large paws are tipped with eagle talons, black and needle sharp. Its head is all oversized eagle. Its hooked beak is open wide, blasting a high-pitched shriek as its ten-foot wings pull it up into the air above me and then propel it straight down like a two-ton mortar round.

While pulling one hand back, readying a strike, I raise the other toward the griffin, willing the wind to catch its wings. The giant creature should have been catapulted away.

But it continues to dive toward me.

There isn't even a breeze.

And I am out of time.

I fall back, flat on the grass. A second later, the griffin lands over me, its lion paws framing me on either side. Its eagle eyes lock onto mine, looking down at me. Its beak hangs open, as though in surprise. A bead of purple blood slips down the lower beak, gathering at the end and dangling above my forehead.

Nephilim blood can heal a human being, if its severely watered down. Fresh from the body, even a small amount is enough to kill. Most Nephilim heal before they can lose too much of it, but this is not a normal demon-child. The lower beak is filling with the purple fluid.

The dangling drop stretches out slowly and then breaks loose. My eyes cross as I follow the bead of blood's descent, but I lose sight of it a moment before it smacks my forehead.

And that's when I feel it.

Nothing.

The fact that these creatures are unable to heal has removed the deadly side-effects of their inhuman blood. Of course, that also means the griffin standing above me, with the bladed end of Whipsnap punching all the way through its neck, is about to collapse.

Pushing hard with my feet, I slide out from under the griffin just in time. The ground shakes as the heavy beast lolls to the side and topples over. Purple blood oozes into the grass around its head.

When the ground shakes again, I spin around and find a stone-tipped club coming toward my face. I lean back, dodging the weapon with just inches to spare. It's a minotaur, all mottled hair and musky stench. The club looks small in its massive arms, but the swing overextends the creature, leaving it open to attack...if I had a weapon. I glance back to Whipsnap, still buried in the bird-lion's throat, and I find two more griffins charging in from behind.

For a moment, I think, *where is Kainda*, but then I'm forced to act. Before the minotaur can recover from its missed blow, I leap toward it. While in motion, I reach into a pouch on my right hip, pull out my homemade climbing claws and slip them onto my hands. The claws, fashioned from feeder leather and feeder teeth, line my palms for climbing and my knuckles for punching. They aren't great for killing Nephilim, but they don't feel good, either.

I leap up to the minotaur's left shoulder, grip handfuls of its course, clumpy hair and swing myself around to its back. The creature huffs in aggravation, but doesn't react like I pose much of a threat. But hunters do not need weapons to kill, nor control over the elements. And since these monsters are Nephilim, I have no reason to hold back. It's like fighting robots. Or zombies. There is no moral roadblock stopping me from inflicting maximum damage.

I wrap my legs around the creature's waist, locking myself in place, and punch the two-inch long, pointed teeth of my climbing claws into its back. The minotaur howls in pain and pitches forward. I twist my hands, carving trenches into its flesh. The giant drops forward, lowering its head like a true bull, just in time collide with one of the two charging griffins.

Several things happen at once. The minotaur's horn—it only has one—pierces the griffin's chest and snaps free. The griffin's wail is cut short when the horn slips through its lung. Meanwhile, the minotaur's scream of pain is silenced when I wrap my hands around its neck and leap away, drawing six blades across its throat. The second griffin collides with the first and the minotaur, and tumbles wildly through the grass, crushing a pair of harpies before coming to a stop.

I land beside the minotaur. Without missing a beat, I snatch his crude club from the ground and rush the second griffin. One of its eagle eyes snaps open just in time to see me bring the heavy stone down on its head. As I turn to face the others, I'm thinking about Whipsnap. If I can get my weapon back, this will be a whole lot easier. But when I face down my enemies again, the chaos of battle I'm expecting is nowhere to be found.

The mythological creatures have gathered in a sort of formation. Two lines of harpies, feathers puffed up and bristling, followed by gorgons and basilisks and then finally a row of minotaurs. The griffins have all taken to the skies and are circling like buzzards.

The giant centaur, its gray-bald head gleaming in the sunlight, stands at the front of the rough-looking formation. It lowers its head toward me, not in reverence, but in emphasis for its mentally spoken word.

Ours.

He motions to his hooved feet. Mira lays, still motionless, in the grass. Her face is coated in dirt and dried blood. Her clothing, an olive-drab green, camouflage, combat uniform, is tattered and torn. Her jacket—if she had one—is missing, revealing a black tank top that's equally torn, showing her brown skin. The tightness of the shirt also lets me get a good look at her back, which rises and falls with each shallow breath.

Still alive.

Thank God.

I am simultaneously filled with relief and fierce determination. I didn't come this far to find Mira, only to let her be killed and consumed by this freakish lot. I grip the club tighter and step toward the centaur.

Its mind hums inside my head, pushing for a weakness.

I take another step forward, working on a battle plan. Centaur first. Take out the knees. Then put this club in its forehead. I'm not certain, but I think that if I can drop the big guy, the rest of the myth-squad will head for the hills.

The centaur rears up for a moment and then stomps its hooves on the ground. The display is very horse-like, but it's coupled with a mental shout.

Mine!

No, I think back, stepping forward.

The mythological creatures stomp and shout, shaking weapons, feathers and limp snakes. They're angry and agitated, but I think there is some fear in there.

The buzzing in my head grows stronger and it happens again. My mind and body disconnect. I fall to my knees, but then a surge of power from somewhere within me repels the giant. The centaur-gatherer rears up, clutching its head and letting out a shrill scream.

I have no idea what is happening to him when he digs down into my mind, but I can't complain. I'd be a mythical-creature readymade meal without it. Whatever *it* is. And while the centaur *has* managed to keep me from using my powers, my body is still under my control.

I step forward again, looking up at the centaur. It's absolutely massive. Its knee caps—my intended targets—are twice the size of a basketball. I'm going to have to hack at it like a manic lumberjack to do any real damage. I glance back to the jungle. *Where are you Kainda?*

Mine! Mine! "Mine!"

The last "mine," is shouted. The voice is high-pitched, almost fragile sounding, but the anger in it is powerful, like a child throwing a tantrum when a toy is about to be taken away. But the shout is coupled by a sudden and jarring psychic attack that drops me back to the ground and makes me shout out in pain.

I can feel the strange force inside me, fighting back, pushing hard, but the centaur retains its grip on my mind. My body twitches and I fall onto my back, looking up at the sky. The earth shakes beneath me as the centaur clomps toward me. Then it looms above me, looking down with those black, almond shaped eyes. Its thin lips are pulled back in a sneer that reveals two lines of rotting, cracked, horse-like teeth. Its eyebrows are deeply furrowed, punctuating the hate radiating from its body—and its thoughts.

It lifts a single hooved foot above my head. All it has to do is stomp, and I'll be dead. The great Solomon Ull Vincent, the last hunter, vessel of Nephil, slayer of Nephilim, destroyer of a good portion of the planet and promised leader of the human race is about to be killed by a centaur-gatherer with the disposition of a five year old.

Honestly, it's embarrassing. But I'm currently unable to do anything about it.

The force inside me rallies, delaying the centaur's attack, keeping its hoof locked in place. *What is going on?* I think. *Is there a mind outside mine that's fighting the creature?*

Luca, is that you? I think, but I get no reply. Before he died, Xin, one of several clones of me, bestowed the gift of telepathic communication on Luca, also a clone, and a perfect replication of me at age six. But while Xin was part gatherer, Luca is all human, and I doubt the child, as strong as he is, could put up much of a mental fight against a creature with thousands of years of practice.

There is no reply to my silent question. Instead, the battle is brought to a very sudden and violent conclusion.

There is a grunt off to my side. I recognize the voice.

Kainda.

But before this can fully register, her hammer flies into view above me, striking the centaur in the side of his hairless, plump head. The weight of the weapon crushes bone and implodes the cranium.

At the very moment the skull is ruined, my body and powers return to me. I roll back onto my feet and the wind carries me away from the now falling centaur. There is a deep, resonating boom as the giant body topples over, its legs jutting straight out, almost comically, frozen by its surprise death.

I turn and face the remaining mythological creatures, who appear enraged and confused.

Kainda wanders onto the battlefield almost casually. She looks at me. "Sometimes timing is more powerful than body count."

I must have a big, fat, "Huh?" written all over my face, because she smiles and explains. "Kat taught me that. Thought it made sense."

She stops by the centaur's head, reaches down and tugs at the hammer. It comes free with a slurp, dripping purple blood. She turns and faces the horde of creatures. They stare at her for just a moment.

I suddenly feel like I'm watching a herd of wildebeest staring down a lion, each creature growing more tense with each passing second until one of them cracks, lets out a yelp and then bolts. Suddenly, it's chaos. The creatures shout and shriek, tearing away in random directions, making themselves even more pitiful and shaming their names.

While the creatures flee, I run to Mira and kneel down beside her limp form. She's still breathing. I feel for a pulse. It's strong. "Mira," I say. "Wake up." I tap her face with my hand. "Mira."

"Harder," Kainda says and then grins. "If you're not up to it, let me wake her."

There's a high-pitched wail from inside the jungle. A moment later, three harpies charge back into view. I lift Mira into my arms while Kainda readies for a fight. But the harpies steer clear of us. They're terrified. So terrified, in fact, that they bolt straight past us and run right off the cliff, plummeting to their deaths.

"I'm starting to see why they were cast out," Kainda says.

A loud laugh wipes the smile from her face.

We both recognize the booming mockery carried by the laugh of a Nephilim warrior. It's joined by several more.

A second shriek rips from the jungle, and the top half of a minotaur sails into the clearing.

More laughter follows. Trees crack. Footsteps rumble. A Nephilim war party steps into the clearing and looks straight at us.

5

The three warriors are short by Nephilim standards. Twenty feet tall, tops. But they're decked out for battle. One carries an oversized scimitar, one an axe and the last a double-sided spear. Each is dressed in similar black leathers, the stylization of which reveals that they are from the Egyptian clan. Blood red hair, matted like a dirty dog's, hangs to their shoulders. Unlike many of the larger Nephilim I've seen recently, none of them have gigantes wings or Titan tails.

"Lesser Egyptians," Kainda whispers, locked in place like me.

We should probably be running, but the moment we move, I have no doubt these warriors will spring into action. I'd like to learn everything I can about them before that moment arrives.

"Scouts," Kainda says. "Too short to be anything else."

"Do you know them?" I ask.

"They would have been below even my station," she says.

Kainda's master had been Thor, son of Odin, leader of the Norse warrior clan. In terms of Nephilim hierarchy, her word once carried a lot of weight, even more than these three. And as a hunter in the service to Nephilim royalty, she wouldn't have had many opportunities to fraternize with lesser warriors. That this is my first time seeing them means they were probably shunned, possibly living outside the major citadels—Asgard, Olympus, or in the case of Egyptians, Tuat.

"Will they recognize you?" I ask.

"If I got close enough for them to see my hammer, maybe," she says, "but their eyes are not on me."

She's right. They're looking at me. And my blond hair makes me easy to recognize.

"Don't worry," she says. "They won't be a problem for us."

As though in agreement, the three warriors take a step back.

Then another.

And as quickly as they arrived, they leave, slipping back into the thick jungle.

Kainda and I look at each other, sharing our bewilderment.

"That," Kainda says, "was unexpected."

"If they're scouts, we're going to have company, soon." I bend down to Mira, give her face another pat. "Mira!" Still nothing. I take her beneath her arms and lift. She's tall, but not heavy. Of course, even if she was, the part of me that is still a hunter would never complain about it. I put her over my shoulder. "We should—"

The ground shifts beneath my feet.

The vibration grows in intensity and is quickly joined by a rumble. A horn blast, deep and powerful, rolls from the jungle. The cracking of tree limbs and trunks that follows sounds like the manic popping of a burning fireplace log amplified through a loudspeaker.

We back away from the jungle, our pace quickening with each step.

"That's a lot more than three," I say.

The jungle explodes. Leaves and branches burst into the air. At least thirty heavily armed warriors charge—all Egyptian, and all larger than the three scouts. None of them have wings or stingers, but really, thirty warriors in a berserker rage don't really need either.

With Mira over my shoulder, this is more than we can overcome.

I turn to run and start to shout for Kainda to do the same, but she's beat me to the punch and she's at least five steps ahead of me. The ground shakes so violently that I fear I will trip. And a delay of a few seconds is all the giants will need to close the distance.

But I forget all about my balance issues when I remember where we're headed. Going left or right is no good—Nephilim could lurk in either direction along with who knows what else. So we're headed back the way we came, which is about a hundred more feet of grassy clearing and then about one thousand feet of vertical space.

As we approach the cliff's edge, a slight grin works its way onto my face. Kainda has not slowed, looked back or shouted her desire for a plan. She knows the plan without asking, and she has complete faith in my abilities to execute it. That kind of trust is rare in the world beyond Antarktos and it's unheard of among hunters. It's a compliment of the highest order.

I wish I had more time to enjoy it, but Kainda suddenly drops from view. For a moment I think she's gone over the cliff, and I prepare myself for the jump, but when I reach the edge of the clearing, I find the stone slope carved by water and peppered with griffin nests. When my bare foot hits the hard, unexpected grade, I stumble and am carried forward by Mira's weight on my shoulder. Before my foot leaves the ground and my stumble becomes an all out fall, I push off. Something in my foot twangs with pain, but then we're off the ground and descending hard. That is, until a gust of wind pushes us up and out, away from the incline.

I soar out and over Kainda, reaching the cliff's true edge a moment before she makes her literal leap of faith. The wind cuts out and I plummet, shifting Mira so that she's in front of me, my arms wrapped tightly around her back. Air rushes past my body, tugging my hair, drawing moisture from my eyes. I turn toward Kainda. Her eyes are on the rapidly approaching ground, still fearless and certain in her belief that we will survive this fall.

Then, a shadow.

I see it for just a moment, shifting over Kainda's back. Then its source comes into view, and passes us. Then again, and again.

Warriors.

Thirty-foot giants with double rows of teeth, six fingers and toes, and a penchant for pain—a display of which we're about to witness. The five giants, who weigh far more than Kainda and me, reach a faster terminal velocity, and reach it faster. They rocket past us, not one of them reaching out to attack or capture. They've streamlined their bodies with the intent of reaching the ground first. But unlike Kainda and me, they won't slow before impact.

Then it happens. The first of the warriors strikes the ground below us in a startling display of gore. Purple blood sprays, bones crack in half, pop from joints and stab out through the tattooed skin. All the while, the monster howls in ecstasy.

It happens again. And then three more times. By the time the fifth and final Nephilim strikes the ground beneath us, the first is standing, his body nearly fully knit back together. Purple blood coats every blade of grass, tree branch and pebble in a fifty foot radius. The very ground beneath our feet will kill us if we land.

When we land.

Hunters should really start wearing shoes, I think, but then I'm on task, looking for a solution in the few seconds before we reach the ground and die on impact, or from overexposure to Nephilim blood, or if that can be avoided, at the hands of the five warriors now drawing their weapons.

We're falling too fast to change our trajectory fully, not without being picked off by the warriors armed with bow and arrows. But maybe we can fly past without changing trajectories.

"Kainda!" I shout, reaching a hand out to her. She takes hold of my wrist and I pull her close. "Hold on!"

She wraps her arms around Mira from the other side. We're face-to-face now, looking over Mira's shoulder. Kainda's eyes burrow into me, searching for a hint of my plan. But there's no time to explain. Instead, I tip forward and we fall the remaining distance head first.

The confused expressions on the warrior's faces is priceless. But there is no way for them to know what is about to happen, and when it does, they just stumble back in bewilderment.

Twenty feet and a fraction of a second before impact, the ground opens up. The hole is just eight feet across, but it stretches down for several hundred feet and is still deepening even as we fall inside, passing the Nephilim as a blur. Darkness consumes us as the land above comes back together again, sealing us off from pursuit.

We fall in silence for another ten seconds when a strong wind from below slows our descent before depositing us gently on the stone floor of a wide cavern lit by an array of glowing blue crystals. Once we're settled and Mira is in my arms, Kainda steps away, hammer at the ready, scouring our surroundings for any hint of danger.

While Kainda slides away into the dark, I lay Mira on the floor and sit beside her. Slowing a fall from 1000 feet is one thing; doing it for three people after opening a several-hundred-foot deep passage through solid stone is something else. Even a few months ago, an effort like that would have knocked me out. I'm stronger now, but I feel like I've just run a marathon.

I lean back on my hands, regaining my strength, and look at Mira. With her eyes closed and her nappy white-blond hair puffed out around her head, she looks so much like the little girl I knew so long ago. The girl that made my stomach twist with nervousness. The girl who made me feel like a normal kid. The girl who gave me hope.

The girl who *is* Hope.

While I'd like to wait patiently by her side and let her heal naturally, that could take time. Days maybe. But what can I—the answer is found on the side of a pouch on my belt. A dark spot. A *purple* spot. At some point during our battle with the Forsaken, a drop of blood must have found its way to my belt. I'm lucky it didn't strike my skin. I draw my blade and scrape it against the purple spot. As suspected, the blood is dried and flakes off into my waiting palm. In this form, it has no effect, but rehydrated... I put my hand beneath Mira's neck and lift. Her mouth slips open and I shake the dehydrated Nephilim blood into her mouth. Most of it misses or sticks to my hand, but a few flakes make it inside. It's not much, but it should be enough. I *hope* it's enough.

Nothing happens. The reaction to Nephilim blood is usually quite sudden and violent. But Mira hasn't flinched. Maybe it wasn't enough? Maybe it loses its healing properties when it dries?

I reach out and place my hand on her cheek. "Mira," I whisper, but I still get no reply. Her skin feels cold. The cavern's ambient blue light is dim, but my eyes have long since adjusted to low and no-light scenarios. I watch her chest for signs of life, and find nothing.

Panicked, I lean forward and place my ear against her chest. I don't hear any breathing, but her heart beat is loud and strong.

That's when I feel a sharp sting on my throat, followed by the words, "Try anything funny and I won't hesitate."

Mirabelle Clark...or Whitney rather, is awake. And I'm pretty sure she wants to kill me.

6

I move back slowly, lifting my hands out to the sides in a posture that reveals I am unarmed and am not a threat. "I wasn't going hurt you."

She sits up, while keeping the knife at my throat. A trickle of warm liquid reveals that she has already cut me, thought not very deeply. Her dark brown eyes lock on to mine with fierce determination. I've seen the look in the eyes of many hunters before. She means business. And after the things she's been through—her mother's kidnapping and rescue, the global cataclysm, battling with the Nephilim—she has a right to be paranoid.

"Enki is dead," I tell her, hoping the news will reduce her anxiety. It does, but only a fraction.

"How do you know about that?" she asks.

"I saw it happen," I say. "You blew him into little bits."

Her eyes flit back and forth as she remembers. "He dropped me."

I start to nod, but don't get very far as the blade cuts a little deeper. She sees me wince and pulls the knife back a little. I could disarm her. It would be simple for me. But that's not how I want this reunion to go. Of course, nothing about this meeting has gone like I envisioned. She clearly doesn't recognize me, which is understandable given the beard and one hundred and thirty pounds I've put on since we last met. But I suspect her memory has been tampered with. Like with Merrill, it might have been a long time since she had any memory of me.

"You landed in the lake," I say. "I saved you."

Her eyes flit again. "It wasn't you," she says, sounding accusatory, "It was..."

"Weddell seals." I step back so that the knife is no longer in striking distance. She keeps the blade pointed at me, but some of the fury has left her eyes. "They're friends of mine."

"Man, I hate this place," she mumbles to herself.

"Your father believes me," I say.

This catches her attention. Her body goes rigid, like a snake's before it strikes.

"Your mother, too," I say. "They're both safe. At a U.S. forward operating base on the coast. They're with Kat."

"Kat?" She's shaking a little bit now, caught between relief and distrust. "But she and Wright..."

"Survived," I say. "With me and my friends. Wright...didn't make it. He saved us. But Kat is alive, as are the other people from your group."

She flinches and her face becomes angry. "You're lying. You're not who you say you are."

"I haven't said I'm anyone yet."

"I saw you change."

She's talking about the shifter who captured her, stole her identity and left her for dead.

"That was a shifter," I tell her. "A Nephilim capable of changing appearances, not to mention stealing and erasing memories. That's why you can't remember me."

"I *don't* know you," she says.

"Your parents said the same thing," I say. "But they remember now. I was part of the Clark Station Two mission. You were there too, and my parents, Mark and Beth Vincent."

"They never had a son," she says. "And you're too young to have been—"

"My name is Solomon," I blurt out. "You liked my name."

She shakes her head, still confused, but then gently says, "King Solomon."

"Yes!" I say.

"Solomon—"

"—Islands." I finish the thought for her. We've had this conversation before and she's taking it in the same direction.

"Solomon Grundy," we say at the same time.

"The nursery rhyme," she says.

"And the evil comic-book zombie super villain," I say, quoting twelve year old Mira verbatim.

"Are you in my head?" she asks.

"Of the creatures on Antarktos capable of doing such a thing, I am not one of them."

"Antarktos," she says and I'm pretty sure it's the only word in my reply that she's heard.

"The Greek for Antarctica," I say, and then I remember the word's true significance. "It's what Merrill—your father—calls this place."

She looks me in the eyes. "You could still be in my head. You could be lying."

"I'm not," I say. Thanks to my perfect memory, I could recite every conversation we had during our time together. I could perfectly describe her house or the way her mother's chocolate chip cookies taste, or I could rattle off a number of 1980s pop culture references, but it could all come from her mind. There is nothing I can say that will make her believe me, at least not without physical contact. "I promise."

It's a simple claim, the kind made between children, and it carries all the innocence and earnest emotion I can muster, which is actually quite a lot.

She smiles, her teeth gleaming white against her light brown skin. "You *promise*? Are you serious?"

I hold out my left hand and extend my pinkie. "Pinky promise."

The absurdity of my request and the goofy smile on my face seems to put her at ease. She lowers the knife some. "You're really one of the good guys?"

She steps forward, raising her pinky.

"Actually," I say. "I'm leading them."

When she's stunned by my wild claim, I close the distance between us, wrap my finger around hers and recite the song lyrics she once sang to me. "Any hemisphere. No man's land. Ain't no asylum here. King Solomon he never lived round here."

I'm dizzied by a pulse of energy that jolts my body before flowing from my hand to Mira's. She jumps back, as though a lightning bolt has passed between us. With a gasp, she stumbles back, hands on her head. She stumbles for a moment, weak and disoriented.

"Mira," I say.

Her eyes lock on to me. She squints, looking me up and down once, but then focuses on my eyes. Her hand slowly rises to her mouth. Tears well up and tumble down her cheeks. "King Solomon," she whispers.

I nod slowly, a smile forming on my lips. "It's me, Mira."

She notices the knife in her hand. It falls from her grasp and clatters to the stone floor.

"Sol!" she shouts, and smiles so big and bright that it breaks my heart. I have waited a long time for this moment. When she charges toward me, arms outstretched, I find myself weak with emotion.

She leaps at me, wrapping her arms around my neck and colliding full force with my chest. Overcome as I am, the impact knocks me back. My Jell-O legs fail me. We fall.

But before slamming into the stone floor, a gust of wind creates a buffer, cushioning our landing. Mira sits up, face radiant. She grips my cheeks in her hands. "It's really you!"

I laugh and nod, feeling almost like myself again. Like little Sol.

She embraces me again, crushing herself against me. Her tears mingle with my own as they drip down the sides of my neck. Then she kisses me. On the cheek. Long and hard. If she'd done something like that when we first met, I probably would have passed out, but the expression of love is very welcome now. She kisses me again, on the forehead. Then the other cheek and I'm suddenly enveloped in a wave of kisses that make me laugh. There is nothing sexual about the kisses. Nothing intimate. We're more like two puppies reunited after a long time apart.

But when Kainda clears her throat, there is no doubt that she sees things differently.

7

I cringe at the way Mira jumps away from my reclined body. It makes us look all the more guilty. But then I see the knife reappear in Mira's hand and she's got it pointed at Kainda. "Get behind me, Sol."

She sees Kainda as a threat, like she did me before her memory was restored. Thankfully, her offer to protect me is probably the best thing she could have done.

I look up at Kainda, and she at me. We maintain our straight faces for just a moment, but then break out laughing. Our voices roll through the cavern, echoing back to us. It's ten seconds before either of us can control ourselves, but when we finally do, and I look at Mira again, she just looks annoyed.

I sit up and hold up my hands, much like I did when Mira had the knife to my throat. "It's okay, Mira, she's with me."

"I'm *with* you?" Kainda says, her tone revealing that she has not forgotten about the shower of kisses.

I get to my feet, clear my throat and motion to Kainda. "Mira, this is Kainda." I shift my arms toward Mira. "Kainda, meet Mira." I turn back to Kainda. "You know who she is and what she is to me." Back to Mira. "Mira, Kainda and I are, you know...together."

She looks at me, not understanding, but then her eyes go wide and she smiles. "Ohh, she's your *girlfriend*."

I start to nod, but then Kainda says, "I still do not know the meaning of this word. Girlfriend. I do not like it. It sounds weak." She steps closer, into the light cast by a collection of blue stones. Her beautiful face, strong body and scant hunter's garb are revealed. "I am his passion."

Kainda speaks earnestly, naïve to the meaning the word might convey to an outsider.

Mira doesn't miss it. She gives a lopsided grin and says, "I bet you are." She lowers the knife and ribs me with her elbow, "Not bad, Schwartz."

"Schwartz?" Kainda says the name slowly. She's never heard the nickname before. And I have no intention of explaining it now, not just because it embarrasses me, but because I'd have to explain the *Spaceballs* movie to someone who has never even seen a television. Winning the war against the Nephilim might be a simpler task.

"Never mind that," I say. "What we need—"

"Wait," Mira says. "I want a few answers, the first of which is, what—exactly—am I to you?"

"Huh?"

"You might have a perfect memory," Mira says, "But mine is pretty good, too. You said, 'you know who she is and what she is

to me.' So I would like to know *who* I am and *what* I am to you."
She crosses her arms. "If you don't mind."

This could take a while, but we're safe here and I get the
feeling that I'm going to have to spill the beans to fully gain
Mira's trust. I might be Sol to her, but she is no doubt rattled by
her recent experiences. I rub my hand through my hair, trying to
think of the best way to start. Do I begin with my kidnapping
and do the chronological thing? Do I jump to recent events? I
slap the side of my face a few times, lost in thought.

Kainda makes up my mind for me. She answers in her blunt
way, delivering the truth like a missile. "You're Hope."

Mira scrunches up her face. "Actually, I'm Mira."

I sigh. "That's not what she meant."

"Then what did she mean?"

"You're..." I wander away, crossing my arms as I remember
those years spent underground, in hiding, with nothing but a
Polaroid photo of Mira and me for company. "You're *my* hope."

She looks even more flabbergasted when I turn around. "You
might want to sit down, this is going to take a while."

I start at the beginning. My birth. I tell her about her mother
and the words she spoke to me at my birth, "You are a precious
boy." I do my best to summarize our trip, my kidnapping,
breaking and transformation into Ull. I'm not sure she's buying it
all, but there are tears in her eyes. Even Kainda looks sullen and I
realize she hasn't heard me tell the whole story, starting from my
birth and moving forward.

When I get to the final test I faced as Ull and reveal that I
was the person who took her mother all those years ago, the tears

disappear. But when I quickly relate what happened next, how her mother saved me and how we've been allied since, the tears return.

"You were just a kid," she says, after I tell how I swallowed the physical body of Nephil, escaped from Asgard and killed the Nephilim, Ull, son of Thor—my master. "That you survived at all is a miracle."

I've always been too busy feeling guilty about my failures to consider that most people would have died. I was strong without ever knowing it. But part of that strength came from the memory of the woman now sitting across from me.

I relate the rest of the story, trying to focus on major events, but I find myself talking for almost an hour. By the time I'm done, she's heard it all. The photo. Tartarus. The Titans. Cronus. Hades. Kainda, Em, Luca and Xin. Everything. Including the angel's proclamation about faith, passion, focus and hope, and my subsequent revelation that those qualities were, in fact, people—Em, Kainda, Kat and now, Mira.

To finish things off, I retell the story of her rescue and how we ended up in a cavern several hundred feet below ground.

After hearing all of this, most of which I fully admit is ridiculous to say the least, her response is to lean back on her hands and says, "Huh," like I just told her the Red Sox traded Wade Boggs.

I assume she's just trying to digest everything I've told her, or maybe trying to figure out if I'm nuts and whether or not she should make a run for it. After several minutes of silence she says, "Let me see if I've got this straight. You were kidnapped, turned into a hunter—" she points at Kainda, "by her father, Ninnis, took my mother, caused the crustal displacement event that killed billions, all because the Nephilim want you to be the vessel for the spirit of Nephil, aka Ophion, their leader. And now you're leading a group of rebel hunters, the U.S. military and a pack of Crylos against them in an attempt to save humanity as we know it. Oh, and you have powers because you're supernaturally bonded to the continent. That about sum it up?"

I look at Kainda, then back to Mira. "Yeah, actually, I think you've got a handle on the situation. But...you're okay with it? You believe it? All of it?"

"I've seen the Nephilim with my own eyes. And the dinosaurs, though I have a hard time believing they've turned nice, and I even kind of remember your seal buddies saving me. But..." She shakes her head. "My father sees patterns. He's grown blunter about it since you knew him. Calls it the fingerprint of God. I normally think he's nuts, but everything you're saying... I don't see any other way around it, especially given the fact that I'm here at all."

"Why's that?" I ask.

"When the crust shifted, I was at home."

"In Portsmouth," I say.

She nods. "I watched as the water slipped out of the bay.

I cringe inwardly, knowing what will happen next.

"And I watched it return. The wall of water slid through the city. It killed everyone, including my friends. And then, it rolled up the hill."

"Prospect Hill," I say. "Two hundred feet tall."

"The water rose to the foundation of my house. It took my neighbors, and nearly took me. I was knocked unconscious, but I survived. And when I woke up, the world was frozen. The house was no longer at the top of the hill, it was the only building still standing on a plain of ice that stretched to the horizon. I survived in the basement for months before heading south, where Wright, Kat and Cruz found me in a church. The point is, I was the only survivor in New Hampshire. The only survivor. And somehow I ended up here, with you, and am now told that I'm one of four women you need to save the world. What are the odds of that happening by chance?"

"Probably zero," I say. It's something I've had to come to terms with, too.

"It's crazy. Borderline stupid. Hell, I spent the last few weeks arguing against the idea with my father. But now, after everything I've seen, and what you've told me, I'm pretty sure I'm supposed to be here. Just like you are." She looks at Kainda. "And you are." She shrugs. "I don't know about you two, but *that* is what gives me hope."

Kainda chuckles and says, "Adoel was right about this one."

I smile so wide it hurts.

Hope has arrived.

8

Now that the three of us are a little better acquainted, Kainda lets
her guard down a bit. She had been pacing during the retelling of
my story, arms crossed and brow furrowed, but she looks more at
ease now, as relaxed as she allows herself to get while in hostile
territory, at least. She sits on the cavern floor next to me,
unclipping her battle hammer and laying it beside her.

I'm sure she still feels threatened by Mira, so I put my hand
atop hers and lace our fingers together. Mira sees the gesture and
frowns.

The part of me that is an average young man wonders if
Mira is actually interested in me still, after all these years. *Things
like that happen*, I think. The idea makes me nervous and
uncomfortable, and I'm a little surprised that I hope that is not
the case. Without meaning to, Mira became a central figure in
my life, but the part of me that bumped feet with her, clung to
that photo and checked off a box in the note she left behind has
grown up.

"I was married," she says, and all of my worry melts away.

"Mirabelle Whitney," I say.

"Did my father tell you?" she asks.

"Remember when you took the boat down the river?" I ask. "From the citadel? Before you killed Enki?"

She nods.

"We were in the trees. On our way to help. You passed just beneath us and I overhead someone call you Whitney. Just put two and two together. Is he..."

"Alive?" she finishes for me. "No. But don't worry, he wasn't, you know...it wasn't the crustal displacement. He was shot, by a robber who wanted my watch. Just over a year ago, actually. Tried to defend me. It was a stupid thing to do."

"What was his name?" Kainda asks.

"Sam." Mira's head dips toward the floor. "His name was Sam. Well, Samuel, but I never called him that."

I'm more than a little surprised when Kainda lets go of my hand and puts two of her fingers under Mira's chin. The touch is gentle and caring in a way that was never modeled for Kainda, so this is all her. She lifts Mira's face so they're looking eye-to-eye. "If he died defending you, and you believe you were meant to be here, then it was not a stupid thing to do. It was brave. That's how you should remember him."

Mira sniffs back some tears and gives a nod. "Maybe, except that he was more like Sol when we first met. Kind of a nerd. Clumsy. Never really stood a chance." She looks at me. "But that's not exactly true either, because look at you now. You're like Tarzan or Ka-Zar, or something."

We smile together.

"Seriously, do you swing from vines?" she asks with a sniff, signifying the conversation about her past has come to a close.

I chuckle and say, "I can sort of fly, remember? Don't really need the vines. But I probably could."

Kainda is once again lost by the pop culture references and looks resigned to wait for the shifting conversation to end. But then Mira pulls her back in. "Can I see that?" Mira points to the hammer lying beside Kainda.

"My hammer?" Kainda asks. I'm not sure she's ever let anyone hold her hammer. Not even me. Not that I've asked, but I think I've always assumed it would be a bad idea. They seem kind of attached.

"Yeah," Mira says. "Looks intense."

"Intense," Kainda says slowly, thinking on the word. "It has tasted the blood of human, Nephilim, crylophosaurs and countless other denizens of the underworld. 'Intense' is a good word." She lifts the hammer as though it weighs little more than a dead branch, and holds it out to Mira.

As soon as Mira has the handle, Kainda lets go and the hammer yanks Mira's arm down. The stone head clunks against the cave floor. Mira laughs and takes the handle with two hands, grunting as she lifts it up. "Holy damn, woman. You're strong."

Kainda beams with pride. Maybe its that the legendary "girl in the photo" is giving her such high praise, or that she could clearly take Mira in a fight, I don't know, but she's enjoying the moment.

But then Mira goes and steers the conversation into a telephone pole. "This looks like Mjölnir, but smaller."

Kainda and I both stare at her, unmoving.

"Mjölnir," she says again. "You know, Thor's hammer. You'd think you two would know this since..."

I can see her mind working. She's figuring it out.

"Since what?" Kainda asks, her face grim.

"You knew him?" Mira asks. "The real Thor, I mean?"

"Yes," Kainda says, taking the hammer back. She stands, clips the weapon in place and starts walking away.

Mira looks to me for an explanation.

"Hunters are trained to use the preferred weapon of their masters," I say.

It takes a second to sink in, but then Mira's eyes go wide with understanding. "She was Thor's...but..." She stands quickly, shouting, "Kainda, wait!"

I know for a fact that chasing Kainda down when she's just stormed away to be on her own is a bad idea. I jump up and head off after Mira, but she's running now and has a good lead.

Also, Kainda has stopped walking. She turns and faces Mira with a look that could make a Nephilim warrior squeal in fright. She's about to say something, but Mira beats her to the punch— luckily, not an actual punch.

"You must have just missed it," Mira says, oblivious to Kainda's dark mood. "Back on the river, when we escaped in the boat, Thor was one of the Nephilim chasing us."

"Then you are truly lucky to be alive," Kainda says and starts to turn away.

Mira puts her hand on Kainda's arm, stopping her.

"Mira," I whisper, but before I can finish my warning, Mira finishes her story.

"Kainda," she says. "We ran Thor over in the boat. The water washed right over him. He drowned."

Kainda whips around toward Mira. "Drowned?"

Mira nods. "Thor is dead."

I have seen the transformation a hunter goes through upon learning his or her master has died. It's like an invisible bond is severed and all the tension and hatred created by the connection is released. I saw it with Tobias, Em's foster father, when he learned that I killed Ull, his former master. But his reaction is mild in comparison to what Kainda experiences.

Her hammer slips from her hand and lands with a thud. She falls to her knees beside it, arms shaking. She looks up at her quaking hands for a moment, clenching them tightly, probably frightened by the intensity of her own emotions. Then a sob escapes her lips and I'm by her side, on my knees, wrapping my arms around her.

Kainda's powerful body wilts under my touch. Her muscles go slack. Her back shakes with each sob and tears, bona fide tears—from *Kainda*—drip onto the cave floor.

I have no idea what to say. Or even if I should say anything. Kainda is more of an actions-speak-louder-than-words type, so I decide to stay quiet. My presence and physical contact are enough.

When I open my eyes and lift my head, I surprised to find Mira kneeling down on Kainda's other side, one hand around her lower back, the other holding their heads together like they've known each other their whole lives. I can hear Mira whispering. She speaks about pain and loss, strength and courage, and about love. I only catch bits and pieces, but I hear my name in there a few times.

When Mira pulls away, all of the tension is gone from Kainda's body. She's no longer shaking and her strength has returned. She sits up, takes a breath and looks at me. Nothing physical has changed, but she looks different somehow. Not exactly a softness, but something...wonderful. While the Jericho shofar freed her from the Nephilim corruption, some part of her must have still been bound to her former master, maybe not physically or supernaturally, but mentally. Perhaps she feared facing him someday. Who knows what tortures he performed on her. Or maybe she feared realigning with him if he commanded it. Whatever the case, that part of her is gone. She is really and truly free.

She takes my hand and gives it a squeeze. Then she's on her feet, clipping her hammer to her belt and acting as if nothing at all happened.

Message received, I think, *don't talk about it.*

I'm pretty sure Mira picked up on the cue, too, because she moves on to a new topic without missing a beat. "So what's next? We need to get to the FOB, right?"

"Yeah," I say. "Your parents will be happy to see you."

Mira gets a concerned look on her face. "Have...you heard about your parents?"

Fear grips my chest. Adoel didn't want me to know, one way or the other, about my parents, but that was right before I was to face Ophion in battle. Maybe it would be alright to know now? But I already know, don't I? If what Mira described about the crustal displacement event is accurate, and I believe it is, then the coast of Maine where my parents lived wouldn't have fared any better than New Hampshire. "They're dead, right? They must be."

"Actually," Mira says. "I have no idea. But...they moved to New Mexico a few years back. From what I understand, the climate is pretty nice there now."

"Oh," I say. "That's...good to know." Once again, Hope delivers. And that's where I'm going to leave it. No more wondering, speculation or worry. If I dwell on the fate of my parents, I'll never be able to focus on what needs to be done next. "We should get going. The FOB is three days from here and we have no idea how long it will be before—

The floor shakes beneath my feet.

I stop and listen.

The shaking returns, this time with an audible rumble.

"Maybe this is a dumb question," Mira says, "But what is that?"

I look at Kainda and see my fears reflected in her eyes.

I sigh.

"Footsteps."

9

"You said we were hundreds of feet underground." Mira glances around the dull blue cavern. I can see a good distance in far less light than this, but she probably can't see more than fifty feet, which is probably disconcerting. "Is something down here with us?"

"Actually," I say, "it's above us, and I'm pretty sure it's still a ways off. Hold on."

I close my eyes and focus on the stone around me. A shiver runs through my body as I allow myself to feel the Earth itself. Strata of stone, veins of water and shifting air. Then a footstep. I feel the compression. Massive. Water is squeezed down through the ground. The air in the cavern shifts. The weight is immense.

As I expand my senses, I hear Mira speaking to Kainda.

"What is he doing?" Mira asks.

"I'm not really sure. He can...feel the land."

"Can he see through it?"

"If the land had eyes, maybe," Kainda says. "It's like the Earth becomes an extension of his body. He experiences the changes on Antarktos the way we might on our skin or in our bodies."

Listening to Kainda's surprisingly accurate description of what I'm doing, I start to lose focus and drift back to the cavern, but not before feeling the thunderous impact of a hundred thousand more feet.

"So that's how he's able to control the elements?" Mira asks. "Because he's part of them?"

"Something like that," Kainda says.

I return to my body with a gasp, shifting the women's attention immediately to me.

"What is it?" Kainda asks.

"I'm not sure," I say. "But I think it's an army. I couldn't tell how many, but some..." I shake my head, trying to comprehend the weight I felt compressing the layers of Earth. "They're so big."

As though punctuating what I've said, the ground shakes. A rumble rolls past, and I suspect the distant sound is reaching us thanks to the cool underground air—which I can't feel, but I know the ambient temperature is somewhere around fifty-five degrees—and the acoustics of the solid stone surroundings.

When the rumble fades, Mira asks, "How far away are they?"

"Ten miles to the East," I reply. "Give or take a mile. Feeling through the continent isn't exactly a science."

"Ten miles, and we're *feeling* their footsteps?" Mira looks mortified, but then she wipes the fear away and replaces it with determination. "Do I need to guess where they're headed?"

I shake my head, no. "The FOB. We might have a week, tops."

"We need to take a look," Mira says.

This catches me off guard. "What?"

"Recon," Mira says. "You know, 'know your enemy.' It's what Wright would do. If we know what's coming, we'll be better prepared for it."

She's right, it is what Wright would say, but I would still argue. "Yeah, but if we take the time to look, we won't reach the base with much time to prepare anything."

"I agree," Kainda says.

I nod. "Thanks."

Kainda raises and eyebrow at me. "Not with you. Reaching the others a few days sooner will not change anything."

"It will give them hope," I counter, though I'm not just talking about Mira. Strangely, I'm referring to the effect my presence will have.

"It does not matter when hope arrives," Kainda argues. "Only that it does in time. Emilie and Kat will have our forces as prepared as they can be."

When I still look unsure, Kainda says, "Perhaps that is why Emilie is called Faith."

It is really hard to argue my point when Kainda is invoking the wisdom of an angel, but even harder when she is acting so differently. Mira's news about Thor's demise has truly given Kainda hope. She's been transformed by it.

I relent with a nod. "Fine. But we're going to have to move fast." I turn to Mira. "Can you keep up?"

Mira crosses her arms. "In case you missed it, I ran a race to the geographic pole of Antarctica."

It's true. She did. Which is impressive, and she's obviously in good shape. Despite everything she's been through—the race, the battles with Nephilim, killing Enki and being taken by the shifter, and then the gnarly band of mythological creatures. She's holding up better than I would have guessed. She was always tough, but it's never easy to tell who can stare down a Nephilim warrior and who can't. Despite all that, she's not a hunter, and I need to be honest.

"This will be harder," I say.

Perhaps thinking I'm just bragging, Mira looks to Kainda, who confirms my statement with a nod and the words, "Hunters are weapons, forged in darkness and agony, and are trained to endure pain beyond imagining. Running for days is a simple thing compared to the tortures endured by most of us." She glances at me. "Some more than others."

Mira has blanched a bit.

"But don't worry," Kainda says, "We understand the softness of outsiders and have learned what it means to be merciful."

This doesn't exactly put Mira at ease, so I translate. "Which is to say, we won't leave you behind. But, you're going to have to push yourself."

The weight of everything Mira has learned in the last hour, including Kainda's intimidating speech about hunters is no doubt weighing on her, along with the fact that this enemy force is bearing down on the FOB, where her parents are currently located. I'm impressed when I see her set her jaw, straighten her back and declare, "Then I'll push."

"I have no doubt," I say, and reach a hand up toward the ceiling. Five of the blue crystals dislodge and fall before being caught by the air. They swirl around in a circle, joining together one at a time until they've been forged into a baseball-sized crystal that's putting off enough light to see by. When the glowing orb lowers in front of Mira's stunned face, she smiles.

"Hearing about what you can do is one thing, seeing it..." She shakes her head. "It's still hard to believe." She reaches through the column of compressed wind holding the sphere aloft and takes hold of it. "What about you two?"

"We can see in the dark," Kainda says.

Mira rolls her eyes. "Of course you can."

"Ready?" I ask of Mira, putting as much seriousness into the single word as I can. A ten mile run through the dark won't be that bad. She's clearly run further. It's what I fear will happen after we've arrived at our destination, and the sprint back to the FOB that concerns me.

"Which way are we headed?" she asks.

I point to the East.

Mira looks to the East, takes a deep breath and starts running.

Kainda looks over at me. "She's brave."

"Yeah," I say. "But sometimes the brave are the first to die."

Kainda's expression sours for a moment, but then she grins, slugs me in the shoulder and says, "Then we're all in a lot of trouble." She sets off after Mira, leaving me alone with my thoughts. But I don't linger, because if I think for too long, I'll have to admit that I already know what we're going to see when we reach our destination.

Only one creature—that I know of—could shake the Earth with such violence.

Behemoth.

10

As we run through the darkness, I realize that my assessment of the Nephilim forces might have been...inadequate. The idea of a behemoth joining the fight had never crossed my mind. Not only because the giant I faced on multiple occasions is now a hollowed out corpse, but I was also under the impression that the remaining two could not be controlled.

It's Nephil, I think. If any Nephilim were powerful enough to control the mammoths of the underworld, it's him. Thankfully, I know that behemoths fear fire, and humans excel at making things burn or explode. If we get back in time, maybe we can have a few jets loaded up and ready to go with napalm.

I nearly laugh at the absurdity of my thoughts. To me it's been five years since Justin and I blew up a toy volcano with baking soda and vinegar and now I'm plotting to use napalm, which burns at 1,200 degrees Celsius and can literally melt people.

Would probably melt Nephilim, too, I think, *ring or no ring on their heads.*

Before my thoughts of war get too dark, I turn my attention forward, reaching out through the Earth as I run. The tunnel through which we have been traveling rises at a slight grade, bringing us roughly fifty feet nearer to the surface with every mile we travel. Having gone eight miles already, we were within thirty feet of the surface. Every giant behemoth footfall shook dust on our heads. But now the land above is growing steep, rising toward a tall rock formation. At first I thought it was a mountain, but now it feels more like a nunatak—a flat sided tower that might have once been a true mountain, or maybe just all that remains of a vast plain after millions of years of erosion and glacier movement. Basically, it looks like Devils Tower in Wyoming, the one from *Close Encounters of the Third Kind*, but wider or longer. One of the two. Of course, Wyoming is pretty close to the North Pole now. Devils Tower might be the only visible landmark for a hundred miles now.

I focus my attention on our path. It's a fairly straight natural passageway that might have been formed by runoff from the tower, or from a natural spring. I follow the path as it bends up, its grade growing steeper until…

What is that?

I stub my toe, stumble forward and fall on my face, all before my senses fully return to my body. With a groan, I roll over onto my back and find Mira standing above me. She's wearing a goofy, one-sided grin. She shakes her head slowly. "Some things never change."

Kainda steps up next to Mira. "What never changes?"

"The first time I met him, he tripped and fell. Smacked his head on the ground. Thought he was going to cry."

Kainda smiles. "He was…smaller before."

I roll my eyes and sit up, pointing a finger at Mira. "I seem to recall you being nicer about it back then."

"Yeah, but you were all small and pathetic," Mira says, which gets a snicker out of Kainda. "Now you're all—" She makes her voice deep and hits her chest with a fist. "—macho and strong. Me Solomon. I ride dinosaurs."

"That's it," I say, focusing on the air around Mira's head. I compress it, and then flare it out, filling every strand of hair with static electricity.

Now Kainda laughs loudly. "She looks like Zuh!"

Mira raises her hands to her head, feeling the pompom of blond hair.

"And this," I say, "is how I remember you."

At first I think she isn't amused, but she smiles, and then laughs. "If only we had a Polaroid. We could take a new photo."

I get to my feet. "Someday we will."

Kainda huffs and pushes past us. "Then he might pine for you again for two years."

Mira looks at me and whispers, "Was that a joke?"

"It's hard to tell sometimes, but I think so, yeah."

"And fix her hair," Kainda calls back. "The enemy will see her coming a mile off."

I quickly pull moisture out of the air and direct it to Mira's hair as a thin mist. She pulls the now damp hair down, but doesn't tie it back.

"I think you broke the elastic," she says.

I reach into my pack where I've got some feeder-leather string that would work, but I feel something soft. When I remember what it is, I take hold of the fabric and pull it out. She kind of flinches when she sees it.

"Is that?"

I hand the blue bandana to her with a grin. "Your father's. I found it on top of a wall. Where I think the two of you escaped from a pack of cresties."

"They nearly got us," she says, confirming the story.

"It's how I knew he was back," I say. "Your father. I didn't know you were here until later."

She smells the bandana. "Smells like Vesuvius."

"Vesuvius?" I'm confused for a moment. The bandana smells like a dog. Then I realize who the dog belongs to. "Of course. Your father's dog!"

"Did you meet him?" she asks. "He's a big Newfoundland."

"I didn't see any dogs at the FOB," I say. "But I wasn't there very long, either."

"Hey!" Kainda shouts from further up the tunnel. She sounds a little annoyed. "You're the one who wanted to rush. So—rush!"

She's right of course. I wait for Mira to tie her hair in place with the bandana, and then we set off up the tunnel, double timing our pace until we rejoin Kainda.

After another mile, the grade increases to the point where even I'm feeling the burn in my thighs.

Mira mutters, "Jane Fonda eat your heart out."

"No kidding, right?" I say.

Kainda doesn't get the reference and even if she did, I doubt she'd find it funny. In fact, when I look up and see her legs—the muscles accentuated by a sheen of sweat—I wonder if she's even fazed by the ascent.

I do a quick reach out with my senses, looking for the aberration that caused me to stumble. It's just a quarter mile ahead. The tunnel, which is fairly straight, suddenly angles and spirals straight up. I start to follow the path upwards, but then Kainda says. "Up ahead. Look."

I stop and peer through the dark, at first not recognizing what I'm seeing, but then the sharp angles leap out at me. "That's unexpected."

"What is it?" Mira asks. "I can't see a thing."

Her orb of blue light allows her to see, but the glow doesn't come close to reaching the end of the tunnel.

"A staircase," I say, then use the momentary pause to follow it upwards, through the mountain. It's just over a thousand feet to the top, probably fifteen hundred steps, but the top...isn't the top. "There's a chamber at the top."

"What's in it?" Mira asks.

I shrug. "I can't sense things at that level of detail. Only broad pictures. There could be anything inside."

"Anything living?" Kainda asks.

"I—I can't tell," I admit. "All the rumbling footsteps outside are making everything kind of hazy. Either way, up is the only way we're going." I head for the staircase and reach it a minute later, pausing at the steps. They're old and worn, hewn right out of the mountain itself. The steps spiral upwards, straight through the core of the nunatak.

It's Mira who makes the observation both Kainda and I have missed. "These stairs were made by people. *For* people."

When the Nephilim build staircases, there are often two sets of stairs, one with four-foot tall steps for the warriors and other large classes, and a smaller set for hunters, gatherers and thinkers. Besides, even without the larger set of stairs, this tunnel was clearly never used by Nephilim. It's far too small. All this and the fact that Kainda doesn't know about this place leads me to conclude, "This was built before the Nephilim controlled the continent. Back before it was frozen over!"

My excitement is crushed when a rumble violently shakes the tunnel.

"We should probably get to the top before they bring down the whole place," Mira says.

With a nod, I lead the way up the staircase, growing dizzy after the first fifty steps, spinning around and around like a human corkscrew. But I don't really pay the dizziness any heed. Or the growing ache in my legs. Or the rising volume of the thunderous footsteps permeating the stone around us. My thoughts are of what we'll find at the top, and who built it.

11

"The rumbling is fading," Mira notes as we near the top of the spiral stairwell. She pauses, placing her hand on the gray stone wall. Its surface is smooth, almost soft to the touch, no doubt as polished as it had been when it was abandoned. "Maybe they've passed?"

I lift my leg and take another step up, which at this point in the climb, feels like a small victory. Steps are supposed to make scaling heights easier, but they really just put all the strain on a few muscles and bones. Had we been scaling a wall, all of my muscles would be sharing the burden. "It's just because we're above them," I say. "The shockwaves are moving down and out, away from the impacts. So the effect isn't as severe if you're above the source of the vibration."

"Thanks for the sciencey, Einstein," Mira says with a touch of sarcasm.

"Thank *you*," I retort, "for making me feel like I'm back in school."

"Please," Mira says, about to launch into some kind of witty diatribe.

"Shut-up," Kainda hisses. "Both of you. I swear you're like a couple of children in need of a few lashes."

My instinct is to look at Mira and share a knowing smile, but the fact that Kainda is likely speaking about the parenting style modeled for her, and which she might actually believe is appropriate, makes me frown. I'd never thought about the possibility of having children some day. And it's still a long way off. But if we survive this war, and really do get married, will she want to raise our children as hunters? Or will their childhoods look more like mine?

A conundrum for the future, I tell myself.

I look up to Kainda, who currently leads our upward charge. "What is it?"

She's just around the bend and no longer climbing. As I follow the curved stairs up, I see the stone just beyond her change from a smooth and steady gray to a column of blocks. One more step reveals an archway.

"We're there," she says.

We gather at the top step, looking into the space beyond, but remain unmoving, like there's an invisible force field preventing us from entering.

The chamber beyond the doorway is vast, with a flat floor and a domed ceiling, all carved right out of the solid stone. Beams of light stream through circular holes punched into the wall every fifteen feet.

"Is that daylight?" Mira asks.

"I think so," I say and finally take a tentative step inside. The floor is as smooth as the walls in the stairwell. It's almost soft under my feet. I scrunch my toes expecting to feel the threads of a rug, but it's all solid stone. As my eyes adjust to the brighter light inside the chamber, I start to see details.

The room is largely empty save for a few pedestals that rise straight out of the floor. I walk to them and count seven. Mira kneels beside one of the protrusions and runs her hand over the top. I look for Kainda and find her walking around the perimeter of the chamber, looking at the walls between the windows.

"It's indented," Mira says. She moves to the next pedestal and touches the top. "They all are." She stands, steps inside the circle and sits atop of the stone towers. "They're seats."

I step inside the circle and sit down across from Mira. She's right. The indentations were worn by human backsides, which means these seat were used for a very long time.

"It's like this was some kind of meeting place," she says. "Maybe for leaders of some kind."

"Or a secretive cult," I add.

Mira frowns at me.

I shrug. "Just saying."

A rumble rises through the nunatak, the stone seat and then my spine, reminding me why we're here. I stand and head for one of the windows. It's round and four feet in diameter. As I get closer, I see that it has been carved through ten feet of stone, at an upwards 45 degree angle. I put my face inside and look up. There's a stone ledge blocking my view of the sky, but its bottom glows with a greenish hue—sunlight reflecting off the green jungle far below.

A breeze flows through the opening. As it washes over my face, I close my eyes and take a deep breath, expecting the sweet scent of a thawed Antarctica. Instead I get a perfume of decay, blood, feces and death—the scent of Nephilim. It's so strong, I feel like I've just licked a warrior's armpit. I reel back from the window, smacking the back of my head against the stone and falling to the floor, stunned.

"You okay?" Mira says, crouching behind me. She sounds more concerned than comical this time around. Probably a result of the disgusted look on my face. She must catch a whiff, too, because she suddenly groans and puts a hand over her nose. "Oh, God. Is that...them?"

I rub my head. "Eau de Nephilim at its finest."

When I look up, I don't see the window. Instead, my eyes focus on the wall between this window and the next. What I see is enough to make me forget all about the stink. "Whoa."

Mira turns to the wall and holds up her glowing crystal, illuminating the scene. The entire wall, ten feet up to where the dome begins and all fifteen feet between the portals, is a collage of images and strange text, similar to those found in Egyptian tombs, but much more simplistic in style. But they're also more complex than what is typically thought of as "cave paintings," which is to say, these aren't the paintings of a lone wandering artist, or even a collection of artists over time—this was a communal effort to create something permanent.

"It's a record," I say, looking at the vivid portrayal of a hunt. Ten warriors dressed in brown and carrying spears are battling a large animal. I point to it. "That's a giant sloth, I think."

The next picture over depicts a celebration. The dancing figures are lit by a bonfire's glow and their shadows are cast on the wall. In Mira's shifting blue light, they almost look real. The effect is really quite spectacular.

"Can you read the text?" Mira asks.

I shift my attention to the lines of text below the art and note that while the art is painted on, the text is carved right into the stone, a far more permanent medium. Whatever the text says was clearly more important to these people, but unfortunately, I can't read a word of it. "I don't recognize the language, but I'm guessing it predates anything we know about."

"Wright once told me about a team of Delta operatives who discovered what they called "the mother tongue," while on a mission. Said it was the language people spoke before the tower of Babel. He didn't believe it, but..."

"Maybe that's what this is," I say. "Anything is possible, I suppose. But the real question is, what were they trying to tell us? What is this a record of?"

"The beginning."

Mira and I both turn to Kainda. She's still on the far side of the room, running her hand over the text and staring up at an image. As we head toward her, I ask, "Can you read the language?"

"I doubt anyone can," Kainda replies. "Not anymore."

"Then how do you know?" I ask.

She steps to the side, allowing me a full view of the image she's been staring at. "Because, you've been there."

I stop in my tracks. "No way."

"What?" Mira asks.

I can't answer. Not yet. The accuracy of this painting is blowing my mind. Every detail is exactly how I remember it. I turn to Kainda, "In all this time, nothing has changed?"

"It would appear so," she says.

I step closer and reach my hand up, placing it on the big tree at the center of the image. I close my eyes and picture myself there again. It was so peaceful. Without pain. Or death. Or any of the horrible things that plague our world. That is, until Nephil found his way there.

"Where is this?" Mira asks, growing impatient.

I pull my hand away, feeling a great sense of longing and loss. "Edinnu."

"Edinnu?" she says. "That's...that's the place you said was Eden, right? Where you met the angel?"

"Adoel," I say with a nod. I point to the grassy hill surrounding the tree. "We stood right here." I turn to the right and see several more of the massive murals. "This is a record of the beginning of human kind. *Before* the Nephilim."

I walk slowly to the right, following the progression of time from Edinnu, to tribal life, villages, farms and eventually war. It's right around that time that the images take on a darker tone, painted in blacks and reds. The style is also different. Evolved. I realize that I've probably just seen the records of a thousand years of humanity's beginning. Maybe more. The artists painting at this point in the massive storybook might not have even known the names of those who came before them. They were just carrying on the tradition, maybe gathering as a group of leaders and artists, sitting in those chairs and deciding what image or collection of images best depicted their generation. Or century.

My stomach twists when the dark images resolve into blatant Nephilim images. Giants can be seen alongside men. Monstrous creations of man and beast, like the mythological creatures we discovered, and a mixture of violent and depraved acts performed by Nephilim and men alike.

With only two fifteen foot sections to go, the style disappears almost completely. The illustration is almost like a Jackson Pollock—smears of red, and black, and purple. I don't miss the significance of the purple, a perfect match to the blood of the Nephilim. Perhaps there was a war, a final rebellion of men against gods. Perhaps it is the time when the Titans and the Nephilim fought for the world. The Titans were driven to Tartarus while the Nephilim claimed the world as their own.

Feeling heavy, I wander toward the final section and leap back when Mira holds her light to it. It's a face. A black and angry face skillfully rendered. Yellow eyes. Double rows of glaring teeth. The whole thing burns with hatred and loathing. While I have never seen him in the flesh, I know this monster.

"Nephil," I say.

"This is him?" Mira asks. "This is the big-wig Nephilim that wants to claim your body, wipe out humanity and live forever as a soulless world dictator?"

"Yes," I say. I'm having a hard time looking at the image. I feel like he can see me through it.

Mira reaches into her cargo pants pocket and steps up to the image. She stands so that I can't see what she's doing, but I think she's drawing. I understand that the image is offensive, but it's also an archeological treasure. "What are you doing?"

Mira holds up her hand for a moment, revealing a small white brick about the size of a soap bar. "Chalk," she says, "In case we had to climb. Never did."

She puts the chalk back in her pants, claps of her hands and leans back to admire her work. "There," she says, smiling widely. She steps back revealing the marred image.

Mira has given Nephil, aka Ophion, the greatest enemy mankind has ever known...a handlebar mustache.

Despite my feelings about defacing this priceless record of ancient man, I smile. And then I laugh. Even Kainda finds it funny. Our laughter grows with each passing moment as the alteration drains our tension.

But the momentary distraction is interrupted by a thunderous boom and a violent quake in the Earth around us.

"They're close," Kainda says. Her hand has instinctually gone to her hammer, despite no one knowing we're here.

I step toward the nearest portal. "It's time to take a look."

The window-tunnel is spacious by underworld standards, so it takes me only a few seconds to reach the top. I squint in the bright daylight as I reach the top of the angled tunnel. Although the sky above is blocked by the ledge five feet over my head, I can now see the more distant sky, and the gleaming, wet jungle below. When my eyes adjust, I quickly see that I'm at least eight hundred feet above the base of a vast, east-to-west valley that's thick with jungle.

And Nephilim.

I look to the right, just before the nunatak rises from the jungle and follow the sea of monsters all the way to the horizon. The ground shakes again, drawing my eyes to the left. My heart sinks. Tears well. My throat tightens.

"What do you see?" Mira asks from below.

The beginning, I think, *of the end.*

12

I have to force myself to not count. Not only would it take a while, but the enemy force below stretches so far that their numbers just blur together into a liquid-like smear across the land. The jungle obscures many of them, but I can see enough to know that this army is hundreds of thousands strong. I see hunters toward the front, slipping through the trees like wraiths. Among them are gatherers and thinkers, perhaps for control, perhaps to take part in the fight. Then there are lesser warriors, greater warriors, and high above it all, the winged upper echelon of Nephilim leadership. All this is expected, but there are some elements below that I hadn't thought possible.

Feeders. A horde of them. The egg shaped monsters with stubby arms and legs, with the teeth of a great white shark, bobble forward, snapping their jaws. Their black, orb eyes seem vacant, but they move with purpose, eager for the fight...or the promised human smorgasbord. I don't see any breeders, the morbidly obese, bird-like monsters that give birth to feeders, but that's to be expected. They can't even walk, let alone fight. That said, given the sheer number of feeders, it's clear that the breeders have done their part to prepare for the fight.

It's hard to tell from this distance, but I think there might even be some classes of Nephilim that I've never seen before. Some are stout and broad shouldered. Others walk on all fours, like silverback apes. I've always understood that there was more to Nephilim society than I sampled in my short time here, but I hadn't considered the idea of there being more classes of lesser Nephilim. Given all the jobs required of any society, I suppose it makes sense.

But all of this is dwarfed by what follows the main force of the army. Behemoth.

Correction.

Two behemoths.

And they're even larger than the one I faced. That creature stood one hundred and fifty feet tall, but these must be twice that height. Their black, bulbous eyes are the size of hills, each emerging from the sides of its head. Behemoths are essentially feeders that are allowed to eat and grow exponentially. They don't die, so their potential for growth is unlimited. Given the size of these two, they might actually be two of the first feeders ever birthed. Their pale gray skin ripples with each step. Their long clumps of red hair reach out, dangling in the air as though held up by strings. Behemoths have feeble arms, much like their smaller feeder counterparts, but the living hair works like tentacles, able to reach out and snag prey. They breathe with mighty gusts— probably where most of the stench is coming from—revealing rows of serrated triangular teeth the size of hang gliders. I have a hard time imagining that these two, who are leaving a flattened forest in their wake, will have any fear of fire. Like their smaller brethren, behemoths can heal, and if these two decided to simply charge the FOB...well, it might be a very short fight.

"What do you see?" Mira repeats a little more fervently.

I turn back to the tunnel. "An army."

"That's it?" She sounds annoyed.

"A *big* army," I say.

She lets out an exasperated huff, and I hear her climbing the tunnel behind me. She squeezes up next to my right side and joins me. "Holy..."

I watch her dark skin turn a few shades lighter before saying, "I know."

Kainda sidles up on my left. She's unfazed by the scene. "What were you expecting?"

"I guess I never really had a clear picture of how many Nephilim there are."

"It's a large continent," Kainda says. "And they've had a lot of time."

She's right about that. In the same few thousand years, the human population has increased by several billions. That there is only a million or so Nephilim actually shows some restraint on their part—that most of them appear to be headed this way, doesn't. They're going for the kill, which again, I should have seen coming. That's what Nephilim do.

"Okay," Mira says, "We've done our recon. Let's get the hell out of here."

"Not yet," Kainda says. She looks like she's counting.

"Are you counting?" I ask.

"The leadership," she says. "Each commander is in charge of ten thousand. So if we count the commanders—"

"We can guesstimate their total number," I say. When Kainda looks confused, I explain without being asked. "It's a made up word. Guess and estimate. Guesstimate."

She closes her eyes and sighs a deep breath. "We face near certain annihilation and you are making up words."

"I didn't make it up, it's...just...forget it." I turn my attention back to the army. A strong breeze carries a scent similar to dead fish rotting in the sun and I stifle a gag. My stomach sours further when I notice the organized march of the Nephilim warriors. I'm not sure why, but militaries always seem more frightening when they're coordinated. "How can we tell the commanders apart from the others."

"Red leathers," she says.

I scan the sky above and the land below. When I've got the number, I swallow and it feels like I've got a stone in my throat. "Done." The word comes out as a whisper. I can't manage much more than that.

"How many?" Mira asks. She sounds afraid to hear the answer, as well she should be.

"There might be a few more that I can't see," I say, which is true, but saying this is more a delaying tactic than anything else, and Kainda will have none of that.

She elbows me in the rib. "*How many?*"

"Eighty-six," I say.

"Eighty six?" Mira says. "There are eight hundred and sixty thousand of those things out there?"

"Probably more," I say. "We can call it an even million and probably be safe."

"Including the two Stay Pufts over there?" She motions to the behemoths.

"If you count them as one each," I say.

"And should I ask how many we have at the FOB?" Mira asks.

"You shouldn't," I say.

"I kind of just did," she says.

"It's been a few days since we were there," I say.

"Solomon," she says, waiting for me to look her in the eyes. "Tell me."

There's no way to avoid telling her the truth, as much as I'd like to. Besides, she's Hope. If anyone can spin the news into something positive, it should be her.

Still, I can't help but try to avoid it one more time. "I didn't exactly count."

"I know the way your brain works," she counters. "You counted whether you tried to or not. So guesstimate."

"Fifteen hundred," I say. My voice is so flat and emotionless I sound like that teacher from *Ferris Bueller's Day Off*. "Maybe two thousand."

She looks ready to pass out. The news is clearly worse than she's expecting. And for a moment, I see hope leave her eyes. This is something I can't stand for.

"But," I say. "We have the Jericho shofar, which reduces Nephilim to quivering lumps. We have modern weapons and heavy artillery. There are Navy ships off the coast. And jets. I'm sure more have arrived since we left to find you, probably from every nation within range."

"There are a *million* of them," she says. "Sure, some of them are human, and some of them are just a little bigger than humans, but they can control people's minds, change shapes, fly and a good number of them are thirty feet tall, again, not counting those two!" She thrusts a finger toward the two approaching behemoths. They're perhaps two miles off to the left, but they're immense, filling up most of the western view. The hunters at the front of the army have entered the jungle where the nunatak begins. It won't be long before they're below us. If we end up behind this army, it could be a problem. We need to leave.

I'm about to say so when Kainda reaches past my face and flicks Mira in the side of the head.

"Oww!" she says. "What was th—"

"They don't have him," Kainda says, nodding to me.

"What?"

"The Nephilim don't have him," Kainda repeats, emphasizing each word. "Which means the very land itself is against them."

I start to smile, but a sudden, jarring impact wipes the smile from my face and sets my head spinning. It comes again, before I can think, striking my forehead. As consciousness fades, my mind registers three things. A hand, dark and caked with mud, my blond hair locked in its grasp, and then a feeling of weightlessness, and wind...everywhere...whipping past my body—

—as I fall.

13

I come to just a second or two later, just in time to see Kainda shove Mira out of the window. As Mira screams, I'm mortified that it was Kainda who knocked me out and threw me, but then she leaps out behind Mira. It's then that I see my attacker as he throws himself from the cliff's edge and plummets down behind Kainda.

Kainda leaped, knowing I could keep us from pancaking on the forest floor below, but this...man—I think he is a man—jumped after Kainda without that knowledge. I quickly decide the man is insane, a theory that is supported by the white froth around his mouth, the wild look in his eyes, and the fact that his mud-coated body is clothed by the smallest of leathers. His hair hangs in long, clumpy tendrils and is coated in mud, but I can see the blood-red sign of his Nephilim corruption here and there.

A gust of wind buffers me and slows my fall, allowing Kainda and Mira to catch up. Mira doesn't stop screaming until I catch her in my arms and say, "You're okay!"

"She threw me!" Mira shouts.

Kainda reaches us, clasping arms with me. "Almost there!" she shouts, warning me of the impending impact with the ground. I'm facing up and can't see the ground, but I can see the man above us, dropping like a bomb. His arms are stretched out toward Mira's back, fingers hooked and tipped with thick yellow nails. His jaws are open wide, revealing teeth filed to sharp points. He's more monster than human.

Kainda looks back over her shoulder and sees the man falling with us. "Let him fall!"

I can't. It's a thought, but Kainda knows I'm thinking it.

"This is war, Solomon!" she shouts.

I...can't!

Whoosh! A strong gust of wind slows our descent and turns us upright. I still haven't looked at the ground, but I feel the tickle of vegetation on the soles of my feet. I lower us down and deposit the now bewildered man ten feet away. We're in a clearing between the jungle and the nunatak's harsh cliff face.

"Weak fool!" Kainda shouts, and her anger catches me off guard. She shoves past me, unclipping her hammer.

"I don't kill humans," I argue, but my voice sounds feeble in comparison, like some part of me knows this is a losing argument. But I don't kill people. That's been my one golden rule. It's why Kainda is still alive, and why her father, Ninnis, who has wronged me in so many ways was able to return fully to himself before Nephil claimed his body. But something about this feels different.

"He is plagued," Kainda says. She takes up a defensive position between the man, who is looking up at the cliff we just fell from, and me. "Check your forehead. Are you bleeding?"

I pat my hand against the skin of my head where the man punched me. No blood. "Nothing."

The man suddenly goes rigid, like his confusion has just worn off. His head cranes toward us with a kind of stutter, like there are gears in his neck. His eyes widen. His mouth opens. He charges, reaching out his hands and loosing a shrill cry. There is no skill in his attack. Only ferocity. This man is not, nor likely has ever been, a hunter.

As Kainda moves to intercept the man, I manage to say, "Don't—" but then it's too late. She sidesteps the man's attack. He turns his head toward her and stumbles as he passes. He looks angry more than confused, or frightened. I look for some sign of humanity in his eyes. I find nothing. And then, Kainda's hammer connects with the back of the man's skull and a loud crack punctuates the end of his life. As he falls to the ground, I note that his eyes don't change. When people die, or even when animals die, you can see the life fade from their bodies, as though the soul seeps out from the eyes themselves. But not with this man. His soul was already missing. Still, I am not in the business of killing men.

I turn to Kainda, anger filling my voice, "Hey!"

"We are at war, Solomon," she says before I can express my distaste. "People on both sides are going to die. I might die." She points to Mira. "She might die. Billions already have."

"Not when I can save them," I say.

"He was infected. He has no mind of his own. Only madness." Kainda wipes the small amount of blood on the head of her hammer off on the grassy ground. "One bite or scratch from him, and you would be no different. A war ended from a scratch. Is that what you want?"

"I—no..." I'm not sure what to say. Was this man really past saving? Is he really that dangerous? "Who was he?"

"A weapon," Kainda says. "Nothing more. Human once, but no longer."

"How?" I ask.

Kainda is scanning the jungle nervously, wary for danger, which she should be, considering we are now in the path of an approaching army. "They are what a man becomes when he is too weak to become a hunter. They are broken...and stay that way. They are kept in the depths and fed filth and refuse. Their madness becomes contagious."

Before I can ask how she knows all this, she adds, "They are a Norse weapon."

Then it all clicks. The Norse history. The madness. "They're berserkers."

Kainda's forehead crinkles as she turns to me. "You know of them?"

"From human history," I say. Berserkers were Viking warriors that some believe took a drug that put them in a fury, and reduced or removed their sensitivity to pain. They'd keep fighting even while they bled out. This man certainly fit the description, but I have no recollection of the madness being transmittable. That increases the threat exponentially...especially if you're trying to *not* kill them.

"Then you know they are to be feared," Kainda says.

I say nothing. I can't condone killing people. Mind or no mind.

"Solomon," Mira says. She looks a little wind-whipped and startled, but her eyes are serious. "You remember how my husband died?"

"Of course," I say.

"If you were there. If you had the chance to kill the man who shot Sam, and spare me that pain, would you have?"

I stumble back, unprepared for the question. How can I say no to that? Mira's husband. To allow his death, if I had the chance to stop it, even if it meant killing a man...could I do that?

Before I can answer, she takes the question further. She points to the dead berserker. "If that man was about to kill me, would you have taken his life? What about Kainda? Could you let him kill—"

A high-pitched wail rings out, drawing my attention up. A man, as wild and feral as the dead berserker, leaps from a nearby tree branch. He's a second away from careening into Mira. His fingers are flexed. His mouth stands agape. Mira would survive the attack, but not without wounds...which means...

Whipsnap comes free of my belt and I twist the nearest end up, shoving it at the man's chest...impaling him with the Nephilim-forged blade. It sinks past his sternum, slips through his heart and catches on his spine. The man's momentum helps me carry him clear of Mira before I fling him down to the grass, dead, beside his kin.

Question answered.

I look at the man's dead body, motionless, devoid of life. I did that. I killed a man.

Whipsnap falls from my hands, landing in the grass. I follow it, dropping to my knees, which divot the earth along with the tears already dripping from my eyes. I feel two sets of hands on my back, both women offering comfort for what I've done. But I can't accept it. What I did was wrong. It was evil. Corrupt.

My eyes snap open and I see the blurred ground a foot below my bowed head. There is a litmus test for corruption, I realize. At least, there is for hunters here on Antarktos. Through spit and sobs, I make my request.

"What?" Mira asks.

I spit and clear my throat, struggling to control my emotions. "My...hair. My hair! What color is it?"

There's a pause as both women lean back from me.

"It's blond," Mira says. "What other color would it be?"

"Check it all!" I shout.

Hands dig through my hair, searching. As they search, Kainda explains my fear. She no doubt understands it. "Red hair is an outward sign of a hunter's corruption, but if Solomon were paying attention, he would have noticed that my hair is also without blemish." She gives my head a shove. "You're fine."

When I stand up and wipe my eyes, I'm a little too embarrassed to look at Kainda. What guy wants to cry in front of his girlfriend? And I was full on sobbing. Probably not the first time, of course. Despite my breaking, and hardening over the years, I'm still kind of a leaky faucet.

Kainda takes my chin in her hand and turns it toward her. "You're heart is still pure, and I would never ask you to risk darkening it again. We are at war, Solomon. Men will die. On both sides. Some by your hands. It cannot be avoided. And if you run from this responsibility, you will put us all in danger."

Her point finally starts to sink in and I dip my head to nod my agreement. But this revelation is interrupted by a sharp scream. I turn to the sound, and I find another berserker standing at the edge of the forest.

The man repeats the cry.

"What's he doing?" I ask, snatching Whipsnap up off the ground.

When a second voice shouts a reply deeper in the forest, and another more distant scream follows, I understand and answer my own question. "He's calling for help."

The sound of running legs, ragged breathing and frenzied excitement fills the jungle to the west. The berserkers are leading the way for the Nephilim army, clearing the path of anything living that might stand in their way, and making so much noise doing it that they won't go unnoticed for long, especially if there are hunters not far behind them.

We can't fight this.

"Run!" I shout. We break for the jungle, heading east, moving as fast as we can with an army at our heels.

14

Within the first thirty seconds of running, I realize that although Mira can run long distances without any trouble at all, she can't do it at a sprint. Or rather, she can, but she's just not very fast. Granted, she's tired, beat up and overwhelmed, so I should cut her some slack, but the shrieking berserkers not far behind us aren't going to go easy on her. Still, I can't make her run any faster. I turn to Kainda, who is ten feet to my left. "We need to slow down."

"What? Why?" she asks.

I motion back to Mira.

She glances back and sees Mira, twenty feet behind us, which is just about half the distance to the nearest berserker. When I look back, I not only see the closest berserker, but I see the fifteen others behind him, counting their number in a flash. But that's not all of them. I can hear many more as they hoot and scream in bloodlust. I have little doubt the army behind them can hear the din as well.

"She sets the pace," I say. "We'll take care of anyone that gets too close."

"Can you do it?" she asks.

It's a vague question, but I know what she's asking: can I kill?

My reply comes without thought. There is no time for it. "Yes."

She slows and drops back.

Every muscle in my body screams, "faster!" But I slow my sprint, falling back with Kainda.

Mira sees what we're doing and grows angry. "Don't wait for me!"

"Just keep running," I say back to her. "They won't get past us."

I say it with such confidence that it surprises even me. And it's true. A hundred of these wild men wouldn't make it past me and Kainda. They lack the skill and cunning to prove a threat to almost any hunter worthy of the title, but I'm also much more than a hunter. I've killed Nephilim. I've beat Ninnis, the best of the hunters. And I've gone head-to-head with Nephil on more than one occasion. These berserkers shouldn't be a problem.

A sharp pain erupts from my shoulder, spinning me with a shout of pain. I look to my flesh first, worried I've been bitten, but the skin is just red. A shout to my side warns of trouble, and I turn to find a frenzied woman charging in from the side. She reaches back and whips a stone at me. This one sails past.

Just a stone, I think with relief, and then I direct a gust of wind to carry the woman away. She's so stunned by being lifted off the ground that she simply clamps her mouth shut and allows herself to be carried away. I cut the connection and let her fall a moment later. By the time she lands, I can no longer see her...or her fate.

"Uh, guys!" Mira shouts.

I face forward and quickly spot ten more crazed men and woman closing in from the front.

We didn't come down *ahead* of the berserkers, we came down *among* them!

"Kainda!" I shout.

"I see them!"

We close in on either side of Mira.

"Just keep running," I tell her. "Don't stop for anything."

The first of our attackers arrives a moment later, but he's intercepted by Kainda and clubbed to the side. The man is dead on impact, but I cringe as his body slams hard into a tree trunk and then to the ground.

The man who attacks on my side fares little better. I bend Whipsnap back and let the mace end fly. The solid metal ball is covered in spikes, but even without them, the man's head wouldn't have stood up to the blow. I turn away from the man just before his life is ended and see that a third attacker is taking advantage of the opening left by Kainda's assault on the first.

I have no choice. Leaping a full stride ahead of Mira, I pull the mace end free of the berserker's head and thrust the spear tip on the other end into the new attacker's throat. And I see every gory second of it. With a gurgle, the man spins away and slumps into a stand of ferns.

Three more rush at us from the front. Too many to take on without slowing down. I reach out with the wind, scoop them from the ground and launch them skyward. It's a different kind of attack, but I've killed them all the same. They'll land in twenty or so seconds, as dead as the others.

It doesn't seem fair that the moment I come to terms with the idea of killing a human being to save the world...or even another life, I'm forced to perform the act over and over, but these aren't just random men. They're an army. And they're going to kill us, and everyone else in the world, if I hesitate, maybe even once.

So I don't.

We run. And fight. And kill.

Some of the berserkers feel the tip of my blade. Others fall under the crush of my mace. And even more are simply cast away into the trees, or the sky, by the wind. These attacks become so natural that some berserkers are flung away as soon as I see them, the wind acting as a kind of offensive reflex.

While we are making good progress and no doubt distancing ourselves from the marching army, we're also making a racket and leaving the world's most easy to follow trail. I have no doubt that hunters will have found the first bodies by now. But will they give chase like I would expect a hunter to do, or will they call for help? Or worse, will they inform their masters?

When there's no more resistance ahead, I realize we've cleared the front line of berserkers and now only have to worry about attacks from behind. In the momentary reprieve, I reach out to the east. A half mile ahead I find our way out.

"There's a river," I say, pointing to the left. "Just over there. It ends at a waterfall. They won't be able to follow."

No one replies, but we adjust our course toward the river.

A loud hooting draws my attention back for a moment. What I see is totally unexpected despite the fact that I shouldn't be surprised by anything any more. There are at least a hundred berserkers. Probably more. They're charging through the jungle's thick growth without any concern for their well being, oblivious to the thorns tearing at their skin, the sharp stones cutting their feet or the branches lashing their faces. By the time they reach us, they'll be covered in infectious blood. Any contact with just one of them could be serious trouble.

I'm not sure we'll make it to the river in time, so I start brewing a wind above us. The trees hiss loudly, bending from the strength of the power I'm unleashing.

"Careful," Kainda says, glancing up. She knows it's me. "If Nephil sees it..."

She doesn't need to finish the sentence. If I use my powers in a way that's visible to the Nephilim hovering like giant hawks, they'll know I'm here. Right now, they might think the berserkers are having their way with some stray humans, or cresties, or even a flock of turquins. The thick canopy hundreds of feet up, does a nice job of hiding us from the sky, but too much wind will act like a flashing neon sign that reads, "Solomon is here!"

As the wind dies down and the hissing fades, I hear a telltale thwack! An arrow has just been loosed! I focus on the air, sensing its passage, and react without looking. I reach to the side and shove Mira. Her head shifts to the side.

The arrow misses her by inches, but its blade still slices skin as it passes.

Mine.

No one questions why I shoved Mira as the arrow stabs into a tree just ahead of us. We just keep running.

I ignore the sting and focus on the hunter behind us. A gust of wind, small enough to go unnoticed, slams the man from behind and launches him from the tree branch a hundred feet from the ground. He might be a skilled hunter, but there's nothing he can do to arrest his fall. To his credit, he falls in silence, not fearing his death.

As my arm begins to sting, I realize that I've just killed a hunter. It was as quick and easy as killing the berserkers, but I know for a fact that the man could have been redeemed. A single blast from the Jericho shofar would have freed him from his breaking and corruption.

But the shofar is not here. And we must live.

"Almost there," Kainda shouts and I can hear the roar of the river ahead.

"When we get to the edge," I say, "don't stop. Just go over."

We break into the sunlight a moment later and run along the rocky shoreline of a fast moving river. The air is fresh here, cleansed by water welling up from some distant spring. As I step into the water, I can't feel its temperature, but I instantly detect it. I take a deep breath as I sense the foul pollution flowing downstream. The river carries the filth and stink of the army following its path. This whole landscape will be in ruins before the day is done. And a part of me, whatever supernatural aspect of my being that is connected to this land, revolts. It's nearly enough to make me turn around and fight right now, but

Kainda's urging keeps me moving forward, though I have to keep my feet out of the water.

Mist rises up ahead of us. A roar loud enough to drown out a shout announces the presence of a powerful waterfall. Kainda goes off the side first. Then Mira, who leaps without hesitation. I follow last, spinning around as I leap. Taking a last look back.

The horde of berserkers, and several hunters with short range weapons, charge along the river banks, through the river and through the trees above. High above them, I note a few of the Nephilim warriors have descended and are circling the scene. To my knowledge, the Nephilim have eyesight similar to people, so I don't think there is any risk of being identified. That is, until what happens next.

I complete the spin, and call the wind to me. Kainda, Mira and I are carried out and away from the cliff, angling down toward the jungle below as though hang-gliding. Despite our whipping hair, the passage down the two-hundred foot drop to the jungle is smooth, and we are quickly concealed once again.

We pause in the shadows to catch our breath. I look back, craning my head up toward the waterfall, and the unthinkable happens.

The berserkers, lost in frenzy or just uncaring, pour over the side of the cliff. Some are in the water and will land in the river. But others, the majority of them, crash to the ground below, broken by tree limbs or slapping wetly against the large flat stones lining the river. Like lemmings, they keep flowing over the side, dying one on top of the other.

Maybe it's their last bit of free will? I wonder. They've lived in nightmares for so long, maybe now that they have the chance to end their lives, and suffering, they're eager. Or maybe they really just have no minds left. Whatever the case, it sickens my stomach.

Kainda mutters a curse in Sumerian. I turn to her, but she's not watching the river of death. Her gaze is turned higher, to the sky. I follow her eyes and see them. Three winged warriors circle toward the ground, no doubt attracted by the scent of blood and the sight of so many berserkers committing mass suicide.

I take hold of Mira's arm, but before I can speak, she says, "You're bleeding."

I look down at the arm and see a one-inch slice. It's not horrible, but it's not going to heal without attention either. Still, there's no time to worry about that now.

"Doesn't matter," I say. "Remember when I said things were going to get harder? That hasn't really happened yet. But it's going to. We need to run again. Faster this time. Can you do that?"

In response, she runs. Kainda and I follow, glancing at each other to communicate the same unspoken fear: *they're going to find us.*

15

Mira is getting tired. She hasn't slowed down yet, but I can see the signs. She's not raising her arms as high with each step. Her breathing sounds shaky. And she's leaning to one side. It's slight, but I'm willing to bet she's running through a cramp, which isn't easy, even for a hunter. Our pace is not sustainable.

On the bright side, the Nephilim pursuing us from the skies above have yet to find us. The jungle canopy has done a good job at hiding us. They've also split up, widening the search, a fact I learned by sensing the air above. Nephilim warriors, with their thirty-foot tall bulk and giant flapping wings, displace a lot of air. Once I found them, tracking their movements became as easy as feeling someone blowing on the back of my neck.

On the not so bright side, the lone warrior still behind us is dropping down toward the jungle. I don't think he's spotted us, I just think he's tired of trying to see through the endless curtain of green leaves. Either way, once he punches through the canopy, we'll be far more exposed. With most of the direct sunlight blocked in this stretch of jungle, the floor is relatively free of growth. We can run faster, but the tree trunks are our only cover. We could head underground again, but I don't feel any natural tunnel systems heading in the direction we need to go, and using my connection to the continent to create miles of subterranean passages will sap my energy to the point where I might need to be carried.

Unless we can channel our inner ninjas and disappear, this is probably going to end in conflict, which shouldn't be too bad. I can handle a lone warrior. But the scent of his blood, as well as his disappearance into the jungle, might garner further attention. I might normally open up a pocket of earth to hide in, but I'm still feeling spent, and I really don't want to exhaust my abilities, just in case they're needed for something even more urgent later on.

"Behind this tree!" I shout, catching Mira and Kainda off guard. Kainda reacts quickly, diving behind the tree, which is eight foot in radius with rough bark, like its something out of the forest of Endor. Mira stumbles, but I catch her arm and yank her hard to the side.

She shouts in complaint, but I slap my hand over her mouth a second before the canopy a hundred feet behind us explodes. Leaves shake free. Branches shatter. And then, as the Nephilim lands hard, the ground shakes. He's a big one.

Loud sniffing fills the air. Then a booming voice. "I can smell you, humans. Reveal yourselves and your suffering will be short. Exquisite, but short." That last bit is followed by a laugh.

Kainda leans in close, cupping a hand around my ear. "I know his voice," she says. "Ares."

Ares! Great. Of all the Nephilim that had to chase us into the jungle it had to be Ares, the Greek god of war. He's not only known for being ruthless and bloodthirsty, but he's also a very skilled fighter. I'm going to have to make this as unfair a fight as possible.

More sniffing. A branch cracks. He's getting closer.

Running isn't a choice now.

"You smell weak," Ares says, sniffing deeply. "Untainted." He laughs again, like he's just heard a great joke. "You will taste delightful."

Kainda tenses, and I sense she's about to charge the giant. I take her hand and squeeze, mouthing the word, "Wait," to her.

Ares's own personal brand of Nephilim stink, which I note includes the scent of human blood, reaches us. He's not far now, maybe twenty feet from the far side of the tree. *Does he know we're here?*

No, I decide. I can hear him shuffling around, looking in all directions. He smells us for sure, but can't pinpoint our location. To make it harder on him, I shift the natural breeze some, pulling our scents upwind. He grunts with the wind shift, no doubt thinking we've begun to move. When he does, I slide to the side and slowly peek around the tree.

Ares is massive. Perhaps one of the largest Nephilim I've seen, both in height and in muscle tone. He's dressed simply, wearing only a tunic, but its blood red coloration, which matches his ponytailed hair, reveals he is one of the commanders in charge of ten thousand troops. Killing him will help disrupt the Nephilim ranks, though not drastically.

His body is facing me, but he's got his head craned to the side and his nose raised. Despite the simple garb, he is intimidating. He carries a thirty foot long spear in his left hand and a shield in his right. I have never seen a Nephilim use a shield before. They generally prefer to absorb blows with their regenerating bodies. The pain suits them. But perhaps war is different, especially when the enemy—modern humans—have things like anti-tank missiles. Then I see the gleaming, razor-sharp edge of the shield, and I realize it's not just a defensive weapon. But the most dramatic statement is his red crested helmet. At first I think that the hair is either his own, or from a feeder, but then I see it move, as though on its own, and I realize the brazen god of war has decorated his helm with behemoth hair.

I'm so entranced by the thirty foot tall warrior dressed like a Spartan Hoplite, that I forget to pull back when his head swivels forward again. But Kainda is still thinking and pulls me behind the tree.

"Ares is no ordinary warrior," she whispers in my ear. "He is not to be trifled with."

A metallic zing rings out from the other side of the tree. A loud clang and a snap follows. I duck instinctively, but nothing happens for a moment. When I look forward, I see Ares's shield embedded in a tree directly across from us...which means...

I look up at the tree giving us shelter. The line of bark has burst outward.

He threw the shield through—a tree! A sixteen foot wide tree! It hasn't fallen yet because the branches high above are thickly mingled with those of other trees. It will likely stay almost upright for a long time to come, or until the behemoths make their way through.

The exploded bark is just a few feet above us. Had he aimed a little lower, we'd all be dead. Thing is, I don't think he wants to kill us. I think he wants to toy with us first.

Which isn't going to happen. I step out from behind the tree. He sees me, but I don't give him time to react or even recognize me. A compressed column of wind strikes his side and lifts him off the ground. The giant's body slams into a large tree trunk, folding around it backwards. Several loud cracks issue from his spine.

The wind lets up.

His body falls.

And then, he heals. Each vertebrae that cracked pops back into place, one by one. And with each pop, the Nephilim warrior moans in ecstasy, relishing the pain. I really hate that these guys enjoy pain so much. Kind of takes away any pleasure I might get out of beating them up. Then again, his attitude will change when he realizes he's going to die. For the soulless Nephilim, death means nonexistence. A permanent end. It's the one thing they fear.

Kainda rushes in, fueled by bloodlust. But Ares has mostly recovered and never let go of his spear, even while his spine was shattered. He sees her coming and growls, "Betrayer!"

Ares thrusts the spear at Kainda, but she rolls around the sharp tip like a football running back and continues her charge. Ares's massive wings give one big flap and he's carried up onto his feet, bringing his head out of Kainda's range, but I think that's what she expected him to do because she's already diving forward, bringing the her hammer hard against his kneecap. I see the bone swivel to the side, making the leg momentarily useless.

Ares shouts in pain, but he's got a big grin on his face. Pleasure, pain or both, he drops to his knees, while the bone repositions itself.

While he's down there, I direct a gust of wind toward his head. The helmet is knocked free and cast aside, revealing the golden ring protecting the weak spot at the center of his forehead.

The giant's laugh becomes sinister. "The prodigal son." He knows who I am now.

"I'm not sure you fully understand the message of that story," I say, walking toward the giant. Mira lingers behind, staying by the tree, which is a good choice.

Ares spits purple blood. The wad lands near my feet. I stop. No need to put myself at risk for the sake of bravado. "You should have stayed in Tartarus."

He frowns at this. I've actually managed to strike a nerve. "We all have to live with our choices," he says, then he glances at my arm. "How are you feeling, Ull?"

I glance down at the arm. The wound looks the same. I ignore the question, and focus on the earth around Ares's legs, willing it to rise up and lock him down. But he's quick and leaps back into the air before I can catch him. For a moment, I think he's going to flee and get help, which would be a serious problem, but this is a Nephilim warrior. He's proud, like a hunter. He won't ask for help, he'll—

"Solomon, watch out!" Kainda shouts.

The tip of Ares's spear resolves in my vision. I drop down and feel the blade pass over my head. A blond tuft of cut hair tickles my back as it falls. The spear slams into the tree, just feet away from Mira who had already leapt to the side.

But how did I not see the spear coming?

How was I not aware he was going to attack?

He couldn't have been moving too fast. Both Kainda and Mira reacted before I did. *It's me*, I think. *My perceptions are slow.*

To punctuate the realization, Ares swoops down, lands in front of me and backhands me. I slide across the jungle floor, cushioned by leaf litter and mud. Had I struck a tree, like Ares did, I'd be dead. Of course, I'm now in so much pain that death might have been a mercy.

I fight against the pain and get to my feet, happy to find everything working and no bones broken. As Ares stalks toward me, Kainda throws her hammer at his head, but the weapon just clangs against the metal ring and falls to the ground. The ring should have come free.

Ares laughs, and my anger surges. I leap into the air, carrying myself up with the wind and tug Whipsnap from my belt. I arc up above the warrior and as I drop down, a focused burst of air strikes the metal ring from below. The plan was to remove the ring and plunge the spear tip into Ares's head, but the ring does not come off. Instead, it simply moves a little. But in that motion, I catch a glimpse of what's happening.

The metal rings worn by Nephilim warriors typically rest on the head, like a metal headband. It's goofy looking, like the headbands worn by some basketball players, but it protects them.

That is, unless you knock it off, which isn't too hard to do if you know what you're doing. But this metal band is held in place by four spikes that have been *driven into Ares's head.* It's not coming off.

A second gust of wind carries me up and over the warrior. As I pass by, his scorpion tail, which was concealed by a long red cape, lashes out and nearly strikes my chest. But I don't see it until it's already retracting for another strike. I survived by dumb luck alone.

What is wrong with me?

I land beside Kainda and stumble.

"Are you all right?" she asks.

"The crown is nailed to his head," I say. "I can't get it off."

"Then you'll have to remove it," she says.

"I just said—"

"Not the crown," she says. "His head."

My eyes widen. How am I going to do that? Whipsnap's blade isn't nearly long enough to do the job. Sure, if Ares laid down and patiently waited, I might be able to hack through his neck, but he's going to heal just as fast as I can swing.

A wave of dizziness swirls through my body. I grunt and stagger.

"Damnit, Solomon," Kainda growls and then leaves my side. When I look up, I see her charging out to meet Ares, who is headed toward us. She dodges two blows and manages a strike against his shin, but he merely kicks her away. I reach out with the wind, catching her before she strikes a tree. Nausea tears through my body as I lower Kainda to the ground.

When she's safe, I fall to my knees and vomit. Hard.

"Feeling ill?" Ares says, stomping closer.

I know he doesn't want to kill me. Nephil will want me alive. I am his vessel, after all. But that's a fate worse than death.

"Shut. Up!" I scream, my voice more of a roar. I'm filled with a rage so intense that I wonder if my Ull personality has once again taken over.

Ares chuckles. "Feeling...angry?"

I grind my teeth, seething with raw hatred. Just as I'm about to leap up and launch myself at Ares, I see the wound on my arm again. It's pink around the edges. Hot. Raw. The arrow wasn't poisoned...it was laced with blood.

Infected blood.

I'm becoming a berserker.

16

No time, I think. Ares is about to knock me silly and I don't think it matters to Nephil whether or not I'm a berserker. He might actually enjoy the rage added to his own. I have to end this threat, fast, and then worry about what's happening to my body. Right now, my rage is certainly growing, but I'm still me. Still in control.

The trees behind me whoosh as the wind rushes toward the back of my head. It rushes past, bending the trees all around, and strikes Ares head on. The giant stands his ground. He can't move forward, but he's also still standing, which was not part of the plan.

Instead of a tightly compressed surge of air, I summoned a broad, sweeping wind, like a tornado. Knowing the swaying trees might attract attention, I stop the attack.

Ares steps toward me. "Give into the madness. The change will be less painful and a part of your mind will remain, for a time."

All I can do is look at the ground. Stabs of burning pain move up my arm, spreading out into my chest.

Ares kneels in front of me, places an index finger on my chest and flicks it out. I sprawl backwards, unable to stop even this simple, humiliating assault. I see layers of green shifting high in the canopy, some glowing almost yellow under the direct gaze of the sun.

"In minutes, the rage will consume you," Ares says. "Then darkness. And when you awake, you will be one of *my* creations."

I let out a groan at the realization that Ares is not only the berserker commander, but also the source of the plague that turns men into mindless monsters beyond redemption.

I've amused him again. "I expected more from you, Ull. But I see now that the growing legend of the boy hunter is...exaggerated. You are weak. A pitiful thing." He laughs. "You are without hope."

As I look up my nose at the giant leaning over me, I see a flash of blond hair covered by blue. Ares rears up, shouting in pain-fueled joy. When he stands, I see a slash across his knee. Then it's gone. I turn my head, following the blur of motion.

Mira.

No...

She's not fast enough.

Ares reaches out for her. If he catches her, all he'd need to do is squeeze. She has faced Nephilim in the past. She even killed Enki. But she has no grenades, and I don't think Ares will bother having a conversation with someone he doesn't need to keep alive.

No!

His fingers are just inches from her back.

"No!" I scream, thrusting my hands out, generating a burst of wind as though it came from my body itself. There's an explosion of purple on Ares's chest, then a circle of light.

I stare up at it for a moment, unsure of what I'm seeing.

Then the image resolves.

Trees.

I'm seeing *trees* in Ares's chest?

Not *in* his chest, *through* his chest! I punched a hole straight through him, using just the wind.

Fueled by rising anger, fear for Mira's safety and the fact that I've just formed an invisible force into a horrible weapon, I stand to shaky legs.

Ares stumbles back. Despite enjoying pain, he must be experiencing so much of it right now that he doesn't know what to do with himself. He's like a kid with a cake to himself who knows, at some level, too much of it is bad for him. He puts his fingers on the wound and looks down. It's already closing, healing the meat and bones that had been torn away, but he's still afforded a clear view of the forest behind him.

He looks up at me, and then to his spear, still embedded in the tree. He runs for it.

I let him, picking up Whipsnap as he runs. With a tug, Ares removes his spear from the tree, turns around and throws it at me. I can feel the spear moving through the air. I can detect its molecules and its origins. The metal, was dug from the Antarctic earth and the shaft taken from a long dead tree that grew in Antarctic soil. My earth. My tree.

With an anger-fueled thought, the spear disintegrates just before striking my chest. It falls to the ground as dust.

As I step toward the Nephilim, a wind swirls around me, bid by my emotions rather than by my will. My hair flails in the air around my head, like living gorgon snakes. A darkness settles inside me and I grin.

Ares sees my cocky smile and balks at the challenge. Then, with an anger matching my own, he roars and charges. He could crush me underfoot. He could bite my head off, or sever me at the midsection with a swipe of his fingernails. He could sting me with that Titan tail or simply thrash me about.

But he'd have to get close to do any of those things. That's not going to happen.

I lift him off the ground and then return him to it with enough force to shake the it. Before he can recover, grunt or enjoy the pain, I fling him against a tree.

Hearing the monster's bones break fuels my own dark rage, and I let out a battle cry of my own. As Ares recovers from his wounds at the base of the tree, I rush in and leap into the air.

He sees me coming and raises an arm in defense. His intent is clear, to take the blow on his forearm and then attack with his uninjured arm. But I have no intention of striking him with Whipsnap. The weapon serves only as a catalyst for my attack. I raise Whipsnap over my head and swing the blade edge down.

I've read about windstorms so strong and intense that people had limbs torn away, or skin scoured off, but for some reason, I've never thought to use the air as anything but a blunt object. Condensing it to the point where it becomes sharp...I'm not sure

I would have come up with that without this berserker blood boiling my insides.

An invisible blade of wind cuts through the air with a sound that reminds me of those 1970's Kung Fu movies and ends with a wet slurp. I have struck Ares's arm right where he intended me to, but the blow is far more powerful than either of us thought possible. Part of the giant's arm and his hand fall to the ground.

I land and watch Ares react. The limb rolls twice, stopping between us. He looks at it with a level of confusion that I find funny. The laugh that escapes my lips sounds a lot like Ares's laugh, only not as deep or resonating. The part of the arm still attached to his body begins to regenerate, but so much is missing, it's going to take some time.

"My legend," I say, but the words sound jumbled, like I actually said, "Muaye leoganada." That I can't seem to speak right sends a wave of frustration through my body. It's all the catalyst I need. With a hate-fueled shriek I slash Whipsnap at an angle, left to right and then right to left, carving a deep X in Ares's chest. It's unnecessary. Some part of my mind recognizes this. But I don't care.

I want him to know pain.

To feel fear.

To beg for his life.

I want to delight in his anguish.

A strand of hair blows across my eyes. It's just for a second, but I see it clearly. It's hard to miss.

Because it's red.

Blood red.

I let out a scream so horrible and loud that my throat stings and becomes hoarse before the air in my lungs is extinguished. When Ares proves that we now share the same dark heart by laughing at my pain, I spin around, strike through the air with Whipsnap and send a razor thin streak of air through his neck.

His head comes off his body with a fountain of purple blood and rolls to the ground. The monster is dead. For good.

But I am lost.

I stagger back as the weakness claiming my body resurfaces. I mumble incoherently, only vaguely aware of Mira's and Kainda's voices. My foot catches on something and I fall back. But I never feel the landing. I simply slip away into the darkness promised by Ares.

17

I awake as something hard pounds into my gut, pushing the air out of my lungs. I wheeze, trying to catch a breath, but the impacts keep coming. It's less severe, but it prevents me from catching a real breath.

I hear shouting. The voices are indistinct. The words warped as though shouted through a tin can. But the tone— hurried and desperate—reaches my ears. I try to move in response to the sound, but I'm unable. Am I too weak or am I restrained?

I open my eyes for a look, but my vision is blurry. Everything is distorted and moving, racing past like trees outside a car window.

Another jarring impact rattles my body. When I clench my eyes shut, spots of light explode onto the backs of my eyelids.

Then darkness again.

****

The car ride is bumpy. Dad tells mom that it's normal, but I know it's the suspension. I think mom does too, but she's just humoring him. I warned him about the problem a few weeks ago, but he didn't believe me. I'm only eight, after all. I'm not even sure if he remembers dismissing me with a chuckle, but I do.

I don't mind feeling every bump in the road. I don't get car sick or anything. But it frustrates me sometimes, when I'm imagining Superman is running beside the car, jumping over signs and trees, or cutting through them with his heat vision. A solid bump can throw me off and my imagination, which is happy to follow its own course, will envision Superman tripping or falling in a heap. It's embarrassing.

To make matters worse, it's early Spring. In Maine. This means the roads have not yet been repaired after being scoured by snowplows all winter. Potholes abound, and if steering a car into every single hole in the road were a sport, my father would be the champion.

To prove the point, we strike a pothole so deep that the impact sends a vibration through the car strong enough to yank me completely out of my imagination.

"Dad," I say, annoyed.

"What?" he says with a shrug. "I didn't see it."

"Mark, it must have been the size of Lake Ontario," my mother says. She sounds annoyed, too, but the way she slaps his shoulder says she's not. I think she finds his inability to spot giant holes in the ground amusing. Or cute. Which is just...yuck.

A moment later, I say. "Better pull over."

"Why?" my father asks. "You have to pee? We're almost there."

My mother turns back to me. "You can hold it for ten more minutes."

I sigh. "I don't have to pee." I nod my head toward the front left tire. "We're losing air pressure."

The slight dip is still subtle, but they'll feel it in a moment.

"Schwartz," my father says like he's about to teach me something. But the *whupwhupwhup* of the now flattening tire and shimmying front end silences him.

We pull over to the side of the road. My father gets out and inspects the tire. As he does, I slide over and reach for the door.

"Sol," my mom says in that tone that says, "Don't."

My reply is raised eyebrows and a stare leveled at my mother. I've always found it fascinating how much information can be communicated through body language and facial expressions. We have a silent argument in the course of three seconds, at the end of which she says, "Ugh, fine. Go."

I open the door and slide out. I pause for a moment, enjoying the warm air—some of the first I've felt in five months. Red buds coat the trees lining the roads. The first strands of green grass are beginning to poke up through the brown. And in a week or so, the lilies in our front yard will push up through the earth and turn skyward. It's my favorite time of year.

I close the door and find my father crouching down by the side of the olive green sedan, inspecting the tire like he's an archeologist who's just discovered the Rosetta Stone.

"You have no idea how to change a tire, do you?" I ask.

He looks over at me slowly. I can tell he's trying to think of something to say. Maybe an excuse. Or a joke. But he gives up and says, "I've never had to before."

"The spare is in the trunk. The jack is on the left side."

He looks at me dubiously. "You've changed a tire before, have you?"

"I read the car manual," I say.

He smiles wide, stands, puts his hand on my head and shakes my hair so blond strands are hanging in my eyes. "You're my hero, Sol."

"Whatever," I say, moving for the trunk.

He takes my shoulders and turns me around. Leaning down so we're face to face, he says, "Seriously, Schwartz, the way your mind works. It's a gift. Wouldn't surprise me at all if you saved the world someday."

I wake again, this time lying on my back. I'm no longer moving, and I can breathe, though I'm quite sore. But my vision feels off, and it's dark. I try to sit up, but can't. And it's not from weakness. I can feel the tightness around my arms and legs. I've been restrained.

A surge of fear races through my mind. Have I been captured? Are Mira and Kainda still hurt? Or dead?

A shiver rolls up through my body, leaving a sickening tension in its wake. When it reaches my head, an all consuming rage flares out, burning my thoughts away and turning my emotions into a howl that explodes from my mouth. But I've been gagged, and the sound is muffled.

My teeth grind at the fabric in my mouth, but before I can chew through it, a canteen of water is emptied onto my face, making me gag and sputter.

A woman looms over me. "Shut up!"

I clench my fingers, reaching for her, intending to tear her apart.

"Hey!" she says, sounding offending. She leans closer and slaps me across the face. The impact is dizzying. "Look at me."

Something about the voice calms me, and I try to look at the woman, but all I see is a vague shape.

"Dark," I say, then growl and struggle some more.

A flicker of orange light illuminates the space...which I still can't see clearly. The woman returns, her body lit, but still blurry. My eyes roll back and she strikes me again, harder. "Solomon! Focus!"

Focus...

The word slowly sinks into my mind like a stone, before reaching the depths where a small part of my sanity still resides.

Focus.

"Kat?" I ask.

"I think he's back," Kat says, stepping away.

Another person slides into view, this one close and gentle. She slides a hand across my face, trusting me implicitly to not bite it off.

"That might not be a good idea," warns someone else. Kainda, I think.

"Solomon," the woman leaning on me says. "Look at me."

I try to see her, but it's like looking through a dirty window.

"He's burning up," she says.

I know she's saying I have a fever, but I can't feel anything beyond a craving for violence.

Kat returns. She grips my mouth roughly, yanks back the gag and drops three small, solid objects in, then pours in water and shoves my jaw closed. I try to resist, but I feel weak now. When she says, "It's Ibuprofen," I swallow.

For ten minutes, the woman beside me bravely strokes my hair. And with each gentle touch, I feel my mania subside just a little. I lose myself for a bit, staring at what I think is a stone ceiling.

"Are we in a cave?" I ask.

"Yes," the woman replies. "We're twenty miles from the coast. Just a day's journey from the base."

I turn toward her. Her face is still blurred, but I think I recognize the shape...and her voice. "Em?"

I hear a sniff, and I wonder if she's crying. Her hand reaches for my cheek and rubs it gently, the way my mother used to. "It's me."

"How?"

"Luca," she says. "He still sees you in his dreams. He sent us to you, Kat and me."

"Luca..." I say, picturing the boy, which is easy, since he looks like me. But then the face in my mind's eye changes. Luca looks angry. Then furious. His eyes go black, red seeps from his skull and stains his hair. He shrieks at me.

Except he's not the one shrieking, it's me.

I hear shouting. And a pain-filled scream.

Something hard strikes my forehead and everything disappears.

18

I'm vaguely aware that I'm moving. I see a kind of red haze, but I'm not sure I'm actually seeing it. I sense that some part of me is able to see, and act, but the real me—the Solomon me—feels small and trapped.

Distant voices reach me. The words are hard to make out and the voices impossible to identify. I feel like I know them, but can't think of names or faces to go with them.

"Look out!"

A shout of pain.

"Here, here! Now!"

I sense a stab of pain, but its more like a memory.

"Down!"

Grunting follows. Then a shout, loud and angry.

More pain. A surge of energy.

"Kainda!"

Kainda? Is that a name?

"Hold on!"

"I'm coming!"

"Hurry!"

"Ready!"

A wave of dizziness spins my fragile consciousness.

Then weightlessness.

"Oh no," someone says.

"I didn't think he could do that."

There's a *whump*, and a surge of energy.

"Solomon!"

A second surge of energy follows.

"Solomon!" The voice is screaming. Desperate. "Solomon, please st—"

Whump!

SOLOMON!

Everything stops.

This voice is stronger than the others. It's unfiltered by the haze.

"Who are you?" I say aloud.

Stop, says the voice. *See!*

"I can't."

Then we are lost.

"We?"

You are connected to Antarktos, and it to you.

I know this. I think.

The earth is your flesh. The atmosphere, your lungs. The water, your blood. You can shape them. Bend them. Control them.

"Who are you?"

Listen! Hear me. As the continent is, so is your body. They are joined. Control your body as you control the wind. Push this evil out. Burn it from your blood. Push it from your pores. Expel it!

"How?" I ask.

Open your eyes.

"They are open," I say. "I can't see."

Then choose *to see! Will it!*

"Can you help me?"

I...must save myself. For another time. But...I will try.

The real world around me flickers into view for just a second, but it's enough for me to get a glimpse of my surroundings, and in the brief moment, I understand everything I'm seeing.

Kainda, Kat and Mira are all lying on the ground, unconscious and bleeding from various wounds. A portion of the surrounding jungle has been bent or broken, all of it leaning away from me. I did this. I hurt my friends. I—

The red haze returns.

I sense my memory of what I've just seen grow distant.

No! I shout inwardly.

The voice said to burn it out. Earlier, Em said I was hot. I remember that now. I had a fever. But Kat gave me some painkillers and the fever was reduced, which allowed the berserker infection to run rampant through my body.

But I can stop it. The voice believed it. I can control it like I do the elements.

Burn, I think, and for the first time in a long time, I start to feel heat. But it's not on the outside, it's inside. I feel the sting working its way through my body. Itchy pinpricks cover my skin as I start to sweat. Chills wrack my body, and I fall to my knees, feeling the impact keenly. I can feel my body again, though I haven't quite taken control of it.

A surge of anger pushes back as though the infection has a will of its own. And it very well might. Created by the Nephilim, this virus might have a supernatural element I don't understand. My perfect memory replays a scene from *The Exorcist*, a movie I watched during a sleepover at Justin's house. It's one of the things in my life I most wish I could forget, especially now that I fear I've got some kind of demon living in me.

But I've already faced that and won, I tell myself. I expelled the spirit of Nephil. I can push this thing from my body.

I double my efforts, cringing into a ball on the ground, clenching my eyes shut and focusing my attention inward, to my core. I don't need my white blood cells to attack the virus, or whatever this is. I can do it myself. It takes intense focus to identify the plague, but once I identify it, I'm able to locate it in my blood, in my organs, in my bones.

With a shout of exertion, I expel the madness from my body. The effort nearly sinks me back into unconsciousness, but I sense the plague returning. I didn't find it all! It's spreading again!

I scream from the effort this time, but it clings to me. It's hooked into me and will come back no matter how hard I push. All the burning and purging in the world can't make it go away.

I've lost, I think.

We're lost.

"I'm sorry," someone says.

I turn toward the voice as the madness reclaims my body once more. In the moment before my vision fades I catch a glimpse of Em. She looks...sad, but determined.

Then I see the knife in her hand.

She snaps her wrist forward, throwing the knife.

I feel a jolt.

My head turns down.

The knife is in my chest, buried to the hilt.

19

Pain explodes from my chest like my heart is the catalyst for an atom bomb. I can't scream. In fact, my senses are so immediately overwhelmed that I just fall, crumpling to my side.

But I haven't lost consciousness.

And the madness has been turned back.

I suppose it has no power in death.

But I'm not dead.

I manage to turn my eyes down and look at the blade. Yeah, it's there. An expert shot. The sideways blade slipped between my ribs and punctured my heart. I'm sure of it because I can't feel it beating.

Any second now, my mind will fade, deprived of oxygen.

But it doesn't.

Instead, my body convulses. The pain in my chest flares with each electric jolt, before I'm slammed back on the ground.

Through the shaking and pain, and the tears in my eyes, I see Em stand above me. She lifts a foot and places it on my chest, holding me down. "I'm sorry," she says again, sounding as wounded as I feel.

I want to tell her it's okay; that I understand. She had to do it or I would have killed them all, been lost to the madness and eventually captured by Nephil who would use me against the whole planet. Killing me and preventing all that makes sense. The human race stands a far better chance of defeating the Nephilim if I am not under their control. The odds are still not good, but last time Nephil controlled my body, just for a few seconds, he managed to kill billions of people.

She reaches down and takes the knife handle in her hand. I try to tell her to leave it, not because I want to die, but because I know it's going to hurt. A lot. *Take it out when I'm dead!*

She tugs.

I feel the metal sliding out of my body. The sting is intense, and it's followed by a wicked itch and a radiating pain unlike anything I've ever felt before.

That's not true.

I have felt this before...

As the blade comes up into view, a slick of red blood slips down the polished blade toward the tip. But there is something wrong with the blood near the hilt. It's tinged...purple.

My eyes widen with the realization that Em just stabbed me in the heart with a knife laced with Nephilim blood. For a moment, it feels like a vile invasion, but then I remember the blood's ability to heal the human body when used in low doses. I used Nephilim blood to save Kainda's life not long ago. Sure, stabbing me in the heart was a bit extreme, but she knew it wouldn't kill me. She just needed to stop me from killing the others, which it seems I was on a path to do.

I clench my eyes against the pain wracking my body. *It will end soon*, I tell myself. *You'll be okay. You'll live.*

But will the madness return?

I try to get a sense of my mind. I feel like myself. I can remember everything. Literally, everything. I'm in control. I can't even feel it at the fringe of my mind. The Nephilim blood destroyed the plague. Odd that the blood of something so vile could be the cure for a madness created by a Nephilim. In fact, I recognize the blade as Mira's. It's the knife she used to slash Ares's knee. Ares was the source of the madness, and the cure for it. Part of me wishes he was still alive to hear this.

"Solomon," Em says. I can't see her. My eyes are still shut, but her voice is above me.

I'm about to reply when an intense energy blooms in my chest and spreads through my body.

"Something is happening," I say quickly. "Move back!"

An intense pressure covers my body. Wind tugs at my hair. Then a sound like thunder explodes all around me.

As quick as it began, it stops.

I'm not sure what just happened, but a steady wind is circling me, and I can no longer feel the ground. I open my eyes slowly, prepared to find myself airborne, but I'm not remotely ready for what I find.

"Whoa!" I say, panicking and dropping a good fifty feet before catching myself and leveling out. I'm at least two miles above the ground. And I covered the distance in seconds. *That boom*, I think. *I broke the sound barrier!*

I look down and see nothing but jungle, but there is a little black hole in the green canopy directly beneath me. That must be where I came from, but it looks like I kind of exploded out of the tree. I feel no pain on my body. At all. In fact, I've never felt better.

I'm tempted to enjoy this moment, but then I remember my friends on the ground. Kainda, Mira and Kat were hurt, maybe badly. And Em just stabbed her brother in the chest and had him take off like a missile. That's probably not easy to deal with. I'm about to head down, but a shift of movement pulls my eyes to the west.

The Nephilim army.

They're like a black stain. From this height, I can see a trail of destruction behind them winding across the continent. They're at least fifteen miles off, so the behemoths are the only two of the bunch I can make out individually. They look like two giant egg-shaped Weeble toys I had when I was little, bobbing back and forth with each enormous step.

Knowing where the Nephilim are heading, I turn east. The strip of blue water marks the horizon. This is the Southern Ocean, though it's no longer in the South, so maybe the Equatorial Ocean is a better name. I spot a large clearing and what looks like a tiny man-made scar. The FOB. It looks miniscule compared to the incoming enemy force. But there are more shapes out in the water. A lot of them.

The base is roughly twenty miles off.

The Nephilim are just thirty-five miles from the base, I think. I look up to the sun and note its position in the sky. Still morning.

The Nephilim don't grow tired, and the hunters and berserkers they command have been trained to endure long stretches without sleeping. They'll march through the night.

"They'll be there tomorrow," I whisper to myself. We need to move.

I look down, preparing to descend when I spot an aberration sliding over the jungle canopy. Shadows. I trace the angle of the sun up and find the source of the shadows.

Warriors. Three of them.

My exit from the jungle has attracted attention. They haven't spotted me, but they're headed for the hole in the trees.

And my friends.

I cut the wind and drop through the sky. I angle my body downwards, urging myself to reach terminal velocity.

The Nephilim slip into the jungle and disappear, cloaked in shadow.

Terminal velocity isn't going to be fast enough.

I summon the wind. *Faster! FASTER!*

Pressure builds in front of me and I push against it. A white bloom suddenly forms, and then it ruptures with a thunderous *boom*. Free from the sound barrier, I plummet downward. My violent acceleration has created a shockwave that tears a fresh hole in the canopy. I surge the final two hundred feet through the trees to the ground in a fraction of a second.

In that brief moment, I think *I'm going to smear myself on the jungle floor*, but then I remember the lesson learned from the strange voice, which I now think might have been Luca, though it sounded older or wiser. The voice taught me that connection between the continent and my body goes both ways, and in the same way I control the elements of this continent, I can control my body. There are all sorts of possibilities this opens up, the first of them being, I should be able to stick this landing like Mary Lou Retton.

The explosive force of my landing outdoes the sonic boom by at least twice. Which is to say, it's loud. And it's created a genuine two-foot deep, ten-foot wide crater around my body, which is uninjured by the dramatic arrival. I think I probably made far too much noise, but the effect on the three Nephilim is almost comical.

They turn around slowly, wings folded down, tails tucked between their legs and mouths slightly agape with expressions that say something like, "What the...?" and I'm pretty sure that's a phrase never uttered by a Nephilim before, even if just in facial expression form.

Beyond them I see Em and Kainda on their feet. They look weary and wounded, but they have their weapons at the ready. Kat is helping Mira to her feet. But right now, none of them are moving either. They're locked in place, staring at me.

I find Kainda's eyes and grin, doing that silent human communication thing my mother and I perfected. I tell her I'm sorry with my eyebrows. She forgives me with a blink. Then I tell her, "Watch this," with a grin, and I step out of the crater.

20

I find Whipsnap thirty feet away, partially concealed by leaf litter. I don't really need the weapon now, but it's kind of like a security blanket...with a razor-sharp spear head on one side and a heavy spiked mace on the other. I reach a hand toward the weapon. A gust of wind lifts it and flings it toward me. *Luke Skywalker, eat your heart out.*

"It's him," one of the warriors says. Given their black battle gear and square, knotted beards, I believe they are members of the Sumerian clan. I quickly look over their helmets and other distinguishing features.

"I'm not sure who you two are," I say, pointing the spear tip at the two Nephilim closest to me. I redirect the spear toward the warrior behind them. He stands a few feet shorter and is likely the lowest in status. "But he's definitely Ninhursag."

The giants attempt to contain their laughter, but fail. I've just called the small one by the name of the Sumerian version of Mother Earth, which I'm pretty sure is actually a bulbous breeder like Gaia, who played a disgusting roll in my breaking. The small Nephilim tries to charge me, but the other two stop him.

"You must go," says one of the larger warriors, "Ophion must be told."

The smaller warrior doesn't look pleased at all, but I'm pretty sure he's going to consent. Nephil has likely given explicit orders that he be told if my whereabouts were discovered. Sadly for them, I have other plans.

"No one is going anywhere," I say.

The smaller warrior unfurls his wings and leaps for the sky. With two quick slashes, from a distance of fifty feet, I clip his wings. The giant shouts more with surprise than pain as he plummets to the ground and lands in an unbecoming heap behind the two other warriors. The toothy smiles, remaining from my joke at their comrade's expense, transform into sneers. They spin toward me, drawing weapons.

The first wields an axe large enough to chop through any of the giant trees surrounding us with a single blow. It would make short work of me. The second nocks an arrow the size of Whipsnap and draws it back in a massive bow. As the first Nephilim closes the distance and brings his axe down toward me, the second looses his arrow.

They're making this easy.

A quick wind redirects the arrow into the back of the axe-wielder's neck, slipping between the massive vertebrae. I'm not sure if it will kill him, but it drops him to the ground. The giant lands to my left and slides for a few feet.

As the smaller warrior struggles to his feet, his wings slowly regenerating, the bowman fires again and again, sending three arrows at me before the first reaches his target. But not one of them reaches me. They're dust in the air.

The bow dissolves in his hands, leaving him dumbfounded.

While making the Nephilim army's weapons all turn to dust would be fantastic, I doubt I will be able to perform this feat on a grand scale. Reducing a weapon to its various elements takes some serious concentration. But it definitely leaves an impression. Despite being far from defenseless, the warrior staggers back, perhaps realizing that this is a fight he cannot win. I turn my eyes to the metal band covering his head. I hit it with a wind, confirming that it's held in place by spikes driven into the monster's head. I focus on it, trying to melt or disintegrate it, but the metal resists. It's either not made from Antarctic elements or it has some kind of supernatural protection.

It doesn't really change my current strategy. I just wanted to know, because it will affect those fighting alongside me.

Before the giant can recover, I swipe Whipsnap from left to right, using it to direct the course of my wind-blade. A line of purple blood oozes from his neck. The giant staggers and falls to his knees. But he doesn't die. His head, which was completely severed, didn't fall away and has begun to heal. I swipe Whipsnap from right to left, this time striking with more force and a wider blade. The head comes free and falls away. Dead. For sure.

I turn to the smallest of the three. His wings are nearly regrown and when he notices my attention, he tries to fly away again. But the wings are insufficient to carry him up and away.

Seeing the giant beast struggle actually makes me pity him.
For a moment.

Then I remember what they are, what they did to me, and
Kainda, and Em, and Luca, and the billions of people now dead
because of their evil, twisted machinations. Without any further
flair or desire to show off, I remove his head and his presence
from this world forever.

A wet slurp turns me around. The warrior with the axe is
kneeling and pulling the arrow out of his throat. Once it's out,
the wound heals quickly and he's back on his feet. With just one
Nephilim left, I decide to implement the last part of my attack
plan, which is the part that might get me killed. But a little R&D
is sometimes necessary, especially before the beginning of a battle
that might determine the fate of the human race.

The plan is this: no elemental powers. No wind blades. No
chucking rocks, or dropping trees, or tossing the giant around
like a ragdoll. This fight will be man to man-demon. That's not
entirely true. I *am* going to use my abilities, but in a very different
way. If I can really control my body, the way I control the
elements of Antarktos, I should be able to pull this off. If not,
well, I'm not above cheating.

I let the warrior pick up his axe. He's grunting and angry,
eyeing me carefully. This one's not going to be big on the pre-
fight banter, which is fine by me. This isn't a *Spider-Man* comic
book. But, I do perform the classic challenge to fight barehanded
by tossing Whipsnap to the ground and raising my clenched fists.
Sure, the giant hasn't ever seen a movie in which such a scenario
plays out, but I'm pretty sure he understands.

He glances from me to his fallen brethren. He was too busy choking on the business end of an arrow to see how they died, but it's enough to convince him that throwing away his axe would be folly. He lets out a battle cry, punctuating it with a spray of spittle, and leaps toward me. His wings beat the air once, lifting him up, but also propelling him forward. For his size, he's quick. But not quite quick enough.

As his feet touch down and he swings hard with the axe, I sidestep. I don't have to use any special abilities to dodge the blow. Any hunter worth his while could have. It was an obvious attack meant to bring us in close, because once a human being is within arm's reach of a Nephilim, the fight is pretty much over. Avoiding the axe is just the first part of my plan. The second part comes next.

Before the giant can heft the oversized blade from the earth, I turn toward it, draw my fist back and punch. As my fist covers the few feet to the axe, I focus on my arm, bunching the molecules more densely, pulling in atoms from the surrounding air and powering my knuckles with the kinetic energy that fills the very earth of Antarktos.

My fist connects with the six-inch thick base of the metal blade where it intersects with the handle.

There's a loud *clang*, like when a blacksmith hammers a blade.

A throb of pain moves up my arm like a shockwave.

And the axe...

It launches from the warrior's grip as though shot from a catapult. It sails away into the jungle, lost in the trees until it strikes something solid with a distant *bong*.

The warrior is disciplined and wastes no time wondering what just happened. He raises his fists into the air, laces his fingers together and then brings the joined fists down like a mace. The effect of the strike would normally be like a human punching a rotten banana.

I lift my hands up, repeating my focus from the punch and intensifying it, filling my body with all the power I can muster, if only for a moment. The warrior's boulder-like hands land in mine.

And stop.

I feel the force of the strike vibrate through my body and out into the ground beneath my feet...which is technically part of me. The impact presses my bare feet into the earth, and I feel the connection to this continent, and all its vast power, like never before.

The warrior is far bigger than my human body, but what he doesn't know, and what I've just realized, is he's fighting a force more ancient than the Nephilim and larger than the United States.

Actually, I think he's starting to figure it out. He separates his hands and looks down at me. Seems even Nephilim can sometimes have the ability to speak with facial expressions, because this big guy has "how?" written all over his face.

A blur of movement streaks out to my right.

The confused face was a ruse!

No time to move.

Focus!

Whack! The scorpion tail strikes my side. A single sting would have caused me intense pain, and eventually death. Instead, it strikes my ribs, and shatters.

Now the giant is truly stunned. And before he can recover, I leap up, propelled by wind, covering the thirty feet to his head. I grab hold of the metal ring protecting him. Standing on his shoulder, to the side of his face, I pull. He roars in pain and spins his head, trying to bite me with his double rows of sharp teeth, but I'm gone before his jaws close. And I've taken the ring with me.

Purple blood flows from four deep wounds on the sides of his head where the spikes held the crown in place. As the skull and skin knit back together, I wander over to Whipsnap, pick it up and take aim. One good throw and this is all over.

But before I can kill the warrior, something huge roars and pounds out of the jungle shadows. I see a flash of green. And teeth. And then, blood.

21

I flinch back, surprised by the violent new entry into the fray, but then I recognize the green-bodied, maroon-striped dinosaur as Grumpy. He's got his powerful jaws locked over the warrior's head and is thrashing him back and forth. To make matters worse for the Nephilim, Zok, has just stomped out from behind a tree and taken hold of one of the warrior's legs.

The giant doesn't stand a chance against these two, the largest and most powerful of the cresties, now loyal to me. They must have tracked our scents through the jungle since we left them by the river. I've heard of dogs crossing countries to find their masters, but I've never heard of a dinosaur doing that. Of course, they've probably never had the opportunity before.

As the gnawing, tearing and crunching becomes sickening, I turn away. Nephilim blood has no effect on the dinosaurs. They're natural enemies—opposing giants of the underworld, and the cresties relish the chance to feast on the purple flesh. I suspect they might get some sort of kick from the blood, like an energy boost or euphoria, which would explain their hankering for Nephilim, but if they experience any adverse symptoms from eating the supernatural meat, it can't be more substantial than gas, which for a dinosaur, is *always* bad.

With the chewing and slurping behind me, I look down to clip Whipsnap to my belt. A pair of bare feet stop in front of me. They're feminine, but strong, lacking any decoration beyond scars. Kainda. I smile and finish clipping my weapon in place.

I look at Kainda and see a facial expression I wasn't expecting. I look beyond her and find Em, Kat and Mira just behind her and to the sides, all wearing the same expression—a one sided smile and a cocked eyebrow that says, "Showoff."

"I had to know what I could do," I say defensively. The eyebrows inch higher. "Seriously."

"You almost killed us," says Kat. Her words make me see the blood trickling down her face from a gash on her forehead. I look at Em. She's holding her side. Mira has a hand on her opposite arm. They're all wounded because of me.

My smile slips away as I remember the darkness that had consumed me. I became a monster, and not for the first time. With a gasp of dread, I reach for my hair and pull it in front of my face, inspecting it like an OCD chimp mother checking her baby for flees.

"You're fine," Kat says. "Your golden locks are back."

When I confirm this for myself, seeing no trace of red remaining, I look up at my four friends and find them smiling. "Was that—? Were you all teasing me?"

Kainda claps a hand on my shoulder, and I haven't condensed any atoms or anything like that, so it hurts. I wince, but smile when she says, "You fought well."

From Kainda, that might be the highest praise ever.

Em says, "Nicely done, Sol."

My smile widens.

"Wright would be proud," Kat adds, trying to make this sap of a leader tear up.

But Mira rescues me, saying, "I think he's a freak of nature, but that's just me."

We all have a good laugh, letting the tension of the past days seep away. "Are you all okay?" I ask. "*Really* okay?"

"We're fine," Mira says, and if it had been any of the other three, who are more battle-hardened, I would have doubted it, but Mira doesn't have the same kind of tough pride that can't admit injury. She'd say something.

I hear a particularly gruesome bite and swallow behind me. Kat and Mira both cringe. Em and Kainda have seen it before.

"We should go," Kat says.

I nod. "Once they finish eating, we'll leave. They can carry the five of us without any trouble. We're just fifteen miles from the coast. We can make it by sunset."

"And the Nephilim?" Mira asks.

"They'll arrive tomorrow." I say. "Probably in the morning. They feel about ten miles to the west."

"How many?" Kat asks.

I pause, trying to think of a gentle way to break the news. Mira does it for me, not so gently.

"We're pretty much screwed," Mira says.

Kat looks to Kainda, who shrugs and nods.

Kat grunts. "Great intel, guys."

Despite the dire revelation, I smile. "I'll fill you in on the way." I tap my head. "I have all the numbers, sizes, weapons and capabilities up here. When we get to the FOB, you can help General Holloway make sense of how to respond to it."

With a rekindled sense of urgency, I turn around to the eating dinosaurs, intending to disrupt their meal and get us moving. Kainda stops me with a hand on my arm. "Could I speak with you before we leave?" Her eyes flick to the side. She wants a private conversation.

"We'll, ahh, we'll be right back," I say to the others. Kainda leads me away, rounding a large tree. The backside of the tree is lined by thick ferns that come up to our thighs.

"Could be a pack of turquins in here and we'd never know it," I say.

I meant it as a joke. Something to break the nervous tension I'm suddenly feeling. But Kainda doesn't laugh.

Instead, she whirls around and lunges at me. She gets a hand behind my head, grips my hair tightly and uses the surprise to sweep out my legs and drop me onto my back. I cough as the air is knocked from my lungs.

I'm beneath the ferns, looking up at a ceiling of luminous green. Kainda crouches down, sliding through the growth. As she descends, I can't help but notice her more feminine features. Her skin, though mired with mud and her own blood, gleams with sweat in a way that draws my hands. As she slips beneath the thin covering, her eyes lock onto mine. She looks almost predatory.

I smile broadly, but a little sheepishly, too. We haven't really had much time alone since we first kissed. Our intimate moments consist mostly of gentle touches in passing. And before Kainda...I'm not exactly experienced when it comes to interacting with members of the opposite sex. There was that foot bump once, but I don't think that qualifies as a genuine encounter.

"Hi," I say dumbly.

Kainda smiles back, and I swear I feel my insides turn to liquid.

"You fought well," she says.

"You already said that," I reply.

"Should I kiss you, or not?" she says.

My gut churns. "Yes, please."

Her smile looks almost sweet. It's a different kind of look for her. "So polite," she whispers, leaning down. "We're going to have to work on that."

Then her lips are on mine.

We remain still, our lips interlocked. My chest loosens. My mind relaxes. This is bliss.

She leans back slowly. The skin of our lips sticks for a moment, not yet willing to let go. Then she's sitting atop me, leaning over me with her hands on the ground, to either side of my head.

"Whoa..." I whisper. "What was that for?"

"To thank you."

"For what?"

"Everything," she says. "And...I'm relieved you're unharmed." It's a moment of rare vulnerability. It makes me adore her even more. "I thought...when the madness had you. I thought you were gone. When I looked into your eyes then, I couldn't see you. I couldn't—"

I raise my hands to her face, holding her soft cheeks. "What do you see now?"

As she looks into my eyes, a single tear falls free from her face and lands on my cheek. At the moment of impact, I feel its warmth. I can't normally feel *any* temperature, hot or cold, and I'm unaffected by the results of their extremes. I can't be burned, nor can I freeze. But I can feel the warmth of Kainda's tears. There is power in them.

A coolness covers my back. I can feel the earth beneath me!

"What is it?" Kainda asks.

"I—I can feel temperature," I say. "I can feel the ground." I look down and sense the warmth of Kainda's bare legs over my waist. "I can feel you. More than I could before."

I hadn't realized how much I missed feeling temperature. There is pleasure in a cool drink or in the warm touch of a woman. In the Antarctic, and the underground, not feeling was largely a blessing. There were times I should have died from exposure, but I was immune to the effects of below-freezing temperatures.

She smiles at me. "It's a gift."

I start to agree, but then wonder if my powers have left me, too. The ferns shake as a breeze of my creation wafts over them. I relax again and lean my head back on the cool, soft earth.

"Shall I thank you now?" Kainda asks.

"I thought you already did?"

She smirks and leans back, reaching for her belt.

The nervousness I felt before explodes through my body. "I know you're my passion, but I'm not sure this is the best time to—"

She draws a knife, and strangely, it puts me at ease. Like I said, we haven't had much time to get...familiar with each other. What I thought was going to happen would have been a leap forward.

"Relax, Solomon," Kainda says. "Even hunters are not without their traditions. Marriage comes before any coupling."

Coupling. Of course hunters call it *coupling.* There's no romance in the word. Still, that hunters actually get married is strangely heartwarming. I'm sure they don't have elaborate ceremonies, rice throwing or a reception with dancing, but that the institution even exists shows that some part of them retained a notion of purity, even though they might kill someone for suggesting it.

She lifts the blade to her palm and draws it across. The cut is neither deep nor severe. Just enough to draw blood, which drips over her hand.

She hands the blade to me and it's clear she wants me to do the same. I sense that this is meaningful to her, so I take the blade and place it against my palm. I simultaneously feel the warmth of her blood and the chill of the metal, then a sting as I cut my hand.

She takes the knife from me and stabs it into the ground beside us. She holds her hand up to me, opening her fingers.

When I reach out with my wounded hand, she nods. I'm doing it right. We interlace our fingers, squeezing our hands, and our blood, together.

Kainda makes sure I'm looking in her eyes. "Say what I say."

I nod.

"Blood to bind."

"Blood to bind."

"Flesh to join."

"Flesh to join."

"Man to woman."

"Man to woman."

"Woman...to man."

"Woman to man."

"Forever."

"Forever."

She separates our hands, leans down and kisses me again. The sensation is accentuated by the fact that I can now feel the heat of her lips and the warmth of her breath. I'm kind of dazed when she sits up again.

"We have a tradition like this in the outside world," I say, trying to hide what feels like a swoon. "We call it blood brothers, though that doesn't really make sense for us."

She scrunches up her face. "No. It doesn't."

"What do you call it?" I ask.

She leans down again, smiling in a way I have never seen before. She whispers her reply in my ear. "Hunters call it 'the bond'."

"Oh," I say. Not sure why she thought blood brothers was so outlandish. *The Bond* has kind of a similar tough vibe.

She whispers in my ear again, her breath tickling me "You would call it marriage, husband."

22

I scramble out from under Kainda and stand bolt upright, exploding from the layer of ferns like a breaching whale. I turn to walk in one direction, change my mind and turn around, but find I can't bring myself to move at all. My heart races as my mind tries to comprehend Kainda's revelation.

Marriage!

Husband!

The bond!

I don't know what to think. Or say. Or do. Where is Nephil when you need him?

I spin around hoping to be discovered by a Nephilim. A good fight would distract me. It's not that I don't love Kainda. I adore her. But I don't know what to do with the emotions I'm feeling. I've never felt like this before, and honestly, it terrifies me. Everything up to this point has been temporary. I was broken and then healed. I was split in two—Ull and Solomon—and rejoined. I will fight Nephil and one of us will be defeated.

They're obstacles. I can face them, and then move past them. That's what my life has become—a struggle against finite roadblocks, all of which will one day be a part of my past. Or I'll be dead. But this...

Blood to bind. Flesh to join. Man to woman. Woman...to man. Forever.

Forever!

I'm not used to dealing with forever.

"Solomon," Kainda says. I turn back to find her rising from the ferns. Flickers of sunlight, filtering through the canopy, dance across her tan skin. "Are you okay?"

She looks vulnerable. Worried. Beautiful. When I look into her eyes, all of my nervous energy flits away like dust caught in a breeze. I see her with new eyes, feeling the connection between us.

"My wife..."

She nods.

"Forever."

She nods again. "Forever."

I wade through the ferns until I'm standing just inches from her. My mind is still reeling, racing through concerns and scenarios, like worrying if such a marriage is legal, but then I remember I'm technically the sole heir to all of Antarctica and to many, a king. I can write the law. Plus, Kainda and I are both hunters and the laws that govern their culture, as brutal as it might be, are no less valid than those of the United States, a country that is still in its infancy compared to the nation of hunters.

I place my hands on her bare arms and feel her warmth again. All of my fears and concerns are forgotten. None of it matters. I pull her to me and hold her tight. "My wife."

When we separate, I say, "Does this mean you're going to shave your head and walk behind me? That's the hunter tradition, right?"

Kainda shoots me a scowl, but can't hide the humor in her eyes. A year ago, she wouldn't have understood the joke. Still, she lands a solid punch on my shoulder. "Don't push it. We might be married, but—"

A loud gasp cuts off Kainda's words. "What did she just say?"

We turn to find Em standing by the tree that shielded our hasty nuptials, a hand raised to her mouth. Despite how her still-short hair, now something of a bob, makes her look cute, the knives criss-crossing her chest and waist look positively dangerous. But right now, she's neither cute nor dangerous. She looks ready to burst, like a happy face balloon with too much air in it.

In response, Kainda lifts her hand, revealing the self-inflicted wound. Em's eyes grow larger and shift to me. I smile and hold up my hand, showing her the identical wound.

The balloon pops with a squeal of joy unlike anything I've seen from a hunter. She hops into the ferns, clapping her hands and then dives at us, throwing her arms around our necks. She squeezes tightly and then leans back, looking at me. "Brother," she says, and then turns to Kainda, "And now, sister."

Perhaps performing another ritual I am not aware of, the two women lean their foreheads together, hold for a second before separating.

"Sister," Kainda says.

"Sorry to break up the huggy time," Kat says, stepping around the tree, "but we really need to go."

Em whirls around, beaming. "They're bonded!"

Kat scrunches her face. "Not sure I need to know that."

"Married," I say, clarifying for Kat.

"Married?" Mira says, stepping around the other side of the tree. For a moment, I worry about what she's going to say, but then she smiles and laughs, and says, "Could have picked a nicer location."

"Or a better time," Kat says.

"Hush," Em tells her and then waves her into the ferns. "Come here."

Kat resists. "We need to go."

"This is important," Em says.

Kat looks dubious.

Em fills her voice with conviction, raising her arms at the group. "We are a family. We must complete the bond."

Kat stares at her for a moment, looks over her shoulder and then enters the ferns. She stops in front of Em.

"The bond is a tradition among hunters," Em says. "It is one of the few. But it is important. Blood binds so few in the underworld, but the bond is a declaration that replaces it. You are my sister by birth, but there is a different kind of bond that makes Luca and Solomon my brothers, and Tobias my father. And now Kainda my sister."

Kat doesn't reply, but she doesn't leave, either.

Em puts her hand around Kat's head and pulls her down. Kat seems to understand her intention, probably from having witnessed Em and Kainda doing the same. She puts her hand on the back of Em's neck and they press their foreheads together.

"Sister," Em says.

"Sister," Kat repeats, though a little more quietly.

Em steps back and points to Kainda. "Now you two."

The two warriors stare at each other. Both women are hardened by lifetimes of battle and death. They no doubt see this in each other and the compulsion to resist vulnerability increases. But then Kainda steps forward and Kat follows her lead. The put their heads together and say, "Sister."

Kat turns to me. She steps forward, but then stops. "My husband gave his life for you. But...what I've learned about you since... I understand it. And I know he would have no problem doing this himself, so..." She steps forward, takes the back of my head and pushes her forehead hard against mine. "Brother."

I actually have to reign in my emotions when I say, "Sister." My voice cracks. When I lift my head, I notice Mira standing nearby. Her eyes reflect a sense of pleasant wonder, but also of longing. I lift a hand in invitation.

"What?" she says, confused. "Sol, I'm not—"

"You have been with me from the moment I stepped foot on Antarktos, in person or in my heart. When I was lost, you saved me with a memory, with a photo and with a note."

She's surprised by this. "You *found* that?"

"You have supplied me with hope whenever it was needed and though we were separated by space, and even time, the small gift of confidence you gave a scared fourteen year old boy, might have been what saved my life and led me to this very spot." I shrug. "So we're kind of bonded already, whether you like it or not."

With a laugh, Mira accepts my invitation. She walks right up to me, puts her hand on the back of my neck and grins. "Which box did you check off?"

"Huh?"

"On the note."

I know exactly what she's talking about. Every word of it flashes through my mind, perfectly recorded:

Solomon,

I am new to this and I'm not good at writing so I'm going to get right to the point. I like you. A lot. I'm not big on romance. Or flowers. Or girly things in general. So if that is okay with you, I'll overlook the fact that you are clumsy. And smart. And kind. We will always be good friends. I knew it from the moment I picked you up off of my driveway. But maybe, if you're lucky, we can be something more? I'm debating about whether or not to give this to you, because the idea of you turning me down makes me sick to my stomach. Actually, I'm pretty sure that this will make you sick to your stomach, too. So to make this simple I'm going to do something I swore I would never do.

Do you like me? □ Yes. □ No.

Or maybe just sit next to me and put your foot against mine. Grin.
Mira.

I smile, feeling slightly embarrassed, but also safe. This is the history that binds us, and there is no reason to hide from it. "The first."

"I knew you would." Mira smiles. "Looks like we get to be something more, after all."

With a gentle laugh, I pull Mira's head against mine. "Sister."
"Brother," she replied.

Then I feel an arm wrap around me. It's Em. She puts her head against mine and Mira's. Kainda and Kat join in next until all of our heads are touching. It feels like the ultimate cheesy moment, like something you'd see in at the end of a 1980's movie montage, but it also feels significant. This moment is bonding the five of us, and I suspect that Adoel knew it would happen. Hope, faith, passion and focus, united with me. "Family," I say.

The word is repeated four times more, working its way around the circle.

A moment later, a deep, rolling rattle separates us. Grumpy stands by the tree, his muzzle stained purple. Zok, whose snout is also covered in Nephilim blood steps up next to him and repeats the gentle call.

"I think they're ready to go," I say.

My sisters and wife silently agree, and we head for the dinosaurs, all lost in our own silent reflections. The beasts crouch down allowing us to climb on their backs, Kat and I on Grumpy, the others on Zok. When the dinosaurs stand again, I look across to Kainda. "Ready...wife?"

"After you, husband."

I grin, give Grumpy a gentle nudge with my legs and say, "Let's go!"

The dinosaurs take off at a sprint, quickly reaching twenty miles per hour, the speed at which they can run long distance. The jungle passes in a blur, and with every step we take closer to the FOB, my elation over the events of the past few minutes is replaced by a growing dread that we might all be dead by this time tomorrow.

23

The rest of the trip is fairly eventless. With the dinosaurs carrying us, there's no need to stop to rest, though we pause twice for me to use the bathroom. Apparently, getting unexpectedly married has had an effect on my nerves...and my bladder.

I spend the first four hours of our journey speaking to Kat, filling her in on the enemy forces. We cover everything from their numbers, to their various classes and capabilities, how to kill them, their potential tactics, their long history, their parentage and their ultimate goals. By the time we finish, Kat knows everything about the Nephilim that I do. When we reach the FOB, she and I will meet with General Holloway and any other officers that need to be there. I'll answer any questions that come up, but it will be Kat's job to figure out the best military response to each possible situation. I can lead the troops and do some serious damage, but modern military capabilities are something I know very little about.

When we've finally exhausted the topic, Kat goes silent, working out every possible Nephilim strategy and what the human response could be. With my riding partner preoccupied, and conversation with Em, Mira and Kainda impossible as the two dinosaurs weave their way east through the jungle, my thoughts turn inward.

I'm married.

How did that happen?

For a moment, I entertain the idea that this is something I'm not okay with. After all, it was kind of sprung on me. *Sprung* is probably too gentle a word since I didn't even know I was getting married. To be honest, I have never once envisioned what my wedding day would be like. I don't think young men really daydream about that kind of thing. Or at least, I don't. It's not a subject one thinks about much while fighting giants who want to kidnap, corrupt and ultimately possess you.

I try to envision myself dressed in a tuxedo, standing by the altar with Justin, Wright, Tobias and Merrill standing by my side. It's impossible, I know. Some of them are dead, but my closest friends are all women and my imagination already has Em, Mira, Kat and Aimee standing beside Kainda, who I have to admit looks radiant in a white wedding dress. But then she turns to me with a look on her face that says, *I will kill you for this*, and I smile.

A traditional wedding, with a church and rice throwing and the Electric Slide would have never worked anyway. If I'm honest, the whole experience would likely make me nauseous, too.

While I might have been bamboozled into my marriage, it was simple and pure. It might be the one thing hunters got right, if they actually married for love. Who knows, maybe some of them did? When I was split into two personalities, Ull was a hunter to the core. He was cocky, brash, violent and quick to anger. He was passionate. But he wasn't entirely negative. The first time I had feelings for Kainda, Ull was in control. It's why we saved her life. If Ull can show compassion to another hunter because he has feelings for her, then it's possible other hunters experience the same thing, though they would likely never admit it.

Tobias is another good example. He loved Luca and Em enough that they fled and tried to live apart from the Nephilim. And then there is Em. When I look at her, and hear the joy of her laughter and see the cuteness of her full freckled cheeks, I wonder how she could have ever been a killer.

But it's not just hunters. The human race as a whole has the same kind of potential to overcome darkness. And it's happening now on Antarctica. The people of the world came here divided, each hoping to claim a part of this new world for themselves. But now they're united against a common enemy. The old hatreds, many of them created and encouraged by the Nephilim, are falling away.

If the human race loses this fight and is wiped off the planet, at least we'll have fought as one. A hunter would call it dying well, and I think I would have to agree.

Not that I'm planning on dying, or losing the battle. But if it happens...the human race will still have achieved something impressive—unity. It's too bad we couldn't achieve unity without half-demon man-eating genocidal inspiration, but hey, we're flawed.

I glance to my right and see Kainda atop Zok's back as they slip through the jungle. She's dressed in her scant black leathers, hammer clipped to her belt, black hair braided back tight. Her eyes are forward, watching for danger. Her muscles are flexed as she clings to Zok. She's like a sleek sports car decked out with guns—dangerous curves.

This is my wife, I think. *How awesome is that?*

The white wedding dress. The church. The reception. All of that stuff. It doesn't matter. All that matters is that woman. She is my perfect match—strong when I'm not, always by my side, and has seen me at my worst and yet still loves me.

The way we were bonded was perfect. I didn't know it at the time, but there was no better way, or moment, for us to be married. We're both hunters. This is the life we live. We're dangerous with our weapons, and with our hearts. Sometimes we have to kill suddenly, but other times we love suddenly.

Kainda senses my attention and meets my eyes.

Since neither of us is actually directing the dinosaurs, we linger. Despite the jolting ride, the vegetation and the tree trunks flashing between us, I manage to lose myself in her nearly black eyes.

I hear a sound. A voice, I think. But it barely registers.

A dopey smile forms and I feel my body morph into a kind of gelatinous mold of a human being. My parents once told me about the stages of love. Lust, romance and then solid commitment, but I suspect things are a little different for Kainda and I. The way we're wired is a bit different than the outside world, and our notions of commitment, despite also being in what my mom called "the honeymoon stage", is profound.

The voice returns, this time a little louder. I still don't hear the word being spoken. I'm not listening. I'm barely present. But a sharp smack to the back of my head pulls me out of my blissful state.

"Snap out of it, Lancelot," Kat says.

"What? Hey, Lancelot was an adulterer," I complain at the comparison to one of King Arthur's most infamous Knights of the Round Table.

"Whatever," Kat says, "We're—"

"Guinevere was condemned to burn at the stake. The Knight's were divided and the—"

"Fine, bad analogy," Kat says, the urgency of her words reaching my mind. "We're almost there."

I look back at her. She's grim. "That's a good thing, right?"

"Kid," she says, once again forgetting that we're technically the same age, "I called you Lancelot because if you were thinking with your brain, you'd notice that you were about to land yourself in hot water."

The cobwebs of love disintegrate at her warning and I suddenly feel the world around me in sharp detail. "Smoke."

"A lot of it," Kat says.

I lean forward and pat Grumpy on the side of the neck. "Whoa, boy. Slow down. Slow down."

Grumpy huffs in response and our run quickly becomes a slow and careful walk. Zok follows his lead, slowing and falling in line, just behind her pack leader.

"This is close enough," Kat says.

Em walks past us, having already leapt down from Zok's back. She's in a hurry. "Something is wrong." Then she sprints ahead, no doubt concerned for Luca's well-being.

Grumpy lowers himself toward the ground, but Kat and I are off and running before he's all the way down. Kainda and Mira are right behind us, but Em is nowhere in sight.

"Where'd she go?" Mira asks.

"This way," I say, following the barely perceptible trail. I shove aside a low-hanging branch, heavy with leaves that are bigger than me. Em stands ten feet ahead at the edge of the jungle. "Em, wait up."

She turns around at the sound of my voice. Tears are in her eyes. She doesn't have to say anything to tell us something is seriously wrong. Lacking any kind of caution, we push through the brush and fallen trees that mark the border between the jungle and the swath of ground that had been clear-cut in preparation for the final battle.

The first thing I see upon entering the clearing is a black swirling cloud blocking my view. I direct the wind to carry it away, and the air clears quickly. But as the smoke rises, my heart sinks. The forward operating base which was to be the location of humanity's last stand, has been destroyed.

24

When Kat tries and fails to contact anyone on her small portable radio, I start to sprint across the clearing, but Kat snags my arm and stops me cold. "No!" she says. "The first hundred feet are covered with land mines."

A quick look down reveals a mud covered mound that could be a mine...or not. I suppose not knowing one way or the other is the point. "How do we get across?" I ask. I'm about five seconds away from flying myself across the distance when Kat points to a string of tree trunks that cuts across the clearing.

"Seems like a bad idea," I say, "Having such an obvious path across."

"You didn't notice it," Kat says. "And the sniper with a direct line of sight down the path, with high caliber rounds strong enough to punch through five men, would have made a pretty good deterrent."

There's no doubt that Kat would have been that sniper. As I look at the straight line of trees and trace them back to a well protected bunker, it's clear that the path across might actually be far more dangerous. But not for us. I work my way through the jungle to the first tree trunk and climb on top.

Grumpy lets out a deep, but gentle roar. I turn and find the giant's head poking out of the jungle. He wants to come with us. "Stay here," I say, trying to think it at the cresty as well. I'm not entirely certain how the creature seems to understand me, but it does. He grunts in complaint. "Stay. Here."

With a sigh, the dinosaur slips back into the jungle and disappears, thanks to his camouflaged skin.

I climb atop the first trunk and work my way across. Once I'm certain the logs are securely embedded in the mud and aren't going to roll, I run the distance. By the time I reach the end, I'm airborne, spurred by my concern for Luca, the hunters we led here, the soldiers we freed from the Nephilim prison, and all the men and women who have come here since, to fight for the human race.

The rest of the distance flashes past in a blur. I touch down in the center of the base where just days ago I stood with Merrill and Aimee, where I said goodbye to Xin, who gave his life for me and where I killed the shifter posing as Mira. But there's no sign of any of those events or people present.

Including bodies.

For a moment, the lack of dead puts me at ease, but then I remember who our enemy is. Why leave dead when you can eat them? But there are many other clues about what happened, the first of which, Kat points out, when they catch up to me, running through the front gate.

"There's no sign of a fight," she says. "No shells, no blood, no remains. Even if they took the bodies there would still be...parts. The base wouldn't have fallen without a fight. Even if it was a surprise attack."

"No footprints, either," Kainda says, looking at the ground. The easiest way to know a Nephilim has visited, if it's been long enough for the stench to fade, is to look for footprints. The thirty foot goliaths tend to leave deep impressions.

"The heavy equipment is gone, too," Kat notes. "No tanks. No artillery. This was a coordinated mobilization."

"A retreat?" Mira asks.

Hearing the word makes me sick. This is one fight we cannot run away from, even if just the five of us have to fight alone. Kat's silence doesn't bode well, but I come to my own conclusion.

"General Holloway understood the stakes. As did Merrill and Mira, and Luca, not to mention the hunters and soldiers we freed. They wouldn't run away."

"As much as I believe that about my parents," Mira says, "they're not here."

"We just need to figure out where they went," I said, scouring the base for any aberration. Many of the temporary buildings—tents and metal structures—are slowly burning, as is the wall built around the core of the base, and the watch towers. But there are no signs of larger, more violent destruction. "Kat, Em, Kainda, spread out and see if you can find some hint of where they went, and why some of the buildings are burning."

"And what do you want me to do?" Mira asks, clearly not enthused that I've left her out of the search.

"Watch the skies," I say. "We're exposed and alone."

She gives a nod, all hints of disappointment gone. I've given her the most important job—keeping us alive. "If you find a gun or something larger than this knife—" She pats the blade tucked into her belt.

I nod. "I'll look for something, but you've done pretty well with just the knife."

She smiles. "Yeah..." But then forces the grin away and says, deadpan, "Find me a gun."

No matter how grim a situation, Mira has a way of making me laugh. I leave her with a smile, but it quickly fades as I set to work. My first stop is the large metal Quonset hut structure. Smoke billows from its door and windows, but the structure still looks solid. As I approach the door, the smoke parts for me.

Inside is just a cloud of black. I force the soot from the space, and snuff the fires with a thought. Beams of orange late-day sun lance through the wide open space, illuminating the destruction within. Not a thing remains. Every desk, piece of equipment and scrap of paper has been burned. I catch a trace of gasoline in the air.

I step further inside, walking over the embers of whatever was in this building. I'm sure the heat would be burning me if I could feel it, but since that moment with Kainda, I haven't felt any temperature beyond a comfortable ambient seventy degrees. It's odd, but it has its benefits. While the others have been sweating in what is obviously sweltering and humid heat, I've been just peachy.

My search yields no results. Nothing was left behind. No messages. No markings. And nothing that couldn't be burned to a crisp.

I hear a crunch behind me. A quick sniff reveals the scent of sweat and guns. Kat. "Find anything?"

"Just scorched earth," she says.

"What about the radio?" I ask.

She holds the radio to her mouth, pushes the call button and says, in very non-military fashion. "This is Katherine Ferrell looking for General Kent Holloway. If anyone reads, answer now." She lets go of the button and we listen to thirty seconds of static before she speaks again. "They either have no radios or are out of range. My best guess is that they were up to something and didn't want to risk a chance of the enemy discovering what that was, so they bugged out and set the place on fire. Also, the smoke will draw the Nephilim here, at least in part, and they'll still get a good taste of the mine field, which is the one and only thing they *did* leave behind."

"But they knew we were coming back," I say. "And you were just here a few days ago."

She crouches down, picks up what looks like an artifact covered in soot, but it just crumbles in her fingers. "Things change fast in war. And as for you, there was no guarantee you would come back. No offense, but not even I thought it was a guarantee. And let's be honest, you almost didn't make it back."

Well...she's right about that. "So they just up and left without a clue?"

"Didn't say that, but if they left something behind for us to find, it's going to be subtle. I doubt they want to advertise where they went, but I can tell you one thing for certain."

I wait for the big reveal in silence.

"They either went north or south."

Of course. They wouldn't have headed inland. They would lose the support of the Navy if they did. And there is only ocean in the other direction. "Assuming they didn't retreat."

"They didn't," she says.

"How can you be sure?"

"Holloway knows I would hunt him down and put him in a hurt locker."

We leave the husk of a building and split up to search every inch of the camp. On my way to the outer wall, I spot Mira standing still and looking down at a patch of earth. A lump forms in my throat when I realize what she's looking at—Xin's grave.

I find myself walking to her, the wall a distant memory. The earth covering Xin's body no longer looks fresh. It's as dark and muddy as the rest of the ground inside the base. If not for the stone, still in place, there would be nothing to distinguish it as a grave.

I step up next to her, looking at the stone. A single word is inscribed on it, carved by my hand with a knife: Xin.

"The body buried here looks just like you?" Mira asks. I told her the story just once. She has a good memory. Although it's not exactly an easy story to forget.

"We were twins," I say.

"But not at first?"

"At first, he looked like a gatherer. White, scaly skin. Yellow eyes. Moved through the underground like a snake. Nearly killed me."

"Why didn't he?"

"I saved him."

She lets out a laugh. "Seems to be the story of your life."

"What do you mean?"

"All the people following you—" She motions to the gravestone. "—giving their lives for you. They all wanted to kill you, but in the end, your mercy and forgiveness saved *them*." She motions behind us with her head despite there being nothing there. "Including your hoochie mamma wife."

"What's a hoochie mamma?" I ask.

"Never mind," she says. "The point is, well, I don't know what the point is. I guess I'm just glad to know you."

I stand in silence for a moment, absorbing the compliment. I'm about to dismiss myself and continue my search when Mira asks, "What's the arrow for?"

I scrunch my forehead. "What arrow?"

"On the gravestone," she says. "Did Xin use a bow and arrow?"

I kneel down and inspect the gravestone more carefully. It's really just a basketball size hunk of granite I pulled out of the ground. It's smooth, but not polished. I find the arrow etched into its gray surface, near the bottom, almost covered by mud. I didn't make this. Why would someone else? What does it mean? I look in the direction the arrow is pointing and see nothing but ruins and the ocean beyond.

Mira crouches down next to me. "Maybe you're supposed to flip it over. You know, like it's a piece of paper?"

My response is to lunge forward, grasp the stone and flip it over. The other side is devoid of anything interesting, but it's also covered in mud. With a thought, I condense water from the humid air and force it beneath the mud, souring the stone clean. Two strings of numbers are revealed, each with a single decimal point.

Mira and I look at each other, eyes wide and say the same thing, "Coordinates!"

25

As it turns out, they headed south. But there isn't a single tank tread, wheel groove or boot scuff to show their passage. Kat thinks they took helicopters and ships. It would have been a massive troop relocation in just a few days, but doable. The question is, why move at all?

Knowing our answer lies roughly an hour to the south, we head out, rejoining with Grumpy and Zok on the far side of the mine field. With the sky dimming to a deep purple hue, we ride fast and in silence, keenly aware that just hours separate us from a desperate battle for which we are not yet prepared.

But there is one more obstacle in our way. A cliff, rising from the coast and stretching far inland creates a natural barrier that not even a behemoth could force his way through. We stop a half mile away, craning our necks up at the towering cliffs. I see no sign of human defenses at its base or at its top.

"I'm just going to put this out there," Mira says, "just in case any of you tough-as-nails types are thinking it. I'm not climbing up this cliff."

No one argues.

"Heading inland will take us too close to the Nephilim," Em says. "Their scouts have no doubt discovered the ruse and have changed the army's course."

"I could try flying us over," I say.

Grumpy lets out an uncomfortable roar and four women, five if you count Zok, turn to me with looks that say, "Don't even think about it."

"Word to the wise, kid," Kat says. "When you're talking about flying five people and two dinosaurs half a mile up into the air, don't use the word 'try'. Besides, none of that will be necessary. The military is running the show. They wouldn't leave us a way to find them if reaching them was impossible."

"I could open a tunnel through the cliff," I say.

"Save your energy," Kat says. "You're going to need it. And we don't know how thick the cliff is. Could be a mile across at the top."

"Where to, then?" I ask.

She points to the left. "Where the cliff meets the ocean."

Grumpy turns in the direction Kat is pointing, but doesn't move until I give him a gentle nudge with my heels. Then we're off and running, but not for long. The jungle growth here is new and thick. The cresties have a hard time walking through, so we have to dismount and clear a path. Again, I could use my powers, but Kat is right, any unnecessary use of my abilities will drain me some, and we have no idea how long it will be until I need them in a big way.

By the time we reach the base of the cliff, the last light of day is struggling to stay above the horizon. Where the stone wall rises from the sea is cloaked in deep shadow, black as night. Despite the darkness, I have no trouble making out the ledge jutting out over the sea, which is roaring a hundred feet below. It's just eight feet wide, barely big enough for the cresties to pass single file. It's wide enough for a band of humans or a line of Nephilim, but they would be easy targets. And since Nephilim are prone to dying when they drown, the wingless variety would likely avoid this route.

"I can't see a thing," Mira complains. She takes out her glowing blue crystal, but this isn't the inside of a cave, where the light can reflect. It lights our party's faces in dull blue, but that's about it.

"Let me see," I say, taking the orb from her. "The crystals glow because the molecules are active. When they collide, they glow. The color is determined by which elements are dominant in the crystal." Suddenly, the sphere blossoms with light, illuminating the ground, the cliff and the ledge. It's so bright that it hurts to look directly at it.

"What did you do?" Mira asks.

"Sped up the molecules so they collide harder and more frequently."

"It's not going to explode or something?" she asks.

"I don't think so," I say.

Kat laughs. "You really need to work on your declarative statements. Even if you're not sure, sound sure."

I start to sigh, but she cuts me off.

"I'm not kidding. You're going to be sending men to their deaths. If you don't sound confident about the benefit of their sacrifice, or the chance of their survival, they're going to head for the hills. Armies are only as brave as their leader."

"No one is braver," Kainda says, stepping between Kat and I. "Do not insult him again."

"I have no doubt about his abilities," Kat says. "But whatever army we have waiting for us doesn't know him beyond the rumors they've heard, or the show he put on at the FOB. Beyond that, he's just one man. And he hasn't earned their confidence yet. If he's not exuding confidence in the way he talks, or even walks, they're going to see it."

I put a hand on Kainda's shoulder. "It's okay. She's right."

"So let me hear it," Kat says. "Are we going to win this war?"

"Yes," I say quickly, but it almost sounds like a question.

Kat grunts. "Going to have to work on your lying, too." She heads for the ledge, stopping at the edge. The cliff is two hundred feet thick and the ledge stretches the entire distance. But I see nothing to indicate a human presence on the other side.

"How far are we from the coordinates?" I ask.

"Almost on top of them," Kat says, then raises the radio to her lips. "This is Katherine Ferrell looking for General Kent Holloway, does anyone copy?"

There's just a moment of static before a deep voice with a thick Russian accent answers, "Da, we read you. Please state business."

Kat switches to speaking Russian and the conversation flows much more quickly. After a brief exchange, Kat lowers the radio. "This is the place."

"This is where my parents are?" Mira asks.

"Da," Kat says. "Welcome to Mother Russia." With that, she steps out onto the ledge and starts toward the far end. Grumpy and Zok take some coaxing, but eventually follow us onto the ledge. I really don't know if the stone will hold their several ton weight, but if we fall, I have no doubt I can catch us all, despite how insecure my words might sound.

Halfway across, Em says, "This seems too easy. Too undefended."

"There are bombs under the ledge," Kat says.

"How do you know?" I ask.

"They told me," she replies. "Said they would blow us up if we did anything funny."

"And you're telling us now because?" Mira says.

Kat smiles. "That aghast look on your face never gets old."

Before Mira can retort, the same deep Russian voice, no longer distorted by the radio, shouts out. "Is far enough. State your business."

"I already did," grumbles Kat, and I can tell she's about to volley a string of angry Russian in their direction.

"Let me handle this," I say, stepping forward.

"You sure you—"

I shoot her a look that shows how serious I am, and then reach a hand out to Mira. "Light, please."

Mira puts the crystal in my hand. I give Kainda a wink, which makes her smile, and step forward.

With every step I take, the light grows brighter. The end of the ledge is lined with thick brush hiding the Russian from view.

"That's close enough!" the Russian says again, sounding angry now, almost like he's in pain.

"They're wearing night vision goggles," Kat hisses from behind. "The light is hurting their eyes."

I stand my ground. "Are you in charge of this outpost?"

"Da," says the Russian.

"Can you see me?" I ask.

"Da," he says again.

"Do you know who I am?"

Silence.

They're either obstinate, unsure or unconvinced. "You know the name, Katherine Ferrell?

"Da," the man says again, "But we also know of the shifters."

They've been educated. This is good. "Then you know that shifters can't do this." A wind picks me up off the ground and I float closer to the end of the ledge. I set myself down again, encouraged by the fact that I haven't been shot at. I'm just ten feet from the brush when I say, "Show yourself."

To my surprise, the brush stands up. And it's not just one man, it's twenty, each sporting a high caliber weapon. The largest of them, a man who looks like a bush, whose face is painted black, steps forward and removes a pair of night vision goggles. His eyes are bright blue, the kind of eyes I picture women swooning for, but they also look deadly.

He raises an assault rifle at my face. "Your name?"

I speak calmly and confidently. "I am Solomon Ull Vincent, the last hunter and *your* leader. You will let us pass now."

His bright white teeth flash with a grin. He steps to the side and the other camouflaged men pass. They watch us pass with intense stares, but give the dinosaurs a wider birth. Once we're past, the men resume their positions, becoming the forest once again.

Kat slides up next to me. "Good job." I start to say, "Thanks," but she speaks over me. "Lucky they didn't shoot you, though. Spetsnaz aren't known for their patience."

Spetsnaz? While I don't know much about the details of military weaponry, I do know about the major military units. Spetsnaz are the Russian special forces whose training regimen isn't that dissimilar from the breaking of a hunter. It would make Rambo cry like a little girl. In fact, hunters might be the only fighting force on the planet whose training is more grueling.

"Well, I say, if I can impress Spetsnaz, maybe there's hope for me ye—"

I stop in my tracks. We're standing at the top of a hill leading down to a massive clearing where a mind-numbing sight awaits us.

Mira says, "Holy—"

"Now this is more like it," Kat adds.

Kainda says nothing, but she's smiling, and takes my hand in hers, our still fresh bonding wounds pressed against each other.

It's Em who notes the one detail that is less impressive, but perhaps the most strange. "I've never seen that flag before."

She's right. There are several flags billowing in the wind, all lit by a variety of spotlights. They're not any of the most likely subjects: American, Russian, Chinese or any European nation. The first aberration from standard nation flags is that they're mostly white, which normally is a sign of surrender. But there is a splotch of green at the center of the flag. The shape is hard to make out, but there is a single yellow star at the core. A stiff breeze directed by my thoughts holds the flag straight out long enough for me to discern the shape: Antarctica. "It's an Antarctican flag."

26

While the rest of the base is impressive, the Antarctican flag and the unity it reveals makes me beam with pride for my fellow man. It's hard to believe that soldiers from different nations could come together under a single banner, but there it is, waving in the breeze, a symbol of our resistance against the monsters that would not just dominate us, but erase our presence from the planet.

But I don't linger on the flag for long. The base is a beehive of activity and my eyes flash back and forth, taking in every nook and cranny. The strangest thing about the base is that is appears to be a combination of modern fortifications and ancient. It's surrounded by tall, twenty foot walls. Some are gray stone—granite, I think, now braced with steel beams, and some are massive steel plates welded together. There are men across the top, and more halfway down, aiming their weapons through long windows. Several watchtowers overlook the base, once again a mix of old and new construction. I see snipers, so many snipers, keeping watch from the tall lookouts. Within the massive base are a group of modern buildings similar to what we saw at the FOB, but they're surrounding what looks like a Mayan pyramid, beneath which runs a tunnel. Just beyond the buildings are two lines of artillery—howitzers, I think, all aimed toward the distance, their crews nearby and ready to fire.

Closer to the ocean, on a flat stretch of grass, is an array of attack helicopters laden with armaments. I recognize a few, but most are more modern than anything I've seen, and the variety suggests they belong to numerous nations. I quickly count fifty. They're not up and running, but I assume the pairs of men waiting by the open cockpits are the pilots.

My eyes travel further to the left, out to sea, where I see the silhouettes of so many Navy vessels they look like one massive ship, covered in flashing lights. Their numbers are impossible to count in the dark, but at least a few of them are aircraft carriers. I can tell because the air roars with the sounds of patrolling jets.

Looking back to the base, I observe the front lines. Beyond the front wall, which will slow a Nephilim, but not stop it, there is something far more formidable. Tanks. Nearly a hundred of them. Lined up side by side, all aimed toward the west. And more are rumbling into place, arriving in a steady stream from transports at the coast, which gently slopes to the water. In front of the tanks are several long trenches filled with men and weapons. Before the trenches, a field of razor wire, and before that, a clearing that is no doubt laden with mines.

Perhaps the strangest thing about this force lies on the opposite side of the base from where I am now. Cresties. Maybe three hundred of the dinosaurs, lying on the ground, just waiting for the fight to begin. As creatures of violence, hunting and killing every day of their lives in an environment far harsher than this and filled with hunters and Nephilim, this is just another day. They might live. They might die. But either way, they'll fight the Nephilim like they always have. Despite the fact that they can have a taste for human beings, these creatures have done more to reduce the ranks of the Nephilim over the past few thousand years than any man. I'm glad they're here, and I send Zok and Grumpy off to join them.

It's an impressive army. Enough to conquer nations. But while this powerful army of perhaps a hundred thousand, bolstered by the strength of modern weapons, can wreak havoc on a scale of Biblical proportions, they face an enemy numbering a million of *genuine* Biblical proportions, who can heal from any number of wounds and who enjoy the pain. If the two behemoths make it to the base, they'd just have to fall over and much of it would be destroyed beneath their girth.

Still, it's a far better defense than the previous FOB, and our chances of survival are higher, if just by a little. Deep down, I know that the size of the base and number of tanks isn't going to affect the outcome of this battle. That will come down to me. And Nephil.

Solomon!

The voice in my head makes me flinch.

Kainda tenses next to me. "What is it?"

"Nothing," I say, and then smile. "Luca caught me off guard."

I'm vaguely aware of Mira asking about Luca and Em giving an explanation as I focus on my thoughts and reply. *Luca! Are you in the new base?*

Under the temple, he thinks. *It's where the leaders are. General Holloway is here. So are Merrill and Aimee.*

Why are you *there?* I ask. I would prefer that Luca be far away from the action. Someplace safe.

I'm a general, he thinks. *Well, not really, but I'm important. I'm coordinating everyone.*

With your thoughts, I deduce. Luca is just six, but he has my extraordinary mind and a telepathic ability given to him by Xin. A regular Professor X.

I'm not controlling them, though, just giving orders.

Well, that's good, I think to myself. But in the heat of battle, Luca might not fare so well. He might have my mind, but he also has my six year old temperament, which was about as tough as runny mashed potatoes. Of course, he was also raised in the underworld for a time and then trained by Tobias, who was loving, but demanding. He's probably tougher than I was at his age. He might even be tougher than I was at thirteen.

Well, here's my first orders for you to issue, I think to Luca.

What is it? The thought is so powerful that I can actually feel his excitement.

Open the gates and try not to shoot us.

Open the gates! The thought explodes from the center of the base and reaches the mind of every single soldier, including Em, Kainda, Kat and Mira.

"The hell was that?" Kat says, rubbing her head.

"Luca," Em says, smiling.

"He's practically running the place," I tell her and then start down the slope toward the side of the base where a gate is swinging open.

Our pace quickens and we reach the open gate at the same time as a welcoming committee that has hurried out from beneath the pyramid. Mira reacts first, seeing her parents. She breaks ranks, runs the distance between them and leaps into their outstretched arms.

Em runs next, scooping up Luca, who is dressed in green camouflage. If not for the wild, long blond hair that matches my own, he'd look like any other kid from the outside world. Em wraps her arms around her little brother and spins him in the air.

As I pass through the gates, I glance up at the watchtowers to either side. Both contain a mix of hunters and black clad snipers. The ones I don't know just watch. Then I see Adoni, the Australian Aboriginal teacher, now wielding an assault rifle. He gives me a smile and a nod.

Next to Adoni stands Zuh, her pom-pom of curly hair now tied back against her head. She once tried to claim me as her own, vowing to beat Kainda in combat for the right of being my wife. I told her that wasn't going to happen, and she seemed to respect that choice, but just in case it might come up again, I hold my hand up to her, revealing the wound on my hand. She looks momentarily surprised, but then smiles ruefully and nods in greeting.

A man next to Zuh, a big smile on his face, leans over the rail. "Chica!"

Mira waves up to him. "Cruz!"

"Am I glad to see you alive and kicking," he says.

I recognize him as one of the men from the team that raced toward the South Pole and rescued Aimee along with Wright, Kat and Merrill. He sees Kat next.

"Dios mío!" he says. "Kat!"

She nods up to him, stoic, perhaps knowing what his next question will be. But Cruz doesn't ask it. His eyes wander around our small band and he frowns. Wright's absence speaks for itself.

"Relieved to see you in one piece," he says.

"Likewise," Kat says, and offers him a casual salute, which he returns.

General Holloway stops before me, looking me up and down before staring into my eyes as though evaluating my worth. He's got at least a week's worth of growth on his face and bags under his eyes. The man has been pushing himself.

"You look...rested," he says. "Been on vacation?"

"If you don't mind me saying, sir, you've looked better."

This cracks a smile in his grim demeanor. He nods toward Mira.

"Got her back, I see."

I nod.

"The Clarks are good people. They deserved it. But now it's time to get the house in order. We don't have much time."

"How much time?" I ask.

He looks at his watch. "Eight hours. Give or take. We've been tracking them by satellite."

"Then you know what we're up against?"

He sighs and looks defeated for just a fraction of a second. "It's going to get rough, but we couldn't have asked for a better position. We've got cliffs on both sides. If they want us, they're going to have to come straight down the middle. It's a natural bottleneck, a half mile across. Call it the shooting gallery. It's ten to one right now, but we have more men, weapons and vehicles arriving every hour."

"Which nations are involved?" I ask.

"Hell," he says. "Son, you got everyone. Well, everyone in range. The Russians found this place and set up shop early. They never intended on leaving without a fight. But once we all knew what we were facing, well, here we are. Chinese, Arab Nations, the EU, the Brits, Japan, Brazil, the Koreas and at least ten more."

"Whose idea was the flag?" I ask, pointing to the largest of the bunch, flying from the top of the pyramid.

He motions toward Luca, "That would be your brother. Said you would like it. Also said that Antarctica was your land. And that you were the King."

"He was right," I say.

"About the flag?"

"About all three."

We stare at each other for a moment and then he just shrugs. "We can talk about that if we don't die."

"Sounds fair," I say. "Now about Luca."

"I know what you're going to say," Holloway says. "And normally I'd agree. This is no place for a child. But here's the thing. We've got an army made up of folks who speak fifteen, twenty languages. A lot of them can speak English, but at least fifty percent of our force doesn't understand a word of it beyond Coke and Pepsi. It was a real problem at first, but then he figured out that thought has no language. A Spanish speaker receives the boy's thoughts just as clearly as an English speaker. With his ability, he can give orders and direct troops with more efficiency and clarity than the confusing mix of radiomen and translators we were going to have to use. I'm sorry, but the boy is essential."

I look at Luca, still wrapped in Em's arms, excitedly telling Kainda a story while she rubs his hair. "If he gets hurt..."

"He'll be by my side the entire time."

"Beneath the temple?"

"It's the safest place," Holloway says, "Which brings me to my first question. Where will you be?"

I point beyond the wall, to the battlefield. "Out there."

"Solomon!" Aimee shouts, running up and giving me a hug.

Merrill follows her, clapping me on the back. "My boy!" He wraps an arm around me and gives me a squeeze. "We can't thank you enough for bringing her back."

I lean back from the both of them and say, "I just have one more promise to keep. You're all getting off this continent alive and together."

Aimee smiles and shakes her head. "The man you've become. You're parents would be proud."

Would be proud? *Does that mean...* I push the concern from my mind. Being distracted by the fate of my parents, good or bad, will only distract me from what needs to be done.

Over the next ten minutes, I reunite with Luca and share a little bit about what we experienced while we were away. The Clarks and Luca, and even the General listen to our tale, but when it's over, everyone is all business.

We retreat to the temple. A tunnel runs through the center of the structure, stopping at a chamber that has been transformed into a command center. There are thick stone walls all around and above. The tunnel is too small for a Nephilim, the structure too sound to easily destroy. Aside from a behemoth attack, the temple is the most secure location in the base. Despite the ancient surroundings, which were likely built by the same pre-flood human civilization that painted the record found in the nunatak, the space is full of modern computers, weapon racks and cables that snake across the floor before disappearing underground.

A dog barks, spinning us around. A large black Newfoundland charges toward Mira. She drops to a knee and greets the now whining dog.

"This must be Vesuvius," I say, crouching next to the massive canine. He eyes me cautiously, but I hold my hand to his nose and let him get a good sniff. After a moment, he lowers his head and slides it under my hand: permission to pet, granted. I scratch behind his ears with both hands, saying, "You're a good boy." This outside world tradition of greeting friendly dogs with expressions of how good they are feels oddly normal. Feels good.

I spot the Jericho shofar atop a desk that is bolted to the stone floor. It's wedged in a large chunk of foam and covered by a clear case that's hinged to the back side of the desk and locked on the front, like it's some kind of museum exhibit, which it might actually be some day.

Merrill notes my attention. "It's the best we could do to protect it and still have it available."

I nod. Makes sense. But what I'm confused about is the next table over. I give Vesuvius one last scratch and stand. I move to the table, which is covered in what looks like stereo equipment. Several thick cables run down to the floor and out through the hallways. "What's this?"

"The ancient Israelites had several horns and had to sound them over several days for the impact to be significant." Merrill grins. "We have a speaker system pillaged from an aircraft carrier." He points out a microphone. "This is my station. My contribution to the war effort, if you will. I've been practicing with the shofar. It's not pretty, but the effect should be impressive."

"Is the effect the same through the speakers?" I ask.

"I, uh, I don't know," he says.

"We haven't found a red head to try it on," Holloway adds.

"A red head?" I ask.

"It's what they call the Nephilim and hunters," Merrill explains.

"Then I guess we'll find out tomorrow," I say.

We spend the following three hours beneath the temple, developing contingency plans to any number of unthinkable situations. As each plan is documented, it is given a name, and then transmitted into the minds of every soldier by Luca. If he gives the command for contingency Red Bravo, every man on the ground, pilot in the air and captain at sea will know what to do.

With everyone as prepared as they possibly could be, Holloway orders us all to get some rest. Apparently, he was joking when he said I looked like I'd been on vacation, and a few hours sleep, according to him, would work wonders. When I argue that he should rest too, he points out that he'd be spending the following day shouting orders, not fighting thirty-foot tall monsters. So I give in and I'm directed to my personal quarters, which is a sturdy looking tent covered in gray camouflage.

When I enter, I find Kainda already there, waiting in one of two cots that have been pushed together. There might be other items of interest inside the tent, but I don't see them. My eyes don't stray from Kainda.

"I thought outsiders were pre-occupied with comfort," Kainda says. "These could use a few feeder skins."

"Huh?" I say, focusing my thoughts for the first time since laying eyes on her. Despite all I've been through, all the enemies I've faced and horrors I've endured, my nerves churn violently through my gut. This is my wedding night, after all. Kainda smiles up at me and erases all my fears. I remove Whipsnap and my ancient looking Batman-like utility belt, lying them next to the bed where they can be quickly recovered. I climb in bed next to Kainda, pull the blanket over me, place my hand on her cheek, and say, "I love you."

She rubs her hand through my hair—just once—and I'm asleep before she has a chance to reply.

27

"Solomon!" My name, shouted in a way that exudes desperation and encroaching danger, launches me from the cot. Confused by the dull gray space around me, I stumble and trip over Whipsnap, falling to the floor in a heap. As adrenaline fuels the return of my memory, I look up to find the cot empty. Kainda has gone.

Hearing footsteps rapidly approaching, I climb to my feet, pick up my belt and weapon and strap them on just in time to look put together for whoever it is coming to get me.

The tent flap snaps open. It's Em, who is one of the few people I wouldn't mind seeing me sprawled out on the floor. She's seen me at my worst and never thought less of me. Not that she would have noticed. Her eyes are full of concern.

It's begun, I think.

Em confirms it, saying, "They're here."

"What time is it?" I wonder aloud.

"The sun is just rising now."

They made good time.

"Take me to Holloway."

She nods and leads me out. "He's at the wall."

Men and women rush in all directions, hauling weapons and ammo, taking up positions all around the camp, watching the distance and the sky. We work our way through the bustle, past the side of the temple and toward the front of the base. As we approach an ancient staircase carved into a massive stone, I spot Luca by its base.

"What are you doing out here?" Em asks him. "Get back inside!"

"I needed to tell Sol something," the boy says, looking at me.

I kneel down to him and take his arms. "What is it?"

I'm expecting a "good luck," or a "goodbye" or even just a hug, but he levels a serious gaze at me and says. "This is how it's going to work. Think your orders to me, and I'll send them to everyone else. We'll try to use the plans as much as possible—" Luca and I share the same perfect memory. We'll be able to change tactics with a thought. "But there might be some things we haven't thought of. If something comes up, like if you need everyone to focus on a target, just think it. I'll be listening."

Talking to Luca is surreal. He not only looks like me, but he's smart like I was, and for the first time in my life, I can see why people thought I was strange. He seems far too young to be thinking in such detail or with such clarity. It's a gift, I suppose, if you're emotionally tough enough to deal with all that knowledge and the understanding that comes with it. I never was, but Luca seems to be handling his responsibilities just fine.

Then comes the hug and a quick, "goodbye." I watch him run for the temple for just a moment before heading up the stairs with Em. At the top of the wall, I find Holloway, Kainda, Kat and Mira, who now holds a dangerous looking assault rifle. She's wearing body armor and a scowl to boot. When she sees me coming, I say, "Nice gun."

"XM29," she says. "Wright taught me how to use it and trust me, you don't want to be on the receiving end of its explosive rounds."

Holloway turns at the sound of my voice. As I step up between he and Kainda, she takes my hand and gives it a quick squeeze before returning to her vigil. Holloway motions toward the battlefield. "Have a look."

I turn forward, seeing the lines of tanks, which have expanded overnight, the trenches full of men, now aiming their weapons toward the distant jungle, the rows of razor wire and the mine field beyond. After that, I see trees and a distant gap where the two cliffs almost come together. But I don't see any Nephilim.

"Base of the trees," Holloway says.

"Looks like a lot of shadow," I say.

"They *are* the shadows." He hands a pair of binoculars to me, but I dig into my pack and take out the spyglass that Ninnis gave to me so long ago. I raise the telescope to my eye and focus on the distant trees. When I see them, I flinch. They're nearly invisible, covered in mud, but their white eyes almost glow in the morning sun now rising behind us.

"Berserkers," I whisper.

"Those are the people who are lost, right?" Holloway asks. "Not like the hunters who can be—whatever the word is."

"Redeemed," I offer.

"Right," he says.

"But we can try," I say. "We have to try."

"And if it doesn't work?" he asks. "What then?"

The answer hurts too much to say aloud, so my response is to look down at the line of tanks. I can hear the hum of their engines.

"Right," Holloway says.

"I don't see any Nephilim," I say.

"They're still an hour out," he says. "These guys were hard to spot. Didn't even know they were there until the sun came up."

"How many of them are there?" I ask.

He shrugs. "No way to know for sure. Several thousand at least, but the canopy blocks our view from above."

As it blocked my view from the nunatuk. With the number of berserkers unknown, we have to assume the worst. If this is the Nephilim's opening salvo, then they must believe the berserkers are a real threat, which means there must be a massive number of men waiting in those trees.

Merrill, are you ready? I think, directing the question to Luca.

Almost, comes the reply from Merrill. The voice is in my head, and sounds like Luca, but something about it, like a signature, says the thought originated from Merrill.

A hiss of static fills the air, follow by the booming fumbling of a microphone and a whispered, "Sorry. Sorry." Then, in my head. *Ready.*

Stand by, I think.

"How do you do it, General?" I ask Holloway. "How do you condemn men to death?"

"We're not condemning them to death, son," he says. "We're merely providing the means. They're doing all the condemning themselves."

I suppose that makes sense, but it doesn't make me feel any better. I'm the one giving the order. Still, we're doing everything we can.

Go ahead, Merrill, I think.

The speakers are so loud and the microphone so sensitive, that we can hear Merrill take a breath. And then, he blows. The shofar isn't exactly a pleasant instrument to listen to, but Merrill manages to get a robust sound out of the thing. It's so loud that I can feel my insides shaking. Several of the men below, put their hands to their ears. And then the effect kicks in. No one here is directly under Nephilim corruption, but neither is anyone here completely pure. The sound moves through me. Its effect feels something like Christmas morning as a child—magical and peaceful.

The horn sounds for a full thirty seconds before Merrill lets up.

Then we wait.

If the horn has had any effect on the berserkers, we should see them acting strangely. Confused. Perhaps remembering their old selves. Wandering about. But as I watch through my telescope, I see none of these things, just agitation. Then one of the berserkers dashes forward and stops in the sunlight. He's a hairy man, covered in mud from head to toe, so much so that his blood-red hair is hard to see, but its there, corrupt as ever. The berserkers truly are lost.

The man pumps his fists in the air and screams wildly. When he's done, a chorus of voices join in, sending a sound wave of hate and madness over the base that quickly erases the lingering effects of the shofar.

And then, they charge.

The man in front makes it just twenty feet before stepping on a land mine. Then, he's just gone, a mist of a person that the next berserker runs through without pausing, before joining the first in a similar fate.

The flow of berserkers looks like a living black river of mud, flowing from the jungle. They scream in rage, blind to danger, oblivious to anything but a lust for carnage.

But then, among the black horde are specks of white, shorter, wider and bobbing back and forth as they run. I scan the now salt and pepper colored force and focus on one of the white bodies. It's a feeder. Its large black eyes are emotionless, but its massive, shark-like jaws snap open and closed, like it's excited or ravenously hungry. Both are probably true. In some ways, feeders are comical in appearance, but I know from experience that they are savage and deadly, and from the looks of it, there are just as many of them as there are berserkers. Together, they're a dangerous mix.

But we're prepared for this.

Hold your fire. The order goes from Holloway to Luca and then to our multilingual army. For a moment, I wonder if I should have given the order, but then realize I already did, to Holloway himself. He's just carrying it out.

The half-mile long mine field does its dirty work. Thousands of berserkers and feeders meet with abrupt and explosive ends. The shock wave from each explosion tears through me, cutting deeply as another human being meets his end. Sure, many are feeders, whose deaths I will never mourn, but too many are people, who are only here because they were kidnapped and broken beyond repair. I have to force myself to remain stoic. Kat notices my stiff upper lip and gives me a nod. This is what the men need to see. But is this bravery? Is this confidence?

War is a stranger to me.

Despite the field of carnage and the overwhelming death toll, the berserkers and feeders keep coming.

"How many are there?" I hear someone ask. I don't know who it was, but I hear anguish in the question. No one here wants to kill people. But then it gets worse. The last of the mines detonates and the field is clear all the way to the razor wire.

Pick your targets, Holloway orders. *Blue Alpha.*

Blue Alpha is one of the most basic plans. Infantry takes the near ground. Snipers take the middle ground. Artillery and tanks level the jungle.

The tank cannons whir, rising up to fire a ranged attack.

This is it, I think with a sour stomach.

Holloway's next thought comes through loud and clear. *Fire!*

The small-arms fire comes first, popping steadily, but then frantically. Men in the trenches fire first, then more from the walls on either side of me. The staccato pop of automatic gunfire is then accentuated with a less rapid, but far louder crack of sniper rifles. Each shot makes me jump, in part because of the volume, but also because half of the sharp retorts result in the killing of another human being.

But all of the gunfire is suddenly drowned out by a wave of thunder that shakes the ancient walls so hard I fear they might collapse. More than a hundred tanks open fire, leveling the distant jungle along with the men and monsters still pouring out from between the trees. The artillery behind the base fires next, further decimating the enemy ranks.

The enemy numbers are so high that despite all of this power and technology, a few of the berserkers and feeders make it as far as the razor wire. But they make it no further as they become hopelessly tangled, like flies in a spider's web.

The next fifteen minutes is a nauseating blur of uproarious violence that shakes the ground, and my core. And then, the flow of berserkers finally slows. The feeders taper off too, leaving just a few random individuals bumbling clumsily over the dead. The tanks hold their fire. The artillery ceases, too. And then, as there are no enemies within range, those with assault rifles pause to reload and catch their breath. Only the snipers are still firing. But even they soon slow until there is a single sniper tracking the motion of a single berserker. He's screaming, gnashing his teeth, and charging as though his army still existed and victory was assured.

The sniper pulls the trigger, making me jump, and the last man falls.

Silence sweeps over the base.

There's no cheering or congratulations or even relief. Instead, there is moaning. Cries of pain. Weeping. All of it from the battlefield full of the dead and dying.

With a quiver in my voice, I turn to Holloway. "Is there anything we can do for them?"

He purses his lips and shakes his head. "You can pray for them."

When he walks away, head to the ground, I realize the true nature of this attack. The berserkers were never meant to cause us physical harm. Their role was to demoralize us, to make us despair and grieve.

A high pitched wail rises up from the razor wire. A man suddenly lurches forward, pulling himself free and tearing his flesh only to become even more entangled when he tries to force his way through. He shouts madly, rage and confused pain lancing out from his raw throat. A single shot is fired, putting the man out of his misery.

I turn to the shooter. It's Kat. She lowers her rifle and quickly wipes a tear from her eyes.

Round one goes to the Nephilim.

28

Just thirty seconds later, a vibration rolls through the ground beneath the base. The source is distant, but a potent reminder of what is coming, and what might already be here. I take my telescope and raise it to my eye, focusing on the distant choke point where the cliffs come together. Smoke and still settling dust obscure the view.

"What is it?" Kainda asks.

I watch a swirl of dust, rising as though something had just sped past. "Something's out there."

"They're using the smoke as cover," she says plainly, then looks at me. "It's what we would do."

Hunters. With the mine field destroyed and smoke clouding the air, they're pouring through the pass and working their way silently toward us. Unlike the berserkers, the hunters will use strategy and skill. It's possible that some will make it through to the trenches. And if that happens... One hunter with a sword, in a trench—it would be a bloodbath.

Get ready, I think strongly, *but hold your fire. Gold Alpha—with a little something extra.*

I hear grunts of understanding from the nearby soldiers as the orders reach them via Luca. I wait a full minute, while soldiers reload, take aim at a field of smoke and wait. When the stillness becomes intolerable, I start with the little something extra. A sudden wind sweeps in from the ocean, catching the smoke and pulling it back and up like a blanket.

Hunters emerge from the shroud, still and silent, surprised by the sudden and unwelcome exposure. They no doubt believe they are about to be cut down. Some must have seen what happened to the berserkers. Those at the front, hold their ground, waiting at the razor wire. The rest come in slowly, creeping toward us.

They're too close for the tanks, and not far from the first trench. If they can get past the razor wire, and I'm sure they could, things would get bad, fast.

I quickly count three thousand men and woman. Though the berserkers outnumbered them ten to one, this group is far more dangerous.

As the hunters congest together, somewhere from within the group, a man shouts out. He's not speaking any words. It's more of a punchy, three syllable chant that the others take up. And when they are done, to my great surprise, the nearly two thousand hunters inside the base, including Em and Kainda respond with the same, shouted chant.

"What's happening?" I ask in surprise.

"It's a challenge," Em says. "To combat. As Hunters."

"We cannot turn them down," Kainda adds.

"The hell you can't," I say growing angry, and then do my best mind shout, *Gold-Alpha!* Luca does a good job translating the passion of my command and I hear it in my own head a second later.

Kainda turns to me. "It is not honorable. Hunters—"

"We are not hunters!" I shout. "Not anymore."

"Someone must face them!" she shouts back.

I look to the gathering of hunters, who have taken up a formation and look ready to spring into action. "Then it will be me."

I leap from the wall and am carried up and over the battlefield, soaring past rows of tanks and entrenched infantry. I land on the near side of the razor wire, just fifty feet from the enemy. An army's eyes settle on me. I do my best to match their gaze, and then say, "There is not one of you who could stand against me."

A grumble works its way through the ranks of hunters, but no one argues. After my little flight, they all know who I am.

I decide to lay it on thick. "I have slain your masters." I motion to the base behind me. "I have set your brothers and sisters free. And I can do the same for you. The choice is yours. It has *always* been yours."

"I will stand against you," shouts a man. I cannot see him, but his words seem to bolster the enemy rank.

These are hunters, I remind myself. They respect action over words. A demonstration might help convince them. Sure, I could hit them with the shofar, but I'm not sure if that will be enough. If they don't choose the light, they might not stay in it. I have to give them the chance to choose freely first. And if that doesn't work... They might yet see what I can do.

I reach out my hands, directing a surge of wind to snip through the rows of razor wire. Spreading my hands apart, the wire shifts across the ground, forming a clearing through the death trap. I don't really need to use my hands for these things, but I want to leave no doubt that it's me doing it. Feeling a little like a mini-Moses, I walk into the clearing.

"Show yourself," I shout to the hidden man.

There's a distant shuffle and murmur as the man walks forward, shoving his fellow hunters out of the way. As the man approaches, I look at the other hunters in the group. They're clutching their weapons, eager to attack.

Then why aren't they?

Hunters aren't known for their teamwork or patience. Why would they wait for a single man to face me? It's a fight they all must realize can't be won. More than that, why are they not all arguing about who will face me. That every hunter thinks he or she is the best hunter is Underworld 101 stuff. They should all be vying for the chance of killing me, and proving that they are, in fact, stronger than the chosen vessel of Nephil and are the rightful recipient of that honor.

The fact that no one has launched an arrow in my direction shows uncommon restraint.

Why? I wonder again.

As the man reaches the outer fringe, I figure it out, and that split second of realization saves my life.

Merrill! Now!

"Hello, Solomon," the man says, throwing back a cloak that hid his face from view.

The face of Ninnis glares at me with all the hatred and loathing the spirit of Nephil can project.

Black tendrils launch out at me like spears. The first strikes my shoulder, shooting a lancing pain through my body. In that single instant, I feel the darkness seep into my body, its barbs latching onto my very soul. I try to resist it, but it's like trying to lift a behemoth.

Before the burden becomes too great, Merrill puts his lips to the mouth of that great horn and unleashes an ancient battle call that strikes fear into the hearts of Nephilim, not of physical pain, but because for a moment, they can feel the disparity of their own existence. As the first sound wave reaches me, the darkness is repulsed. But it tears out of me, yanking a scream of pain from my lungs.

Ninnis hisses and launches into the air. The sound hits him, causing black tendrils to explode in every direction. He shrieks and flails, lashing out and striking several of his own hunters.

But they're not his hunters. Not anymore. All three thousand men and women fall to the ground, writhing in agony. But it's not pain they're feeling, it's truth. Those who were kidnapped and broken, like me, Ninnis and Tobias, are remembering who they *were* for the first time. Others, who were born in the underworld are feeling the weight of their crimes like never before. A shift of color works its way back through the throng as blood red hair gives way to shades of black, brown, gray, blond and orange.

This happens to be one of the situations for which we have no plan in place. I would have never thought Nephil would risk himself like this, but that was the brilliance of the plan. Who would see it coming? None of us, that's who. So as my reeling mind tries to center itself, I look up at the writhing form of Ninnis, a man who was broken, turned into a monster and is now the vessel of an evil force, and think, *sorry*—and then—*fire!*

When the first bullet flies, striking Ninnis's leg, the demon-possessed man flinches and seems to snap out of his agonized state. The wound drips purple and heals quickly. With a hiss, he launches himself up and away, carried by frenzied tendrils. The gunfire chases him for a moment, but it's clear no one will hit the man. Still, a tank gunner tracks Ninnis's retreat toward the valley's choke point and fires off a single shot.

The distant cliff explodes, showering Nephil with debris and knocking him sideways with the shockwave. He lurches to the side, but then disappears. The attack won't injure him. He heals like a Nephilim now. But the lingering sting to his pride will make him think about exposing himself like this again.

With the danger momentarily waned, I turn my attention to the hunters. Those that remember previous lives will also remember their time as a hunter. They won't be confused by what has happened, but they will certainly be conflicted by it. Some of these people have been living in darkness, literal and figurative for far longer than they lived in the outside world.

One by one, they stand. I nearly laugh when I see some helping others to their feet. But will they stay this way? Or will they choose to remain in darkness?

Then it happens. A single man runs away, his hair turning redder with each step.

Then another.

And another.

And then, no one else.

Let them go, I think. We have shed enough human blood for one day.

A footstep behind me catches my attention. I turn to find Kainda strutting up confidently. She steps up next to me and addresses the freed hunters. "I am Kainda, daughter of Ninnis, servant to Thor."

The group reacts with a mixture of fear and tension.

"But I am now free," she says, quieting the rising talk. "And my master is dead."

Those still speaking, fall silent. They have been freed from the bondage of their hearts and minds, but the threat of physical bondage to their Nephilim masters still very much exists.

"And I fight the monster Nephil who controls the form of my father. All of this is possible because of this man." She motions to me.

Inwardly, I'm caught off guard and thinking, *Who? Me?* But on the outside, I stand confident and bold. I know what I have to do, even if it makes me feel uncomfortable. Despite being freed, these people are still hunters, like Kainda, and Em...and me, despite my previous denial.

"I am the Last Hunter," I say loudly. "I am Solomon Ull Vincent, the first and only Antarctican, leader of the human resistance against the Nephilim, and...*I am your King!*"

To my surprise, and I'll admit it, delight, a cheer rises up. It's just one person at first—Em, I think—but then it moves through the base behind me and the hunters before me.

As a smile spreads on my face, I think, *round two goes to the human race*, though it nearly didn't. I glance down to my shoulder, where the black tendril burrowed into my flesh. There's no wound, but I can still feel its lingering effects, and the raw power of its attack. Had Merrill waited just an instant, the darkness might have claimed me. And if that happened, all would be lost.

29

Em, Adoni, Zuh, I think, letting Luca know who I want my orders to be transmitted to, *split these hunters between you. Get them settled inside the base. Do your best to explain how we're organized and how we are communicating. Put them in defensive units with hunters already among us.*

Luca can send my orders to these new hunters just as easily as everyone else, and they'll understand, but they need to be prepared for the mental intrusion.

Em speaks up from just behind me. She must have already been on her way out. "Hunters, I am Emilie, daughter of Tobias—"

"The daughter of Tobias," a woman hunter says in surprise. She's tall and slender with long curly, light brown hair that hangs wildly to her shoulders. She's holding a double edged sword that looks like something a Roman centurion would carry in one hand and a long spear in the other. "Was he not slain by Ninnis, *father* of Kainda?"

Em frowns and nods. "He was."

"And yet you stand beside her?"

I think I understand the gist of this questioning. In hunter culture, the slaying of one hunter's kin by another might result in some sort of blood feud, or at least a deeper than average hatred.

Em steps up next to Kainda, who's at least a foot taller, and looks up at her. "We are as sisters. The sins of our past, and those of our fathers, are forgotten. As they are for you, as well."

To say the hunters are surprised is an understatement. The news travels quickly toward the back of the throng. It's clear the conversation is about to expand and while I would love to explain the depth of their new found freedom, the rumbling beneath my feet is a constant reminder that we have no time.

"Hunters!" I shout. "Time is short. You all know what is coming. Explanations will come, but only if we survive the coming battle."

"And if we don't survive?" the woman hunter asks, sheathing her sword.

"Then you will die nobly, and free," I tell her.

This seems to placate the crowd enough for Em and Kainda to get them moving toward the base. I notice many of the soldiers following the hunters with their weapons. *Lower your weapons*, I think, *they are with us now*. A moment later, the soldiers comply.

You're doing well, I think to Luca.

This is harder than I thought it would be, Luca admits. *Speaking to you is easy. Speaking to more than a hundred thousand other people is not. I'm getting tired.*

Me too, I tell him. The darkness took its toll. I'm far more tired than I should be. *But we must persevere. This will all be over by the time the sun sets again.*

Okay, he replies.

But, I think, *if you ever feel like you can't handle it, or are worried you can't reach everyone, you let me know.*

I will, he says.

As the woman with the Roman sword passes me, she offers a slight bow and pauses. She glances back toward the valley's bottleneck. "It won't be long." She speaks perfect English with a Southern California accent.

"I know," I tell her.

"We're just a small group," she says. "There are far more—"

"I have seen," I say.

"Then it *was* you in the jungle?" she asks. Before I can answer, her face becomes serious, but then relieved. "We found Ares."

I look at the sword hanging from her waist, and then to the long spear in her hands. Not Roman, I realize. *Greek.* "He was your master."

"No longer...thanks to you." She offers her hand and I take it, shaking it slowly. She motions to the hunters filing past. "They call me Deena, but you can call me Jennifer. I was a roustabout working at McMurdo. Must have been forty years ago. Don't remember exactly what happened. Had too much to drink one night, woke up in the feeder pit. You know how it goes."

Feeling a little bit like a politician on the campaign trail, I thank her and start to pull back my hand. She holds tighter, the calm visage of Jennifer replaced suddenly by the hard stare of Deena. "Can we trust you?"

I match her serious gaze and say, "I would die for all of you, or one of you."

She holds my eyes for a moment, perhaps judging the sincerity of my words. Then she lets go of my hand and steps back. "Let's hope it doesn't come to that."

When the shaking ground intensifies, I urge her to follow Kainda and Em and she complies.

As the last of the hunters walk past, I bring the razor wire back together. I can't weld the strands back together, but I bunch and overlap it enough that the jutting razors entangle and hold the two sides together. Standing at the front of my army, I look toward the end of the valley. No one yet fills the gap, but I know they soon will. Nephil will react to being wounded and chased off with blind rage. On one hand, this benefits us because rage is often absent strategy. On the other hand, it means they will likely rush our position en mass, which is the one strategy that is most likely to succeed. If that happens, the only thing that will slow them down will be the bodies of their own dead.

I stand still, listening to the rumbling footsteps. Distant battle horns sound out. I reach out, feeling the earth and the air. There are so many that I cannot distinguish a human footfall from a behemoth. It's all just one giant force, crushing the land and trampling the jungle.

Five minutes, I think. *They'll reach the bottleneck in five minutes.*

The thought was intended for myself, but I hear a soldier in the trench behind me whisper, "Oh God," his voice filled with terror. Luca must have transmitted the timeframe to the entire camp, which is probably good, but the twinge of fear I felt was also sent to everyone.

Sorry, Luca's voice says in my mind. He sounds small and apologetic, no doubt realizing that my thought wasn't intended for public consumption.

Its fine, I think, *we're all afraid, and I need to say something about it. Ready to give a lecture?*

I can feel him smiling. *Ready.*

Making a note to watch the intensity of my personal thoughts, I turn around and face the base. An army stares back at me. Men from the trenches, from the tanks, and the walls. But there are many more inside the base, waiting by the choppers, manning artillery and crewing the distant ships who need to hear what I have to say, too.

After taking a moment to collect my thoughts, I project them through Luca, to an army.

The Nephilim are mankind's oldest and most vile enemy. They have ruled us, enslaved us and broken us. Our ancestors worshiped them as gods and they became immortalized in our history. You know the eldest of them as Zeus, Odin, Osiris, Enki and so many more names that have been distorted by time and intention. They seek not just dominion over the planet, but the extinction of the human race, of whom they are jealous. For it is we who were given souls that live on after death, it is we who are more powerful and it is we who are protected by a grand design beyond understanding.

They are large. Huge. They inspire fear in all who see them. They attack without hesitation or remorse, and they delight in pain because they can heal from most any wound. Some will fly with outstretched wings, others will sting with scorpion tails, and still others will attack our minds with their own. Our enemies are the heroes of old, men of renown, and they are to be feared.

But the human race has defeated them in the past. Long before we had guns, tanks and warships, an army of men stormed the city of Jericho, a Nephilim stronghold. Using sword, spear and the blast of horns like the one that just freed three thousand men and women from the Nephilim's corrupt grasp, men conquered that city, vanquished the monsters inside and sent the Nephilim scrambling to the underworld where they have hidden for thousands of years.

In that time, they have grown stronger, and they have plotted against us. Their hatred has grown. And now, freed from the ice, they are once again on the cusp of destroying our world. But once again, an army unlike anything in the history of mankind has been brought together. It is we who stand in their path now, and it is we who will stop them. But this time we will not simply turn them away and send them back to the underworld. We will destroy them. We will scour them from the face of the planet. We will end their soulless existence so that they can never threaten the human race again.

I pull Whipsnap from my belt and hold the now iconic weapon over my head, letting out a battle cry, both mental and physical.

As my army shouts back—including the cresties—charged and ready to fight, a rumble rolls beneath my feet so strong that I know the enemy is just seconds away from filling the bottleneck.

Prepare yourselves, I think, and then give the order that sets everything in motion. *Jericho-Alpha.*

30

The first thing I need to do is get out of the line of fire. Although a part of me wants to lead the charge, that's not the strategy we're playing. This is, in effect, a tower defense. We're going to sit tight, hammer them with everything we've got until we run out and if that's not enough, then we'll charge. If I were to storm the enemy, shaking my weapon boldly, it might be inspiring—until I took a tank round in the back.

With a leap, I cover the distance between the trenches and the wall, guiding and slowing my descent with the wind so that I land back in my spot next to Holloway. The General gives me a nod, which is about as much a compliment as I'm going to get at the moment.

The air behind the base fills with the reverberating thunder of rising helicopters, their rotors chopping the air. They lift from the ground and take up hovering formations three hundred feet above and behind the line of artillery. They're armed with an array of small missiles and chain guns that shoot bullets so fast they're kind of like laser beams.

Even louder than the choppers is the roar of jets lifting off from several aircraft carriers. Each jet will fly in a holding pattern until they're called on. They pack a serious punch and can outrun any flying Nephilim, but our real firepower comes from the Navy Destroyers. Not only do they have some really big guns, they can launch missiles designed to flatten buildings. There are also several submarines lurking in the depths. *Nuclear* submarines. While they won't play a role in the coming battle, they're our contingency plan: Cleansing Fire. If we lose the fight, and the fate of the human race is at stake, they will launch their nuclear payloads, essentially erasing the battlefield along with everything in and around it. The plan belongs to Holloway, and while the idea of it makes me cringe—I read the books and saw the pictures of Hiroshima when I was a kid—I couldn't argue with the logic.

But it's not going to get to that point, I tell myself. *I won't let it.*

A rumble beneath my feet pulls my attention forward. Despite the din of modern war machines, a kind of peace settles over the troops as we wait for our enemy.

Rumble.

C'mon, I think, *where are you?*

And then, it's impossible to miss. A behemoth steps into the gap, nearly filling it. Its massive white body gleams in the rising sun. Its long tentacles of red hair writhe around its body. It's solid black, orb eyes, a blank like a shark's so that you never really know if it's looking at you while at the same time, you have no doubt that it's looking at you. The top of its head tilts back, the mouth opening wide to reveal teeth the size of sailboat sails.

Ropes of drool ooze down from the top like waterfalls. And then it lets out a bellow that's high pitched and a deep rattle all in one.

Yeah, I think, *Nephil is angry.* But he's got a decent strategy, too. I have no doubt that this behemoth will be followed by a mad rush of Nephilim. But this is also our chance to slow them down and kill their momentum.

Behemoth-Alpha, I think. *Go.*

As though in response to my mental command, the behemoth takes a giant step forward. And then another. A third brings it just inside the bottleneck and a fourth, all the way through.

But then, six fighter jets whose make and models are unknown to me, but which look really sleek, streak past overhead.

The behemoth takes a fifth step and I realize that just fifteen more will bring it to our doorstep.

The six jets unload with everything they have, launching missiles and peeling up and away. The missiles twist and swirl through the air, leaving white contrails in their wake, like long tails. And then, one by one, they find their target in the midsection of the giant beast. A ball of fire and billowing black smoke obscures the giant, but its wail reveals the strike caused it pain.

I watch in silence, waiting for some sign of success. I don't wait long, but what I see is not success. The behemoth takes another step. It slides out of the black curtain of smoke revealing its prodigious belly. If the missiles caused it any harm at all, there's no evidence of it. The monster has completely healed.

"How the hell are we supposed to take off that thing's head," Holloway mutters.

"We might not have to," I tell him. To my knowledge, only warriors need to be decapitated, or have their weak spots pierced. Other variations of Nephilim can heal, but not as quickly, or as completely.

"How do you mean?" Holloway asks.

"We don't give it time to heal," I tell him, and then I send an order to the tank gunners, helicopter crews, artillery crews and fighter jet pilots. *Fire!*

This time, I have to put my hands to my ears. The volume of this many tank cannons, artillery shells, missiles, jets and helicopters is more than my ears can bear. Unless... Yes, I think I can— *Whump!*

"What just happened?" Holloway asks me, and I can hear him perfectly. He didn't even have to shout.

"I turned down the volume," I say. He looks at me like I'm crazy. "I created a dome of compressed air over the base and the trenches. The sound waves are either being slowed to the infrasonic range or they're being redirected."

A bright flash turns our attention forward. The continuous volley reaches the behemoth. I can see it roaring in pain, and can even hear it some, but my ears are spared.

I quickly communicate the reason for the strange silence to the troops, so that they're not disturbed by it. When I'm done, Holloway says, "*Now* it makes sense."

More missiles pass by. These are larger, the kind that no fighter jet could carry. I'm not sure what they are, but they're big, and powerful. And there are twenty of them racing from the Destroyers at sea toward their impossible-to-miss target.

Explosions rock the valley. Despite the sound being muffled, I can still feel the force of each blast. These last twenty dwarf even the footfall of a behemoth. Rock slides race down the sides of the distant cliffs. The human race is dishing out some serious might.

And yet, the behemoth staggers forward. But it's not immune to the attack. Volcanoes of purple blood erupt from each wound. Chunks of boulder-sized white flesh, the same stuff I subsisted on during my first months underground, fall to the ground.

Another step.

The wounds are healing. This isn't going to work. It's going to stumble forward until we're out of ammunition and then just roll its fat body over us.

Behemoth-Beta! I think.

The jets arc away, while the rest of the big guns hold their fire. If this next trick doesn't work, we'll be in real trouble.

But then I add a second order, *Backfield-Alpha.* The jets moving away from the fight turn in a wide arc that brings them around toward the back of the valley. Missiles launch and lines of tracer fire glow orange as they shoot at targets on the ground *behind* the choke point. The planes will continue to strike the backlines of the Nephilim forces, returning to the aircraft carriers to rearm, refuel, and then head back to the fight.

The artillery opens fire again, having taken time to adjust their aim. A fresh volley of rounds arcs up and over the battlefield, dropping down behind the cliffs and striking even more enemies that are out of sight.

While all this is happening, a single jet, which I actually recognize as a Russian MiG fighter thanks to *Top Gun,* cruises through the battlefield from the south. It cuts beneath the soaring artillery shells, yet above the behemoth. The pilot has guts.

As it passes over the behemoth it drops a single bomb. The silver cylinder glows blue for a moment because of friction, and then strikes the behemoth's head and detonates. At the moment of impact, white phosphorous inside the bomb ignites a gel composed of benzene, gasoline and polystyrene. This highly flammable mix sprays out in all directions, coating the behemoth in a fiery slurry that will burn, white hot, for ten minutes.

The monster's shrill cry pierces my dome of dense air and makes me cringe. Were this any creature but a Nephilim, I would feel immense pity. The creature stumbles forward and then topples over. It crashes to the ground, sending a wave of pressure through the earth that rattles the base and knocks over some of the structures and piled supplies.

I kick up a strong wind from the ocean to keep the dust cloud at bay, forcing it back and down to the earth from where it came. As the behemoth twitches and burns, I watch its flesh fight to repair itself. It's a slow battle between fire and flesh, but after nearly a minute, the rocket-fuel's fire wins. With a groan, the behemoth lets out its last breath and seems to deflate.

As the body shrinks in on itself, several of the long red stands of its living, hair stretch outward. At first I think it's simply twitching as the body dies, but then I realize it's a last act of defiance. The long, python-like hair sweeps in a wide arc, striking the rows of razor wire. The sharp coils of metal tangle with the hair like Velcro and are torn away. In a single attack, the monster removes all but one row of razor wire, effectively destroying our first line of defense. Then it stops moving completely.

"It's dead," I say, honestly a little surprised.

"Napalm tends to do that to things," Holloway says.

Before we have a chance to celebrate, the behemoth moves. Its belly twitches and jerks as though something inside is fighting to get out. No, not *as if*... It's *exactly* like something is trying to get out.

And then, it does.

31

A wet tear punctuates the emergence of a massive sword from the insides of the behemoth. It slides through the thick flesh horizontally, carving a neat line. A second sword emerges. Then a third, all slicing the monster open like a Tauntaun on Hoth. It happens fast. In seconds. And in that short time, I'm too stunned to react.

The cut flesh separates, but there's no blood, nor fluid of any kind. Instead, there is a battle cry. A human battle cry. Three sets of Nephilim hands lift the flesh up, supporting its weight on their unfurled wings, while all around them, an army of hunters surges out.

A Trojan horse. Nephil wasn't overreacting, he's simply one step ahead. And his tactics, while gruesome, are effective. The hunters leaping from the insides of the behemoth, are within striking distance of the trenches and only a single coil of razor wire stands in their path—an insignificant obstacle.

As the first of the hunters closes in on the razor wire and easily leaps it, I think, *Merrill, shofar!*

The horn blasts immediately, but is muffled. Remembering my sound dampening effect, I free the compressed dome of air and allow the full power of the shofar to go roaring up through the valley.

The attacking hunters fall to the ground, the red beginning to fade from their hair. The Nephilim inside the behemoth shriek and shrink back, letting the giant folds of behemoth skin fall atop hunters still climbing out.

This will be another victory for us. Our army will grow once again and Nephil will be forced to stop using hunters against us.

When the horn blast stops, the sound of shouting voices, pounding helicopters and roaring jets take its place. But I barely hear them. My attention is on the few thousand hunters still on their knees.

I'm about to call out to them, to welcome them as freed brothers and sisters when the unthinkable happens. A splash of red appears and then washes over the group like a giant invisible painter is brushing their heads with blood. *All* of them are reverting back to their corrupted selves.

Merrill! Again!

The horn blast sounds, long and powerful.

The hunters resist. There is the occasional flicker of normal hair color, but it doesn't last long.

I don't understand! Why is the shofar not working?

"On the cliffs!" someone shouts when the sound of the shofar fades again.

I glance up to the top of the cliffs. Winged warriors line the precipices on either side of the valley, their wings outstretched.

Their presence is ominous and hellish, but they're not what holds my attention. It is the much smaller, much more numerous, force of gatherers that catch my eye. There are thousands of them, each between six and ten feet tall. Their skinny gray bodies are almost invisible with all the rising smoke, but their black, oval eyes cut through the distance.

Gatherers have the ability to communicate telepathically. That's how Xin, who was part gatherer, gained his ability, which he somehow passed on to Luca, who is fully human. But gatherers can also manipulate minds, implant thoughts, erasing them or controlling their targets completely. And right now, high up on the cliff, they're out of the shofar's range, even amplified as it is.

They're keeping the hunters corrupt, I think.

Along with this realization comes a droning buzz inside my head. They're trying to control us, too!

Guard your thoughts, I shout mentally to my troops, warning them of the danger. *Resist their control!* From such a great distance, my unwilling force should be hard to control completely, but the distraction could prove fatal. *Snipers, clear the gatherers from the cliffs.*

A second later, the first sniper round is fired. I see a single gatherer drop to its knees and tumble over the side. Gatherers can heal, but much more slowly than warriors. If the bullet didn't kill it, the impact with the ground should. More snipers follow the order and a constant stream of bullets fly toward the cliffs, followed by a constant rain of gray bodies falling down. But there are so many gatherers, that each death counts for little.

Solomon.

It's Luca.

I can feel them. They're trying to find me.

He's talking about the gatherers, I'm sure. They can probably sense his presence. Maybe even feel his thoughts and understand what he's doing for us. If they were to somehow interfere with Luca, or hurt him, we would lose our ability to communicate quickly and universally to our multilingual force. The result would be chaos. But I'm not sure what more we can do, aside from killing as many gatherers as possible. We could napalm them, I suppose, but my lungs already sting from the first toxic cloud produced by the first bomb. And our supply is limited. We need to save it for the second Behemoth. Missiles are an option, too, but we could create a rockslide, covering the battlefield, or our base, with mounds of stone, a condition that would benefit our much larger adversaries. I hate it, but Luca is going to have to fight, too.

You're stronger than they are, I tell him.

But there are so many.

Not for long, I think. *Fight as hard as you can.* I send an order through him to the helicopter pilots, directing them to climb and strafe the cliffs with their chain guns.

Before I can think of another countermeasure for the gatherers, a battle cry tears my attention forward again.

The hunters are charging.

Merrill, keep it coming!

The horn sounds again. A few hunters stumble, but the effect is negligible. The gatherers are keeping the shofar's effect at bay.

This is the unthinkable moment I have been dreading.

The lead hunter, who is past the single row of razor wire, charges toward the trenches, sword raised.

My mind, for all its brilliance, can only think of one solution. And with just seconds remaining, I give the order.

Fire.

A barrage of bullets fly from the entrenched soldiers.

Scores of hunters fall, their human blood soaking the soil of Antarctica, but more take their place. So many more. The Nephilim inside the behemoth have reopened the wound, allowing more fighters to emerge. The warriors are screaming in pain, writhing against the sound of the horn, but I suspect that they too, are getting outside support.

A shadow draws my eyes up.

As the helicopters rise toward the top of the cliffs and open fire, lines of gatherers fall before their modern might. But the winged warriors with them quickly take action. Several stand in the way of the streaming bullets, using their bodies to shield their brethren, enjoying the pain and quickly healing from the wounds. Others take to the sky, attacking the choppers.

A scream pulls my attention forward again.

I spot a hunter in the trenches, slashing back and forth with a long sword until he's shot. But the damage was done. Ten of my men are dead along with him, and more hunters are closing in, charging in columns protected at the front by hunters wielding large shields strong enough to deflect bullets. Seeing that there are just seconds before the trenches are overrun, I use my powers, which I've been reserving for the even more difficult battles to come.

A gust of wind slams into the front line of hunters, tossing them into the air like feathers in front of a fan. Even before they land, more take their place. I cut the wind, allowing my men to fire again. And then, when the hunters get too close again, I knock them back. We could sustain this tactic until all the hunters were dead, but danger is coming from all directions.

"Look out!" Holloway shouts. He tackles me from the side, taking us both off the wall. We drop, twenty feet toward the ground, but I manage to arrest our fall before we land hard. Our feet never reach the ground. An explosion rips through the wall, sending us flying. I catch a glimpse of a ruined helicopter as it strikes the wall and explodes. People and shrapnel fly in all directions. The wall crumbles beneath the chopper's weight. I once again manage to catch us with a gust of wind, but the sound and the force of the nearby explosion has sent my head spinning.

Back on my feet, I stagger and release Holloway from my arms. But while I'm unsteady on my feet, Holloway is limp. He falls to the side, landing hard. I dive to his side, putting my hand on his back to steady him. But my hand doesn't reach his back. A large chunk of metal shrapnel is in the way. I look at the wound. Some random chunk of helicopter protrudes from his back. It's large and embedded deep, next to his spine.

Holloway grips my arm. That he's still alive is a miracle. I turn him slightly and look into his eyes. "Fight," he says, and blood drips from his lips. "You fight." His voice is filled with fury. "To the last man. To the last woman. With everything you have. Fight!"

Holloway goes slack in my arms. The General is dead. But his words still ring in my ears.

Fight!

I place the General down, pull Whipsnap from my belt and scream, with my mouth and my mind, "Hunters! Attack!"

32

I run toward the front wall, driven by anger over the death of Holloway. I didn't know him well, but he always struck me as a good man. And the world needs good men, now more than ever. Reaching the wall, I leap into the air, lifting off the ground like one of the helicopters.

As I soar up and over the wall, I remember that we have planned for this moment and mentally issue the order: *Duck and Cover.*

The battlefield comes into view beneath me. In the time I spent laying Holloway down, the battle has shifted. Hunters are pouring into the trenches. Many fall to gunfire, but others are cutting through my men. Not for long, though.

The rows of tanks lined up in front of the base, unable to fire at such close range targets without injuring our own forces, roll forward. The soldiers duck down as the sixty-seven ton armored vehicles drive over the trenches. One row at a time, the tanks park above the trenches in tight formation, sealing off the men below from the rushing hunters, who swarm over the tanks like army ants over beetles. Some of the hunters whack at the tanks with their weapons, but they have no effect. The men beneath them are now retreating into the base through a tunnel I formed.

With the men beneath them protected, and no friendly forces in front of them, I give the order to fire. Just once. Thunder rises from below as I cross over the tanks. The hunters on top of the vehicles stumble and fall, clutching their ears in pain. Others, unlucky enough to be in the line of fire, simply cease to exist. Most of the tanks aimed for behemoth and the Nephilim still holding the beast open. The giants are quickly reduced to pieces from which they cannot heal. The mammoth body folds in on itself again, trapping thousands of hunters that had yet to vacate the hollowed cavity.

Still airborne, I look up. A Nephilim warrior attacks a helicopter, striking out with its sword. The massive blade cuts through the chopper like it was a flying tomato. The attack sends the rotor blades flying and one of them returns the favor, severing the giant's wings. Helicopter and Nephilim both fall, toward the base. Inside the base.

But Merrill is still blowing the shofar and the base is full of fighters who have been trained to kill Nephilim. I'll have to trust that they can handle it. I have to take care of this hunter swarm first. Because I'm sure there will be no delay in what comes next.

To prove me right, a horn sounds in the distance, and I catch a glimpse of Nephilim warriors charging into the bottleneck. Just before landing, I direct the tanks, artillery and Navy vessels to focus their efforts on the bottleneck, while the Air Force jets continue their assault on the forces still out of sight and the helicopters clear the cliffs.

My entire flight, everything I saw and every command given takes just ten seconds. Then I'm approaching the ground on the far side of the tanks, dropping down toward a throng of several thousand hunters all working their way toward the base. And they will have no trouble scaling the walls. Just before landing, I see bullets tear through some of the hunters. Men on the wall are still firing.

Hold your fire, I think, directing my thoughts to anyone firing from the walls. Then I land and put all of my anger and desperation into it. The earth buckles beneath me. A shockwave bursts away from me, moving through air and land. Every hunter for a hundred feet in every direction is knocked down. Those within twenty feet don't get back up.

With every human death, on either side, my anger rises, tenfold so when I am the one responsible for their deaths. But the hunters leave me no time to mourn the deaths of their brothers. They rush me from all sides, and I charge to meet them.

As they close in, I spin, swiping Whipsnap around, focusing a burst of wind from its tip. Men fly away from me, cast hundreds of feet in the air. At least I won't see them die. An arrow whistles past my head, and I quickly form a protecting swirl of wind around me, deflecting several more projectiles being launched in my direction.

They've practiced this, I think. By making me focus on defending against arrows, knives and darts, they're keeping me from attacking. Any lapse in my defense could mean a quick death.

Unfortunately for them, I've been practicing too.

The hunters come at me again with little regard for their own dead, stepping around and on their bodies. As they close the distance, I wait, deflecting the steady stream of projectiles. And then, when the closest attackers are just fifteen feet away, I will the ground around me to rise up. A wall of stone forms around me. It does an even better job of protecting me, but that's not its purpose.

It's a weapon.

For a moment, secluded in my dome of earth, I close my eyes and say a prayer for the men and woman I'm about to kill. At one time, they weren't hunters. They were teachers, photographers, scientists and explorers. They had lives, and loved ones. Some, like Ninnis, were married, or had children. They were good people once. And somewhere, deep inside them, they still are.

But not right now.

And I've done everything I can to prevent this. Right?

My doubt disappears when Holloway's words come back to me and my perfect memory remembers the expression on his dying face. *Fight!*

"To the last man," I say and then, with a focused burst of air, the stone around me shatters explosively. Fragments of stone shoot in every direction, cutting through the horde of hunters flooding toward me.

Men and women fall, clutching their wounded bodies and dropping their cherished weapons. They have known hatred and violence for as long as they can remember, but now...they're free. Really free. And unlike a Nephilim, they have souls that will live on. This gives me some consolation. If I can't free them in life, I can free them in death.

As I survey the battlefield, I find myself growing tired. The combination of strong emotions and exertion are taking their toll. I'm not yet useless, but I still need to watch how frequently I use my abilities, especially in unnatural ways, like turning the earth into a big grenade.

A battle cry spins me around.

A wall of hunters is nearly upon me.

I raise my hands, intending to knock them back with a homemade tornado, but then I see the hunters leading the charge—Em, knives in hand, and Kainda, hammer raised. These are *my* hunters.

As they reach me, I turn and run with them, raising Whipsnap and shouting. The roar of my hunters that follows fills me with energy, and I throw myself into battle against men and women fighting for themselves, rather than a cause they believe in. Their selfish motivations are weak compared to the convictions of my hunters, and the battle turns in our favor.

I try not to think, or feel over the next few minutes. Both ends of my weapon quickly become stained with human blood. And as more and more hunters fall to my skill, but also to the raw power with which I can now infuse my body, I try not to count.

But not counting is impossible for me.

A sword strikes my back, but I see it coming and tighten the molecules of my body. What would have been a killing blow clangs off my shoulder blades before a hammer drives the man to the ground.

"Watch yourself!" Kainda shouts at me.

Em appears by my other side. She whips a knife, dropping a charging hunter and draws a fresh blade before the body strikes the ground. "You shouldn't be here!" she shouts at me. "You're too important."

"We're all important," I argue back, lifting a group of five hunters from the ground and using the wind to send them flying into their comrades. "Especially, you two. I will not leave you."

"Then fight harder," Kainda urges.

Fight harder? Hasn't she been watching? She quickly strikes down two hunters, quickly and efficiently. *Probably not watching,* I decide.

"Our people are dying!" Kainda says.

That's when I realize that it's me who hasn't been watching.

While our force of hunters is formidable, we're actually outnumbered, and though our hunters are killing more, they have more lives to spare. But if I use my abilities against humans, how much will I have left for the Nephilim?

It won't matter if there is no one left to fight, I think.

Em must see my inner conflict reflected in my face. "You can do it, Sol."

Faith, I think.

Kainda grips my shoulder hard. Her touch is like electricity.

Passion.

I look at my wife, the power of her words and presence filling me. Then I leap away, rising above the battle and landing just beyond our front line. With a pulse of air, I clear the area around me. And then, I focus.

It doesn't matter if I kill a hundred or a thousand, I tell myself. This is a fight the human race cannot lose, no matter the cost. Like Luca, I must push myself to the limit and beyond to achieve that end, even if it kills me. *This is for you, Holloway*, I think.

Then I strike.

With a spin, I swing Whipsnap around my head like I'm striking a combatant. But there isn't anyone within range—of my physical weapon. But I am not striking with Whipsnap, I am striking with the very air of Antarctica itself.

A blade, nearly a half mile long and razor thin, follows Whipsnap's path as I swing. With my eyes closed, I finish the strike, careful not to extend it into our own ranks. For a moment, I fear that my attack has failed. Every hunter I struck thus far provided resistance—a subtle tug on the blade as it severed their flesh. But there was no resistance this time, no tug, no indication that I struck a single enemy. That is, until I open my eyes.

While I have left the enemies to my back alive—perhaps a few hundred hunters—the thousands between me and the fallen behemoth are now dead.

Thousands.

God, no.

I fall to my knees. The weight of genocide falls on my shoulders like a cartoon anvil.

This is what Nephil wants.

This is why he sent hunters first.

To destroy my soul.

But he has misjudged me. He has already used me to kill billions. And I found forgiveness for that, and the burden lifted. Cronus's words return to me. "Forgiveness cannot be earned. It can only be granted and received." The Titan leader living in Tartarus, knowing I needed to hear the words, then said, "Solomon, for your crimes against your fellow men, for the darkness of your heart and for the evil thoughts of your mind, you are forgiven."

And I was.

As I am now.

Hands grip my arms and pull me up. I recognize the feel of Kainda's hands and don't resist. As I stand, I look back and find the enemy hunters defeated. I have lost at least a thousand of my own hunters, but those that remain look strong and steadfast.

"I did it," I say, mostly to myself, but Kainda responds.

"And you will need to again," she says.

I look toward the bottleneck, but from this vantage point on the ground, so close to behemoth, the giant's body keeps me from seeing the enemy. But I can feel them. The Nephilim.

Their true assault is just beginning.

33

Cresty-Alpha! I think, sending out a command that gets a loud roar in response. The cresties, natural fighters and killers have no doubt been impatiently waiting for their chance to join the fray. Well, now they're going to get it.

With a thunder that matches that of the approaching Nephilim, the dinosaurs race out from around the base, joining the front line of hunters. Grumpy finds me and lets out an annoyed sounding grunt. He's not happy about being sidelined for so long.

"Quit whining," I tell him and he crouches down. I climb onto his back and I'm happy to see many other hunters and cresties joining forces as well. Em and Kainda climb onto Zok's long back, ready to continue the fight. But we can't see what's coming from here, even from the back of a thirty foot tall cresty, and that's not a good thing.

"Fall back to the tanks!" I shout, and I then remember to think the command. As one, the force of dinosaurs and hunters races back toward the tanks, which are still firing over our heads, smiting the distant Nephilim forces. Before the concussive force of each fired tank shell becomes almost too much to bear, and before we put ourselves in the tanks' sights, I turn Grumpy around and the rest of my army follows suit.

Further away from the behemoth, I can see the bottleneck again. It's a mess. Nephilim bodies litter the area. Some are clearly dead, the shapes of their bodies barely discernable. Others are moving still, healing from wounds that would have killed a mortal. But the wave of monsters flooding into the valley continues...as does the barrage keeping them at bay.

A never ending stream of missiles and high caliber tank and artillery shells rain down on them, rocking the valley with thunder and cloaking the scene in smoke. But the effort is paying off. Not only are many Nephilim dying under the force of the barrage, but the number getting through and continuing the charge are manageable.

Hold your positions, I tell my front line. *Save your strength.*

During the momentary reprieve, while trying to regain some of my own strength, I turn my eyes upward to the cliffs. The winged warriors are all airborne, battling with the helicopters in a deadly aerial dance. The warriors outnumber the choppers by a large margin, but the helicopters are fast and can strike from a distance. Despite the modern advantages, it's still a losing fight. As I watch, a warrior with little regard for his own safety, perhaps empowered by the knowledge that he will heal, or simply looking forward to the pain, tackles a helicopter. He slams into the side of the chopper, flips it upside down and as the rotor blades propel the vehicle toward the ground, he hangs on for the ride, laughing sadistically all the way down. The pair slams into the side of the temple where the helicopter explodes. I can't see what happens next, but I think I hear a fresh spat of gunfire over the din of the continuing battle.

Are you okay? I ask Luca.

What was that? he asks, which I suppose means he's fine.

Don't worry about it, I tell him.

Getting light headed, Merrill thinks, joining the mental conversation. He's been blowing that horn non-stop from the beginning of this battle. Without a breather, he could pass out. Luckily, he's not alone under the temple.

Have Aimee take over for a bit, I tell him.

Then, to Kat, I think, *what happened with the Nephilim on the temple?*

Mira got him, Kat replies. *XM-29. Explosive rounds. It was messy. If too many more of these guys bite it inside the base, we're not going to be able to maneuver.*

She's worried about the Nephilim blood. If it gets on anyone's skin, it will result in a horrible death. That said, the blood could also be diluted with water and used to quickly heal our wounded. *Just don't walk through it barefoot,* I think to her, and then I transmit my thoughts about using the blood for medicinal purposes to the medics set up beneath the temple.

Kid, Kat says. *You're doing a good job. If things go south, I'm proud of you.*

I don't have to think my thanks, she can feel it through Luca.

As for our current predicament, Kat thinks, *the cliffs are clear.*

Have the snipers take out the big guys' knees. Then you can take them before they get up.

Before she's even done thinking the idea, I shoot the order off to the snipers gathered from around the world and sense their aim shift as one.

Just in time, too. The first Nephilim warrior—a mammoth specimen wielding a mace that looks more like a spiked wrecking ball—leaps on top of behemoth's loose body and then off again, shaking the ground with his girth. He bellows at us, trying to put the fear of his demon fathers in our souls. But we stand strong and wait.

Undeterred by our lack of fear, the giant charges. Through the symphony of explosions, both near and distant, the scream of jets and missiles, and the staccato pop of several thousand guns, I hear Aimee take a deep breath through the speaker system. It's followed by a blast of the shofar that dwarfs Merrill's practiced efforts. I feel its supernatural cleansing effect sweep through my body.

The wave of sound strikes the big Nephilim head on. He flails wildly, dropping the axe and sprawling to the ground with all the grace of a younger me. A lone cresty without a rider takes advantage, charging ahead and descending on the giant with all its primal fury. The giant, unable to defend himself, is quickly dispatched as the dinosaur snaps its jaws down over the warrior's head, twists and pulls.

The line of cresties roar in response, as though cheering on their comrade.

But the dinosaur's victory is short-lived. Five more Nephilim warriors arrive. Then ten. The cresty manages to escape their grasp, but only because Aimee's shofar blast is still sounding.

Suddenly, the power of the shofar is reduced. The volume drops by twenty-five percent. I glance back and see one of the speakers, a giant arrow piercing its black case. A second arrow cuts through the sky, piercing a second speaker. There are a total of eight speakers lining the walls and towers. At this rate, they'll all be destroyed within the minute. I look up and find the culprit. A winged warrior hovers high above, ignoring the helicopters, which are almost all destroyed or out of ammo. His aim is uncanny, even for a Nephilim. Given his wings, scorpion tail and blood red attire, he is one of the higher echelon warriors and likely known as a god. The bow and arrow helps identify him. Apollo, Greek god of archery. The giant nocks another arrow and lets it fly. Before it can strike a third speaker, I divert its course with a gust of wind. The arrows strikes one of the armored tanks and shatters.

I turn to Kainda and Em, pointing up at Apollo. "I need to stop him!"

"Go!" Kainda shouts. "We can handle this!" She leaps from Zok to Grumpy, claiming my prehistoric steed as her own. "Go!"

"Be careful," I tell her.

I can see that my worry aggravates her, but then she softens and says, "You, too."

I launch skyward, propelling myself past the sound barrier with a boom that drowns out the cacophony of explosions. Apollo lets another arrow fly, ignoring my approach. I snap it in two with a blade of air, protecting the third speaker yet again.

Whipsnap cuts through the air, projecting an invisible blade toward Apollo. My aim is true, but I'm struck in the side and the blade fades to a blunt wind just before reaching the archer-god.

My body plummets while my dazed mind regains its senses. When it does, I look up to find Apollo, but my view is blocked by outstretched wings. A warrior wielding a long spear drops toward me. He's got one eye, which is odd for a Nephilim, but it reveals his identity: Odin, grandfather of Ull, who was my master until I killed him.

The spear surges toward my face, but I manage to duck to the side. But the attack was a ruse. The true attack comes from the right. I tense up, coiling my atoms to form an impregnable layer of skin, but I'm a moment too late. The tip of the weapon pierces my side and an all consuming fire billows through my body.

I scream in pain, still conscious, still in control, but in absolute agony. I don't have to see the weapon to know what has happened. I've been stung by Odin's scorpion tail.

Odin circles and comes back for another attack, but he's not alone. Twenty winged warriors are with him and they are a veritable Who's Who of the ancient world, identifiable by their weapons, headdresses and garments. The Greek gods: Zeus, Poseidon, Hephaestus and Hermes. The Norse: Tyr, Heimdall and Baldur. The Egyptian: Ra, Anubis, Horus and Osiris. There are several more, but the one that really stands out is the Sumerian god, Enlil, brother of the slain Enki and leader of the Nephilim warrior clan in Nephil's absence.

This group is basically the Special Ops of the Nephilim. They are the oldest and most skilled of their kind. And each and every one of them has their killer eyes set on me.

I swing Whipsnap toward the group, intending to cut them from the sky, but the movement causes a flare of agony to explode from my stung side. The air-blade is never even formed.

I cannot win this fight. Not yet. So I flee. And as I do, another speaker is destroyed.

Then another.

The sound of the shofar dwindles by half. It will soon disappear. And when it does, our advantage will be lost, and maybe the human race along with it.

34

I fly up, keeping ahead of the monsters at my heels. I can focus on flying as it takes minimal effort to control the small forces affecting me, but I won't be able to fight until the stinging poison is flushed from my body. Luckily, I am capable of repelling it from my body, I just need time.

I find it in the clouds.

A curtain of white cloaks my body. Out of view, I angle my ascent, pick a random spot and stop, hovering in the upper troposphere. I can hear the frantic wing flaps of the Nephilim searching for me, but visibility is zero. They'll have to run into me to find me.

With the sound of the raging battle echoing below, I clear my mind and focus my attention on my own body. I can feel my muscles, bones and blood. And I can feel the toxin injected into me. First, I isolate it, separating the foreign fluid from my own, and then I force it back, through my veins, through the meat of my muscles, and push it back to the wound through which it was injected.

I clench my teeth tightly. The poison fights me, clawing at my body, burning with the fury of Odin himself. With a last push, the toxin seeps from the wound in my side. I glance down and see the clear, water-like liquid drip down my side. Using the wind, I scour the fluid from my body and dissipate it into the atmosphere.

Cleansed of the poison, I feel my strength return, but I'm drained. The hunter in me gets angry. *Ignore your pain,* I think. *You are immune to it.*

Then I remember who spoke those words to me. I was still young and recently freed from the feeder pit, begging for scraps of food and obeying his commands like a dog. Immunity to pain was one of the first lessons he taught me. I find it disturbing that his advice could help me now, but I employ the lesson.

The clouds thin as I descend. Then they fade and I am exposed.

The warriors are on me immediately, but they're expecting a wounded adversary, not capable of defending himself. What they get is something else entirely.

I swipe Whipsnap around, directing a blade of wind at the first two warriors to reach me—the Egyptians, Anubis and Horus. Their ancient style helmets, fashioned to look like the jackal and falcon, fly free, along with their heads. Their bodies topple from the sky, limp and lifeless.

As the others emerge from the clouds and soar toward me from every side, I rush out to face the nearest—Odin. The ancient giant screams something at me, presumably in Norse.

I have no idea what he's said, but I reply with a shout of my own. "I'm going to send you to meet your son and grandson!"

The insult here is that there is no afterlife for Nephilim and joining his slain offspring is impossible, unless you count oblivion. He roars in response, thrusting with his spear, trying for a repeat of the tactic that worked before. But this time when he goes to sting me, the tail is missing, removed by the very air around him. Directing the wind with my thoughts, I dismantle the angry warrior and let his pieces fall from the sky, but the wind catches his massive spear.

I turn toward the shout of another god, rushing in. Odin's spear flashes past me, flying toward Tyr, no doubt out to avenge the Norse clan's fallen leader. Instead, the spear finds its mark at the center of Tyr's head, striking the protective metal band with such force that it cuts straight through.

Another warrior falls from the sky.

Then two more.

Then four more.

Those that remain realize that I cannot be taken and flee toward the ground and the battle below. As I give chase, I see that the situation on the ground has become dire. The force of cresties and hunters has been reduced by half. The wall of warriors attacking them is thick and growing in number with every passing moment. A flood of warriors are surging into the valley, no longer hindered by missiles or shelling. And those that are on the front lines, fight at full strength. The shofar has been silenced.

As I drop from the sky, Luca's thoughts reach me again. I hadn't realized I was out of range. And it's not just Luca's thoughts. It's *everyone*.

"Out of ammo," I hear from an artillery gunner.

"Going down!" a pilot thinks in fear.

"Under attack!" a ship captain says, turning my attention to the sea, where several flying warriors are assaulting the ships.

"Fall back!" This one comes from a hunter at the front line, and I shout against it. *No!*

Fight! I urge.

Ground-Beta!

Thankfully, the men and women below haven't lost their senses and are still responding to my orders. Gates to either side of the base open and soldiers from a dozen different nations flood out, carrying an array of weapons—assault rifles, machine guns, rocket propelled grenades, anti-tank missiles and flamethrowers. And they come out shooting with whatever ammunition they have left.

The remaining warriors descending ahead of me must sense me closing in. They break hard for the back of the valley and I think they want me to follow. Ignoring the trap, I drop straight down, aiming for my original target.

As I flash past, I doubt Apollo even feels his own death. One moment, he was targeting a cresty, the next he was cleaved in two.

I return to the battlefield, landing in front of Gumpy. I push at the Nephilim with the strongest wind I can muster and launch fifty of them flying back. I turn and look over my shoulder. Kainda is still atop Grumpy. She has a bleeding gash on her forehead, but she's suffered far worse. Em is still here too, but she's on foot.

I look for Zok and find the dinosaur twenty feet away, slumped over on her side. The massive chest no longer rising or falling. Another casualty.

Modern soldiers swell our ranks, using their long range weapons to stumble the approaching warriors. Mira and Kat arrive with them, both carrying the XM-29 assault rifles.

"Any bright ideas?" Kat asks.

"Working on one now," I say, only half present.

"Make it snappy, kid."

I ignore her, reaching out to the elements around me, setting something in motion that nearly drains me to the core. I fall to my knees and clench my eyes shut. It's like lifting an elephant. Then it's done. The thing is set in motion and takes on a life of its own. No longer fully exerting myself, I recover some.

"Just a few minutes," I say weakly.

"Here they come!" someone shouts. I look up to see an endless horde of warriors charging toward us. Sun glints off their massive weapons and bathes them in a holy glow that feels blasphemous.

"Can you do anything?" Mira says, placing a hand on my back.

I try to stand, but find my legs unwilling. "Not yet," I say.

"Behind us!" someone else shouts. "They're coming from both sides!"

How is that possible? I wonder as I turn around to look. There were a few warriors at sea, but not enough to instill the level of fear I hear in the man's voice. Then I see them. Twenty-five of the giants, each carrying another, for fifty total. The force pounding down on us from the front is far vaster, but these fifty, attacking our rear, will crumble our defenses.

But there is something off about these Nephilim. They look...too big. Taking my spyglass from its pouch, I look at the approaching force.

I gasp, sounding like Em. *Hold your fire,* I think to what remains of the human resistance. *The force approaching from the east is friendly!*

Just as the thought reaches my army, they arrive.

The winged giants release their cargo, dropping twenty-five Nephilim dressed in white. The thirty-foot warriors, gilded with golden armbands, belts and protective head gear, are striking, almost glowing. The ground before me rumbles as the largest of the group lands nearby. He turns his head to me, looking me in the eyes.

Cronus!

The Titans have left the refuge of Tartarus, risking oblivion to save the human race. And they're not alone. There are twenty-five gigantes, the two-headed monsters who stands at least sixty feet tall and delight in killing Nephilim the way Nephilim delight in pain. The gigantes descend into the Nephilim horde, swinging thirty-foot swords in both hands.

A large gigantes settles to the ground gently, just fifty feet away, slowing himself with his massive wings. Gigantes are one of the most repulsive creatures I've experienced in the underworld. Their skin wraps around their bundles of muscles and their organs individually, so you can see gaps between sinews and dangling, skin-wrapped guts. Their two heads are concave on top, like their brains were scooped out. Their teeth chatter loudly, manically, and air hisses through the gaps in their cheeks. Their solid black eyes are unnerving and their three-fingered hands and feet have thick black talons. They are hideous, and I've never been more glad to see one.

The big one turns its two heads toward me, each speaking one word at a time. "Little one, get up and fight."

I sense that it recognizes me. This is the gigantes I faced in Tartarus, the one that pulverized me and took pleasure in it. My stomach twists, but then I shout at the thing. "We've been fighting. It's your turn now!"

The gigantes snarls at me, but then lunges forward, casting down a strong wind as it leaps several hundred feet and lands among a mass of startled Nephilim, cutting them down.

Cronus shouts back to me. "Solomon! Where is the shofar?"

"In the temple," I shout back.

"We must have it!" he says. "It is the key to everything!"

"It won't work," I argue. "There are too many of them!"

"It only needs to work on one," he says, and then stands. He raises his sword high into the air. "Humans!" His voice is thunder itself, the voice of Titan. "Attack!"

Cronus charges, heading for the Nephilim army, with twenty-four warriors and thousands of humans by his side. Now that, is leadership. In the wake of this furious charge, this final charge, I find myself alone on the ground, weak and unable to move.

I want to join the fight with every fiber of my being, but I'm worn out. I can barely stand.

Shofar, I think to no one in particular. *I need the shofar...and a shot of adrenaline.*

If there is a reply, I don't hear it. Maybe Luca is unable? Maybe the strain finally got to us both? I try to stand, but a wave of dizziness keeps me down.

"Don't move," a woman says.

"Regain your strength," says another.

I feel a hand on my back. Mira.

I look up and find Mira and Em kneeling by my sides and Kat and Kainda standing guard.

"I'm coming!" I hear another voice cry out.

I recognize it immediately. I should, I heard it for the first half of my life. "Luca," I mumble. "No."

I turn to find the small boy sprinting around the line of tanks, the shofar under his arm. Merrill and Aimee rush out behind him, clearly trying to subdue the boy and return him to safety, but they can't catch him.

"Go back!" I shout to him. "Go b—"

Something in the air shifts, like a wave of pressure, returning my attention to the battle.

Our force, even strengthened by the gigantes and Titans, have been repelled. They're retreating toward us, pursued by countless Nephilim still pouring through the bottleneck. Beyond the bottleneck, I see the second behemoth, closing in, to the seal the gap or simply trample us. I reach out with my senses. It's almost here.

The timing is right, but I'm too weak do anything but kill us all.

Luca, I think. *Hurry!*

35

Luca arrives just ahead of the retreating forces. "Here's the shofar!" he says, gasping for air. He holds the ancient horn out to me, but it's not what I'm interested in.

"The adrenaline," I say. "Did you get the adrenaline?"

"I don't know what adrenaline is," he says, and I mentally slap myself in the head. Of course he doesn't know what adrenaline is. He grew up *here*. I look up to Merrill and Aimee, but their hands are empty.

"What is it?" Em asks, seeing my despair.

I don't reply. I can't bear to tell her. But then I see Cronus among the retreating force. He's fleeing backwards alongside the remaining eleven Titans, fighting as he backs away from the encroaching Nephilim force. He's taking wounds and healing quickly, bleeding purple.

The Titans are Nephilim that have had the burdens of their past misdeeds lifted in Tartarus. But they are still Nephilim.

Cronus, I think, hoping Luca will still redirect my thoughts. He does, but I can see the strain on his face. *Cronus, I need you!*

The giant reacts to my words quickly, leaping over the retreating human force and arriving ahead of them. He kneels down beside me, sees the shofar and looks relieved. But his concern returns when he hears what I have to say.

"Your blood," I say to the giant. "I need your blood."

He flinches back. "It will kill you."

"I can handle a drop," I tell him.

"There are other ways," he says. "We will—"

"There is no time!" I shout, and thrust a finger east, toward the ocean.

The Titan's eyes widen. His face, lit by the sun, is suddenly cast in shadow. As the shadow casts the battlefield into darkness, all eyes turn up. Even the Nephilim stop and gaze.

A hundred-foot tall wave races toward shore, passing harmlessly beneath the Navy ships. But when the shoreline shallows, the wave grows taller still. It's just moments from washing all of us away.

"Just a drop," I shout.

Cronus quickly pricks his finger with a clean dagger, which is bigger than a human sword, and collects a single drop on its tip before the wound heals. He lowers the blade to my head. I grasp both sides with my hands, cutting the flesh. I lick the blood from the blade and am launched backwards, onto the ground where I thrash and writhe in agony. I can feel the power rushing through my body, so strong that I nearly burst.

The wounds on my hands suddenly heal.

The persistent ache in my body disappears.

A boundless energy, like rocket fuel, surges from my heart, out to my fingers and toes and back again like one of those old Popeye cartoons. My pain-filled scream stops abruptly. The air gathers around me and lifts me to my feet.

Gather close, I think to the retreating force and then notice the gigantes still locked in battle with the Nephilim. I urge them to move, to flee into the air, but they do not respond.

Cronus seems to hear the mental command and turns to me. "They came here to fight, and to die. They will not flee."

I don't like it, but I have no choice but to accept this as reality.

Fueled by the blood of a Titan, I reach out to my wave. It's traveled several miles to get here, gathering speed and size along the way, but now that it's here, I need it to not drown us all. I reach my hands out and feel the wave's power. Its immensity nearly knocks me down, but I push against it with my body and mind, urging the water and air to obey my will.

The tidal wave crests.

The water rises and bends, curling over the base, over the temple, and then directly overhead. The wall of water flowing above us is lit by the sun, glowing in surreal blue, the light shimmering down around us like we're inside a giant aquarium.

I turn with the wave, directing its course. My arms shake from the weight of it, pulled downward by gravity, but repulsed by my connection to the continent. And then, I allow gravity to do its thing. The water at the front of the wave falls, crashing down on the front line of Nephilim who can drown just like anyone else. The pounding water races forward, propelled by the girth of the wave still rising and descending like a solid blue rainbow.

Using all the strength granted to me by Cronus, I push the wave back through the valley. As the cliffs come together, the water deepens and races faster, exiting the bottleneck with explosive force, slamming into the second behemoth and taking hundreds of thousands of Nephilim warriors with it.

Sun strikes us again as the last of the wave passes overhead, slams to the valley floor and flows into the distant, now-flattened, jungle beyond the bottleneck. Then, the water is gone and the battlefield has been scoured clean. Humans, the Nephilim, the gigantes—even the behemoth corpse—are all gone. It's like a battle had never been fought here.

Weakened again, I stagger and I'm caught by Kainda. She helps me stand upright and catches my eye. She says nothing, but it's clear she approves.

As does the rest of my surviving army. Cheers rise up all around.

It's a perfect moment. My dear ones are all here, and living. The battlefield is cleared. The sun warms us like a blessing from some higher power.

And then all of that goodness, every last ounce of it, is erased.

First by the circling shadows above. Then by the army once again filling the gap of the bottleneck.

The wave delivered a serious blow to the Nephilim numbers, but they are an army of nearly a million.

And now we are an army of a few thousand—wounded, tired and beaten.

The approaching Nephilim are no longer charging. They're marching, confidently. Despite my improvised weapon of mass destruction, the battle—the war—is theirs. Their numbers are too great.

To my army's credit, the mix of hunters, soldiers, cresties and Titans stand their ground and wait. I step out ahead of them and walk to the center of the group, followed by Kainda, Em, Mira and Kat, who are in turn followed by Luca, still holding the shofar, Merrill and Aimee. I couldn't be more proud of all of them. Cronus brings up the rear of our small group, carrying more strength than all of us, and strangely, an unwavering confidence.

"How can you be so confident?" I say to the Titan.

"We are not yet beaten," he says.

"It's more than that," I say. "You know something."

"Adoel sends his greetings," the Titan says.

Adoel? The angel? "Is he here?"

"He cannot leave Edinnu," Cronus says. "You know this...but I visited before coming here."

"Then what?" I ask. "Is it the Tree of Life? Do you have its fruit?"

He chuckles, actually chuckles, despite our circumstances.

"We...said goodbye," the Titan says.

"Goodbye?" I ask, growing worried—*more* worried.

"My end will mark a new beginning," Cronus says. "Those were the last words spoken to me by Adoel. The words that helped save me in Tartarus. And it is those words that will soon come to fruition."

I'm about to press him for more. I'm not a fan of vague answers and he knows it. Before I can speak, he says, "It has been an honor serving with you."

And then, a voice, from the Nephilim.

"Solomon!" The voice is small. Human. And old.

Ninnis.

But not Ninnis. This is Nephil—the dark god Ophion—speaking to me.

The marching horde stops a hundred feet away. I can feel the tension of the small army behind me, just waiting for the order to charge and fight to the death.

Winged warriors land at the front of the Nephilim, lining the front of their massive force with ancient, blood-red clad gods. Enlil is among them, burning with anger at having been turned away by me. Enlil, and Zeus beside him, fold their wings down. From between them, a lone man wanders out.

Ninnis's body still looks old, but the beard has been shaved, along with his hair, and he stands more upright than I remember. His eyes, once dark, are now yellow and more Nephilim than human. As he walks, tendrils of black snake out from his body, lifting him into the air.

As Luca clings to my side in fright, Cronus kneels and whispers. "He is more powerful than ever."

Not helping, I think.

The giant continues. "He has bonded himself to the very essence of his brethren, drawing strength from their life force."

"I don't see anything," I say.

"You can't see it," he says impatiently. "But I can feel it, tugging at me, trying to claim me as one of his own."

"Will he?" I ask.

"I have always been stronger than Ophion," Cronus says with a grin that reveals his sharp teeth. "But his strength is of no consequence. It is the connection that is important. He has made himself the capstone."

The capstone is the central stone in an arch. With the stone in place, the arch can withstand intense pressure. But if you remove the capstone, the arch and everything supported by it, will crumble to the ground.

"How do we remove the capstone?" I ask.

"Return it to the earth from whence it came," he says.

"You know I hate the cryptic—" I start to complain, but then I figure it out. *Tartarus.* Nephil, first Nephilim, has a spirit, unlike most Nephilim. He can live outside his body. Not forever, but he could easily take the body of one of his warriors, or even another human if Ninnis is killed. It's what he plans to do to me. So we must return him to Tartarus, which is in some ways a fate worse than non-existence. Unable to turn from his evil ways, Tartarus will be a prison of unending torture, and without Nephilim on the outside to set him free, he will never leave it again.

"But how?" I ask, and then once again find the answer, this time pressed up against me, clutched in the arms of Luca.

The shofar.

Now we just need to get close enough to use it.

"Solomon!" Nephil shouts again. "Come! Let us talk."

Problem solved.

36

Enlil and Zeus break rank from their giant army, standing to either side of Nephil. Enlil is dressed in red leathers, but the armor over his chest is fringed with black, the preferred color of the Sumerian clan. He has a long red rectangular beard held in place by beaded twine. His red hair is parted down the middle, braided and held back by a ribbon I suspect is made from feeder skin. Long earrings dangle from his ears. All classic Sumerian styles. He carries a large sickle sword in each six-fingered hand. Zeus, also wearing mostly red, reveals his Greco-Roman flair with a golden fringe that is basically bedazzled with glowing crystals from the underworld. While his hair is the same blood-red as Enlil's, it is flowing and strangely clean looking for a Nephilim. Where Enlil exudes military precision, Zeus carries himself like a nobleman. Even his beard is trimmed. He carries a sword with a jagged blade. A thunderbolt, I realize.

I step toward the trio and find Em, Kainda, Mira and Kat walking with me. While Nephil's delegation has only three members, I don't think they'll consider the four women a threat. Not only are they human, but the Nephilim are thousands of years old and without a doubt, sexist. But all three look unhappy when Cronus follows us. After all, Cronus is responsible for trapping the Nephilim in Tartarus the first time and keeping Nephil contained there for so long. Though they might not like it, the three god-demons are too proud to complain. They would look weak in front of their subjects.

Luca, I think.

What are you going to do? the little me replies.

Put the shofar behind your back, I tell him. *Slowly. Hide it from view. But be ready.*

For what?

I'm not sure yet.

Done, he thinks.

"You have fought bravely," Nephil says to me when I stop twenty feet away. "You have inflicted casualties worthy of your hunter heritage, despite your..." He touches his hair, but he's talking about mine. "...condition. Ninnis would be proud."

He's trying to goad me into action. Draw me closer. If he does that, he could take me while his army charged. If they attacked now, I could still escape. He must know this. So he has to trap me, or convince me to surrender. But two can play this game. He needs me alive, which is basically a get out of jail free card.

I turn to Zeus. "Do you call it Thunderbolt? The sword?"

He smiles a toothy grin and says with a powerful voice, "It is a name that—"

Krakoom! A lightning bolt snaps from the sky, striking the ancient god-man. Smoldering, he falls to his knees, and then to his face.

The Nephilim horde erupts with laughter. They approve of this kind of grandstanding.

Nephil, on the other hand, looks at me the way a crocodile does a dangling hunk of meat. He longs for this power of mine. It would make him unstoppable. A true god among men.

Zeus recovers from the lightning blast and pushes himself up with a groan that becomes a roar. He lifts his jagged sword from the ground and prepares to throw himself at me. But before the giant can lunge, a black tendril blocks his path.

"You would not make it ten feet," Nephil says. It's not a threat from Nephil, but a warning. He eyes me, and then Cronus. Zeus isn't a match for either of us.

Zeus sneers, but stands and retakes his place by Nephil's side.

Nephil moves a little closer, propelled by the dark tendrils. He stops when Cronus tenses, ready to attack. "If we are done with the theater, Ull, I would like to make you an offer."

I wait in silence.

"Your life," he says, and then he spreads his arms out toward my army. "For theirs."

"You would spare them?" I ask, not believing it for a second. "You would spare the human race?"

"The human race? No," he says. "But what little remains of your army will be spared. Your comrades. Your friends. And I dare say—" He glances at the four women standing to my sides. "—your loved ones."

"You'll make them hunters?" I ask.

"Naturally."

"And use them to hunt and kill humans around the world."

He shrugs. "A likely scenario. But *they* will live until the natural end of their days."

Given the fact that we've managed to save or kill the vast majority of Nephil's hunters, I think his offer is genuine. Until the global human genocide is complete, the Nephilim will need hunters to go where they can't.

I look to Kainda and Em, finding uncompromising glares. I find the same from Kat and Mira.

The choice is obvious, but not.

You must trust me, I think to them all.

I see Kainda glance toward me, fighting not to show a reaction. But Nephil notices her.

"Ahh, dear daughter," Nephil says.

"I am *not* your daughter." Kainda's voice is actually more intimidating than Nephil's.

"He loved you, you know," Nephil says. "Your father."

Kainda tenses.

"He hid it well. From everyone. Even you. Sometimes himself." Nephil lowers himself closer to the ground, making himself an easy target. "Have you ever wondered what your life—"

"Enough!" I say. He knows that eventually, Kainda will attack, and if she does, I will be drawn in with her. But it's not necessary. I'm going to go willingly.

I step forward. When Kainda walks with me, I turn to her and say, "You must stay. Let me do this."

"Solomon," she says, her voice uncommonly fearful. Her fear is understandable. Not only am I her husband, she is also keenly aware of what my sacrifice means. She will live, but as a hunter, broken again in servitude to the Nephilim. She would rather die.

"Trust me," I say, and then, "I love you."

"Forever," she says.

"Forever." She lets go of my hand and I walk five paces closer to Nephil. "Let them live and you can take me."

He stares at me, no doubt believing I would fight to the last man.

"You would sacrifice yourself for this lot?" Nephil says, sounding doubtful.

"Are you trying to change my mind?" I ask, "because I could be on the other side of the continent in less than an hour and we can do this all over again in a few months."

He slides closer to me, within striking distance for sure. He stares into my eyes for a moment, perhaps looking for betrayal. Instead, he finds something unexpected.

Mercy. Forgiveness. Love.

He settles to the ground and the darkness coils inside his body. We're just two men now, standing face-to-face. He speaks quietly so that only I can hear him. "There was a time when I respected your kind. You're capable of things my brethren will never understand. And you, Ull, are the best of them. You remind me of a man, Ziusudra. He led a human tribe, like yours, the last of his kind. The world was nearly ours. The human race was no longer human. And then, a flood. Ziusudra's tribe survived. Your kind was spared."

Nephil turns his head toward the sky. "But the skies are clear and not even your power is enough to drown us all."

"But together," I say.

Nephil smiles, revealing Ninnis's remaining rotted teeth. "Together, we will remake the world."

I sigh and say, "Just get it over wi—"

The blackness explodes from Ninnis's body and pierces mine like a thousand bee stings. My body arches back and is lifted off the ground.

"The body!" Nephil shouts. "Bring it to me."

My mind reels. My consciousness twists through my brain, experiencing one sense and then another. For a moment, I can hear, but not see. Then I can smell, but not feel. I am losing my body.

I feel something in my mouth, soft and squishy, like old pudding. Then I suddenly taste it and know exactly what it is. Nephil's body. After consuming this small remnant of Nephil's physical being, he will be able to bond with me permanently. I thought the body would be lost after I vomited it up the first time, but they have managed to save it all this time.

When both my sense of taste and touch fade, it's a mercy, but when a surge of energy thunders through my body, I know that I've swallowed the flesh of Nephil once more.

Wait, I think to Luca, desperately hoping the message will be received and sent to everyone else.

The darkness snakes through me, filling my body with waves of nausea. My mind is assaulted as Nephil's consciousness spreads into the deepest recesses of my mind. *It's time*, I think. *He's gone far enough. Now!* I shout out with my mind, but the thought echoes back. Darkness surrounds me.

I waited too long. Nephil has taken my body!

37

"Goodbye, Ull," Nephil says, and I feel him pushing on me, forcing me from my own mind and into the oblivion that awaits Nephilim. I won't die, I'll simply be trapped in this dark place for the rest of time, or until an asteroid destroys the planet or the sun becomes a red giant and absorbs the Earth.

Before I wink out of existence, I feel a building pressure. It's not Nephil, it's *opposing* Nephil. *Resisting* him.

And it's *not* me.

As the pressure behind me builds, a searing pain ignites in my mind and I feel, more than hear Nephil's surprise.

Push him back, Solomon!

The voice screams at me, focusing my thoughts as I focus on the name of the one speaking to me. *Xin!*

This was his gift.

His consciousness has been buried in my head, waiting for this moment, defending my mind against the one who could take it.

Push him back, but do not expel him.

Then what? I ask

Control him!

Bind him!

And then—I start to ask, but the answer comes to me.

As the wall of darkness is pushed to the fringe of my mind, I feel my body again. I can sense the world around me. I hear my own voice, screaming, but I also hear Nephil, screaming through Ninnis. He's connected to both of us!

Zeus and Enlil look on. I doubt either knows what to expect from this bonding. They have no idea that Nephil is being repelled. *Not repelled*, I think, *contained*.

"Now Solomon!" Cronus shouts, then I hear him scream to his remaining Titans, "For the King!"

Through foggy vision, I see Cronus charge past, sword drawn. He leaps at Zeus and with one swing, lops the surprised giant's head from his shoulders. His second swing is parried by Enlil and the Nephilim horde rushes in, held at bay by twelve Titans, hacking and slashing with a bravery that sets my mind to the task.

Luca, I think, *the horn!*

I turn to find the small boy lifting the horn.

Over your head, I tell him

He holds it high.

As I reach out to the elements, I feel Nephil grow stronger. He's pushing Xin and me back. But then, the wind obeys and explodes through the shofar with a force beyond that of the amplified speaker system. The valley vibrates with its power. The Nephilim army shrieks and wails. And then, all at once, the shofar shatters, the last of its sound echoing off the valley walls.

Nephil's darkness tears out of me, retreating to Ninnis's body. But he finds no refuge there.

Ninnis...is himself.

His intense eyes lock onto mine and we come to an understanding. Ninnis twitches and screams as Nephil fights for control. He falls to his knees, clutching his chest. Tendrils of darkness squirm out of him, but are pulled back inside.

"I have him, boy!" Ninnis shouts and then screams again. "I can't hold him for long."

Ninnis's strength is beyond comprehension. The combined consciousnesses of Xin and I struggled to repel the monster, but Ninnis is binding him on his own. Knowing what to do, I walk to Ninnis, but before I reach him, I fall to my knees. My stomach revolts, roiling. Then I vomit, a single glob of coagulated purple blood, coated in bile splatters to the ground.

Free of Nephil's body, my strength returns. As it does, my sense of Xin's presence fades. *I will see you again, brother,* he thinks, and then he's gone. Again. But there's no time to mourn the brief return and loss of Xin. I quickly focus on the globe of flesh below my face, removing the fluid from it with a thought. With the body of Nephil reduced to dust, I crawl to Ninnis and wrap my arms over his back, lending my strength to his. The darkness cuts through us both now, and together we fight.

But not alone.

I feel a hand on my back. Then another. I look up and find Kat and Mira supporting me. Ninnis raises his head, too, feeling the hands on him as well. "Daughter!" he says, surprised to find Kainda's head just inches from his own.

"I'm here, father," she says, her words full of compassion.

Ninnis's lips tremble. When he looks the other way and finds Em, he sobs. "But—I killed your father!"

"And I forgive you," Em says. She turns her eyes to me. "Do it."

Finding strength in the faithful resolve of these four women, my hope, faith, focus and passion, I turn my thoughts to the Earth, to my larger body. I reach out, further than ever before, for hundreds of miles, until I feel the deep dark void that was the first behemoth's home.

With a scream of exertion from me, the ground beneath us opens up and swallows us whole. We descend on a disk of stone and soil, rocketing downward at an angle like we're on a rollercoaster fashioned in hell. Strata of Antarktos flash past in a blur as we descend through millennia of time, back toward the very beginning of mankind, of Nephilim and this ancient conflict.

Nephil reaches out, struggling to leave the confines of Ninnis's body. One by one, we shout in pain, feeling his dark touch. But Nephil finds a united front and a cage of unwilling hosts.

And then, we arrive. We drop through the cavern's ceiling. It takes a supreme effort to slow us before we strike the ground, but I manage. Nephil realizes where we are before the others do and he explodes with fury, screaming, "No!" through Ninnis.

The darkness swirls out of Ninnis, striking Kainda, Kat, Mira and Em away. They sprawl across the cavern floor.

The tentacles quickly fade again, reeled in by Ninnis. "Quickly, Solomon!" He looks over his shoulder to the gates of Tartarus, which oddly enough, already lie open.

I throw his arm around my shoulder and we hobble together toward the gates. As we walk, Ninnis speaks through grinding teeth. "Solomon. I cannot thank you enough. You have saved me."

"And now you, us," I say. "We're even."

"Not remotely," he says, grunting in pain. "My daughter. You will care for her?"

"She is my wife," I tell him, and he manages a pain-filled laugh. He places his forehead against mine and whispers, "Son."

Despite all of the horrible things Ninnis has done, all of the people he has killed and the anguish he has caused, I find it in my heart to forgive him again. "Father," I whisper.

He barks loudly, and I can't tell if it's a laugh or a sob, but it transforms into a shout of pain. "Gah!"

I'm thrown away by a curtain of black.

Nephil has taken control again. He turns to face me, just a foot away from the gaping blackness of the open gate.

I catch myself with a cushion of air.

Ninnis's eyes appear for a moment, filled with concern, not for entering the gate, but that Nephil might yet escape.

I summon a wind, throwing it at Ninnis. Black tendrils shoot out, embedding themselves in the floor. Hurricane force winds slam into Nephil, but he resists, rooted like some ancient tree. He's shouting at me, but his words are lost in the wind.

Unfortunately, Nephil is fueled by rage, anger and hatred. Exhausted from the battle, and our journey through the center of the Earth that would boggle Jules Verne, I am growing weaker. Fast.

I fall to my knees, urging the wind to grow stronger, but I can feel its force ebbing along with my reserves. On my hands and knees, I can now hear Nephil laughing, fully possessing Ninnis once more. I turn my head up and look at him. I'm sickened by his smile, by the look of victory in his eyes.

So close, I think, *we were so close.*

Tears roll down my cheeks.

The world is lost. Nephil has w—

A pair of arms slip out of the darkness behind Nephil. They're human, but strong. Before Nephil can react, the arms wrap around Ninnis's throat and lock together in a perfect chokehold. The black tendrils flare wildly, but they cannot assail their attacker. To do so would mean passing through the gate!

The darkness grips the cavern floor like an angry squid, but while Nephil is spirit, Ninnis is human, and his beet-red face, now turning purple reveals a desperate need for oxygen. As Ninnis's eyes flutter, the tendrils lose their power and one by one, they slide free from the rock.

Then, all at once, Ninnis falls back and is yanked through the gates of Tartarus, taking Nephil with him.

I sit up, staring at the gates, unbelieving. *That's it? We've won?*

I look around, finding Em, Kainda, Mira and Kat, all climbing back to their feet, staring at the gate with the same look of disbelief frozen on their faces.

Em looks at me and laughs.

A smile creeps onto my face despite the pain waging a war on my body.

"We did it..." Mira says, sounding relieved.

When I turn to Kainda, I'm surprised to find tears in her eyes. Then I remember that is was Ninnis, her father, who ultimately saved us. Returned to his true self, he became the man I always knew he was, and probably the man that Kainda always wanted him to be.

It's Kat's reaction that really catches me off guard. She walks toward the open gates. Then she runs.

"Kat!" I shout to her. She doesn't know what lies on the other side. She doesn't—

She shouts, and I flinch at the word. "Steve!" She shouts again, desperate. "Steve!"

Just as she's about to dive through the gates, the arms emerge again, and then the body they belong to. Kat shouts her husband's name again and dives into his arms, nearly tackling them both back through the gates.

"Wright!" I shout, and I'm on my feet and running. When I reach the pair, I wrap my arms around them both. "You're alive!"

He laughs and pats my shoulder. "I'm not easy to kill."

"But the hunters," I say, remembering the dire situation we left him in.

"Were only interested in you," he says. "They left me to die, but I found my way here, to the gates."

"But how did you open them?" I ask.

"I didn't," he says.

"I did," says a booming voice from above. Cronus drops through the hole in the ceiling, his wings unfurling to stop his fall.

"You're alive!" I say, surprised. "But Adoel—"

"—is even more cryptic than I am," he finishes with a grin. He turns to the gate and finding no sign of Nephil, says, "You have done well, young King. The dark lord Ophion was still connected to the warriors above when he left this world."

"You mean—"

He nods. "His army is in ruin." He steps toward the open gates, takes one and closes it. "But your work as King has only begun. The lesser clans are scattered, but living, as are those hiding among men. Battles await you in the future, but mankind is saved."

He reaches for the second door and begins to close it, stepping toward the darkness. It's now that I notice there are no other Titans present. "The other Titans?" I ask.

"Fallen," he says. "I am the last. The keeper of Tartarus. Guardian of Ophion."

"You will be alone," I say.

"Adoel would say that one is never alone in paradise," he says. "But I will have company."

Ninnis, I think. "Before you go," I say, reaching into a pouch attached to my belt. I pull out my very used, first edition copy of The Pilgrim's Progress, and hand it to Cronus. "For Ninnis. It will help."

He takes the book, offers a nod, and says, "Farewell, young King. Peace be with you." And then he slides into the darkness of the gate and closes the giant door behind him.

Kainda, Em and Mira gather around Wright, Kat and me.

Mira gives Wright a hug and says, "Glad you're alive, boy scout."

"Likewise," he says, then nods to Kainda and Em. "Thank you for taking care of my wife." He kisses Kat's forehead. "I'm not exactly an expert on this, but I think we should get topside before we miss the next year."

He's right. If we stay much longer, the day above will end before our return.

I lead them to the circle of earth upon which we descended into the depths. With everyone standing atop the stone, I look at each of them—Em, Kat and Mira, my sisters, Wright, my brother, and Kainda my wife. My family. My dear ones. I want to say something, but I'm at a loss for words.

"Just take us home, kid," Kat says.

I laugh, turn my head to the ceiling and we rise. Through the air. Through the earth. Through Antarktos, the land that is me and is now, after thousands of years, free.

EPILOGUE 1

It's been six months since the human race stood up against impossible odds and survived. In that time, the world has changed a lot. Nations are coming together to form a global alliance in which the new resources of Antarctica are shared responsibly, but also in the tracking down of any surviving Nephilim. The warriors are all but wiped out, but the other classes: gatherers, thinkers, breeders, feeders, shifters and more, are still living and active in numbers, though now in hiding. The most dangerous are the shifters, who hide in plain sight, looking like any other human being.

But we will find them all in time.

In addition to working together, world leaders have also recognized my individual claim to Antarktos. And when the hunters proclaimed me King, the outside world cheered. Videos and images of the final battle, how it was fought and won, have surfaced. I didn't even know it was being recorded. But the whole world knows what happened and understands the sacrifices that were made. They also know what I can do, and of my connection to the land, which I suspect has a lot to do with their accepting my leadership.

After all, if someone decided to drill for oil on Antarktos without my permission, I would know just as easily as I would feel someone prick my skin with a needle. With every passing day, my connection to the continent deepens, and grows easier to control. The land is fertile. Life is plentiful. And the human population that has chosen to relocate to Antarktos, is happy.

Not that everyone wants to immigrate. Many prefer to stay where they were, comfortable in their own homes and a safe distance from Antarktos, where the supernatural world, dinosaurs and an underground labyrinth is all part of everyday life. And that's why I'm here. In New Mexico.

As we left Antarktos, roughly thirty miles from the coast I felt my connection to the continent fade. It's not gone completely, so I have no fear that the connection won't come back in full upon my return, but my abilities have all but vanished for now. I feel a bit naked. And vulnerable. Not that I'm alone.

Wright and Kat, dressed in black, carry assault rifles. I wasn't sure we'd be allowed to carry weapons once we got to the U.S., but I've been granted diplomatic immunity, pretty much everywhere. One of the perks of saving the world. Em and Kainda, who are dressed as average American civilians in jeans and T-shirts, carry their hammer and knives, unwilling to part with the weapons. They did change their clothes, though, which was surprising. Back on Antarktos, we still dress as we did as hunters. We're accustomed to it, but given the tropical climate, it's also more comfortable. For them. I still don't feel the temperature...though I'm feeling it here. The summer heat, which is far more humid than New Mexico would have been before the global shift, is like a warm blanket, comforting me in this time of great stress.

I have faced many things over the past few years...but I don't think anything could prepare me for this.

Mira, dressed like Em and Kainda, heads for the ranch's front door. Like me, she is unarmed. Her weapon of choice these days has been the camera. She's back at work, taking photos, sharing the wonders of Antarktos with the world through her camera's lens.

As for me, I feel uncomfortable in cargo shorts and a T-shirt, but I manage. At least I can remember what it feels like to wear normal clothes. Em and Kainda never had the experience. My hair is still long, but it has been trimmed, and washed. The hardest change was actually wearing shoes again. I opted for flip flops. Whipsnap is in the car; I didn't think carrying the weapon to this meeting would be appropriate.

Mira stops in front of the door and looks back at me. "You ready?"

I nod. I'm too nervous to speak.

She knocks.

"Coming," a voice shouts in reply. I nearly break down in tears right then. The last time I heard this voice, it was being impersonated by a Nephilim creation, birthed by a breeder, and I was forced to kill it. My own mother.

The door swings open and there she is. Her hair has grayed, but only partially, and it's just as wavy as I remember it. "Oh," she says in surprise when she sees the large number of people standing outside her door. Then she notices Mira and her face lights up. "Mira, dear! How are you? We've been following your journeys. Mark keeps a box full of your photos. Seems like we have to add to it nearly every day."

Mira embraces my mother. "Thank you, Beth. May we come in?"

My mom looks at the group again, this time meeting my eyes and showing no recognition. Her memory of me has been blocked, just as Merrill's and Aimee's were. The Clarks are living in Antarctica now, in what Merrill has deemed Clark Station Three. They're studying the ancient human cultures that lived on the continent before it was buried beneath the ice. Merrill nearly passed out when he saw the paintings inside the nunatak.

"Sure," my mom says. "I'll get you and your friends something to drink."

"Did I hear Mira?" my father says, rounding the corner into the hallway. His hair is still black and curly, but it's receded to the sides and back of his head. He's healthy and hale. His face lights up when he sees Mira. After giving her a big bear hug, he stands back and looks at the group. Once again, I'm not recognized. Though he is excited to see us. "You must be her friends from Antarktos! Come in, you have to tell me everything."

Kainda puts a gentle hand on my shoulder. She knows how hard this is for me.

My dad leads the way through the front hallway. This house looks nothing like the one I grew up in. The style is all

Southwestern. In fact, I can't find a single relic of my past life. That is, until we pass the living room.

I stop in the doorway, staring.

The painting looks out of place. The lighthouse, and seascape are in stark contrast to the New Mexico feel of the home.

My father notices my attention on the painting when everyone else enters the kitchen with my mother.

"What is it, son?" he asks.

My heart skips a beat, but then I realize he's using "son" as a generic term. He stands next to me. "It's an ugly thing, that painting. But Beth likes it. Reminds her of the old house."

"Why did you move?" I ask.

"I—I really don't know." He shrugs. "One day...it just didn't feel like home any more."

I turn to my father and ask, "Do you know who I am?"

He shakes his head, no.

"My name is Solomon."

After a moment, his eyes widen. "*The* Solomon? The...the king?"

"Yes," I say, exasperated by this response. "My full name is Solomon Ull Vincent."

"Vincent?" he says, confused. "My last name is—"

"Vincent," I say. "I know. I'm—" I stop. Trying to convince him is pointless. Even if he believed me, it wouldn't change anything. I take his hand and recite a random sentence, spoken by my father in the past. "Summer in Antarctica begins in about seven weeks."

He looks at me, dumbfounded. "Isn't it always summer in Antarctica now?"

It didn't work.

I had two fears about this trip. The first is that it wouldn't work here. That I'd have to somehow get my parents to Antarctica to restore their memories. My second fear is that it wouldn't work at all, no matter where we were. Xin gave me that ability to restore memories erased by the Nephilim, but maybe that gift only extended to the Clark family.

While my father is still impressed enough by my celebrity to not be worried about my strangeness, I say, "Mr. Vincent, can you have your wife join us? I'd like to ask you both something."

"Uh, yeah, sure." He heads for the kitchen.

While I'm waiting, I turn around and look at the painting again.

The painting!

I rush over to it, and pull the painting from the wall, revealing a safe. The *same* safe!

I turn the dial left and right, entering the combination: 7-21-38.

"Hey," my father says, more confused than angry. "You can't open that. It needs a combo—"

The safe door swings open silencing my father.

"Mark, what is he doing?" my mom asks.

The others have gathered around them. Nearly losing my mind, I rifle through the safe, spilling its contents on the floor until I find it. The pouch. Immediately, I know that something is different. There had been a photo inside, of my parents and the Clarks. It was inscribed with a note from Merrill, congratulating my parents on my birth. The Nephilim who erased me from history were thorough.

But the small, hard lump remains. I shake the stone out of the pouch. When it hits my hands, I feel a surge of power, not unlike the first time I held this stone, this fragment of Antarctica.

"Are...you okay?" my father asks.

Regaining my composure, I hold the stone up. "This is a part of Antarktos, a part of me." I walk to my dumbstruck parents. The King of Antarktos has just broken into their safe and retrieved a small chunk of granite. "Just as the both of you are."

Holding the stone beneath one thumb, I hold my hands out to both of them. "Take my hands."

They look at each other, confused by the request, but Mira encourages them, saying, "It's okay."

They tentatively take my hands. I swallow, take a deep breath and then speak the words my parents said to me exactly seven thousand five hundred and thirty one times during the thirteen years I was with them, "I love you."

EPILOGUE 2

Belgrave Ninnis stepped into the chilly darkness. His skin rose with goose bumps, and his bare limbs shivered. It had been a long time since he felt the biting chill of the underground. But it was not yet entirely foreign to him. A hunter never forgets these things. Of course, Ninnis wasn't just a hunter. He was a husband. A father. And a man of honor.

He was also old, a fact that he was reminded of with every step of his upward journey. He walked without stopping, spurred onward by anticipation. Remembering his own training, he pushed through the pain until at last, he felt warm sunlight on his face. He stepped from the cave and found himself surrounded by lush green in every direction.

Without a location in mind, he set out, eating fruit from the land and drinking greedily from the clear flowing waters that he seemed to find whenever he grew thirsty. He walked for days like this until he found a stone path winding through the jungle. He looked in both directions, unsure of which direction to follow.

A distant thrumming grew louder. He recognized the sound and search for a place to hide. But it was upon him too quickly. He turned to face the predatory dinosaur, but there was no need to fight. The dinosaur had a rider—a man with thick dark hair. The man gave a nod and removed his dark tinted sunglasses.

"You're pretty far from anywhere useful," the man said. "You want a ride?"

"On that?" Ninnis said.

"Are you new to Antarktos?" the man asked. "Are you lost?"

"No, but I'm afraid, yes."

Accepting the man's offer, Ninnis climbed onto the dinosaur's back, finding a vacant second saddle waiting for him. They rode in silence for a long time, and Ninnis admired the jungle, the lushness of it, and the life. It reminded him of the place that had been his home for the past year.

As the sun began to set, the man finally said, "I never asked you where you were going?"

After a pause, Ninnis said, "To see the King."

"You're in luck, then," the man said. "So am I."

Not ten minutes later, a mountain citadel came into view. It was unlike anything Ninnis had ever seen before, in his time before Antarctica, as a hunter in the underworld or during his time in Tartarus. It occurred to him then, that far more than a year had passed. Nervousness swelled as he feared he was too late. "How many years has it been?" he asked as they rode through the city gates, and were greeted with friendly waves from an assortment of people. "Since the war?"

The man looked back and said to himself, though Ninnis heard him clearly, "Man, I hope my memory doesn't go some day."

"Please," Ninnis said. "How long?"

"Twenty years," the man said.

Twenty years. Thank God.

The man tied the dinosaur to a post where several others were drinking from a fountain. "This way," he said, leading Ninnis past a graveyard. Ninnis glanced at the stones. Some names meant nothing to him: Brigadier General Kent Holloway, Lieutenant Elias Baker, First Lieutenant Victor Cruz, Zok, Vesuvius. But others plucked at his heart, threatening to return a burden he had managed to leave behind in Tartarus. He read their names, one by one: Xin. Tobias. Cerberus. Hades. Zuh. Adoni. Men, women, and Nephilim who fought for what was right, against him, and sacrificed everything.

Ninnis looked up at the tower above. Its smooth surface, lacking any ornate décor, reflected the late day sun, glowing orange. The tower was surrounded by walls lined with trees, staircases and walkways. A flag blowing in the wind caught his attention. White, with an image of Antarctica, a single gold star at its core. He remembered seeing it on the battlefield, a symbol of mankind's unity. Everywhere he looked, he saw people, living their lives in safety.

The sacrifices of the men, women and creatures lain to rest in this graveyard were not made in vain, Ninnis thought.

He paused by the last two sets of gravestones. He only knew one of them, but he knew who the others were and what they meant to Solomon. *Dr. Merrill Clark and Aimee Clark, beloved parents who fought for us all.* And then, *Mark Vincent and Beth Vincent, beloved parents returned to the King.* Wiping tears from his eyes, Ninnis noticed the dates and found all of them to be more recent than not. It wouldn't make up for the years he'd stolen from the boy, but it was something.

"Can you handle a few stairs?" the man asked.

Ninnis nearly laughed. He'd already climbed out of the depths of the underworld. A few stairs wouldn't hurt. But there were more than a few. He had to stop twice to rest.

"Need some help?" the man asked, sounding genuinely concerned and less sarcastic.

Ninnis sighed. "If you wouldn't mind."

They climbed the rest of the stairs together. "Where are we going?" Ninnis asked when they reached the top flight of stairs. A pair of large wooden doors, arched at the top. Over the top of arch was a capstone engraved with the words, *None Shall Remove.*

"To see the King," the man answered.

"You can just walk in and have an audience with the King?" Ninnis asked. It didn't sound logical or safe.

The man smiled. "No. I just happen to be his constable."

"But..." Ninnis said, "I'm just an old man you plucked from the side of the road."

The constable stopped with a hand on one of the doors. "Actually, he sent me to get you."

"Sent you? Who?"

"The King, of course."

The man shoved the door open and Ninnis froze. There before him was the last thing he expected to see. It was a banquet. An enormous bounty. But it was the people...hundreds of them, standing, staring at him.

The constable smiled and waved him inside.

Ninnis took an unsure footstep. Then another, lost in the sea of faces, until he stopped on one he knew. Solomon. The boy stood just ten feet away. But he looked so young, as though little time had passed. "S—Solomon?"

"No," the boy chuckled. "I'm Luca. Sol is up there."

Ninnis followed the young man's finger to the center of the room, where a strong man with long blond hair, broad shoulders and a full beard stood smiling. Beside him was a woman whose strength radiated like the sun. Beside them sat several children, a veritable brood of them. As his eyes scanned to the side, he saw other faces he knew, aged, but living. These were Solomon's friends, the ones who helped him save the human race.

Solomon cleared his voice and nodded to the constable, "Thank you, Justin."

Solomon turned to Ninnis and smiled. "Welcome home, father," he motioned to the children beside him. "Grandfather."

Ninnis stared at the children, his *grandchildren.*

The emotion of it all weakened his weary legs. He feared he might fall, but a strong grasp held him up. He turned to find the blazing eyes of his daughter, Kainda, the Queen, who had left her spot by the King. She held him up like he weighed nothing at all. "I have you, father, and I will not let you go."

He smiled at her, tears in his eyes, and said, "Nor I you."

With a loud voice, Solomon proclaimed, "Tonight we celebrate the return of Belgrave Ninnis, who was dead, and is alive again. Who was lost, and is now found. We welcome him not just as father and grandfather, but as the man who lost his life, who endured torture, the breaking, and enslavement, and in the end, when the world was on the brink, managed to find a strength that is impossible to comprehend. He bound the darkness and removed it from our world."

Cheers and clapping erupted around the dining hall.

King Solomon raised a glass in a toast. "To Ninnis! The man who saved us all."

AUTHOR'S NOTE

Dear Reader,

You have just finished the final book in *The Antarktos Saga*, which I believe is my best story to date, and I wanted to take a moment to thank you for reading and for sharing the life of Solomon Ull Vincent with me. I hope you have enjoyed the journey and that you will come back for more adventures. If you did enjoy the book, please show your support by posting a review online (Amazon, B&N, etc). Online booksellers work on algorithms, meaning the more people review my books, the more those stores will recommend them to other readers. And the more that people buy my books, the more I get to write them, which is a good thing for both of us (assuming you enjoyed the series). While other indie authors are paying for five star reviews, I'm depending on you, the actual reader, to voice your opinion. So hop online when you and tell the world what you thought of this book.

    Thank you, again.

    -- *Jeremy Robinson*

ABOUT THE AUTHOR

JEREMY ROBINSON is the author of thirty novels and novellas including the highly praised, SECONDWORLD, as well as PULSE, INSTINCT, THRESHOLD and RAGNAROK the first four books in his exciting Jack Sigler series. His novels have been translated into ten languages. He lives in New Hampshire with his wife and three children.

Connect with Robinson online:
www.jeremyrobinsononline.com

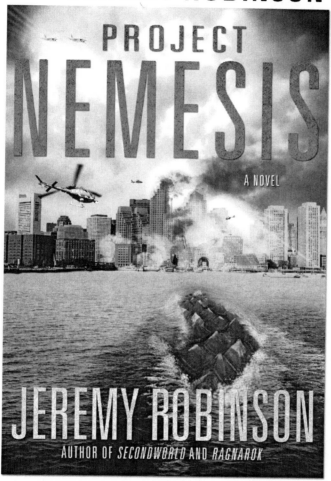

CPSIA information can be obtained at www.ICGtesting.com
Printed in the USA
LVOW131605271212

313476LV00006B/822/P